Dan Abnett

Eric Brown

Tony Ballantyne

Tim C Taylor

Lauren Beukes

Adam Roberts

Ian Whates

Andy Remic

Philip Palmer

Kim Lakin-Smith

Stephen Palmer

Steve Longworth

Gareth L Powell

Colin Harvey

Andy Bigwood

Further Conflicts

Further Conflicts

Edited by Ian Whates

NewCon Press
England

First edition, published in the UK April 2011
by NewCon Press

NCP 035 (hardback)
NCP 036 (softback)

10 9 8 7 6 5 4 3 2 1

ISBN: 978-1-907069-25-3 (hardback)
978-1-907069-26-0 (softback)

Cover art and design by Andy Bigwood

Invaluable editorial assistance from Ian Watson
Text layout by Storm Constantine

Printed in Great Britain by MPG Biddles of King's Lynn

Contents

Further Conflicts
An Introduction

Ian Whates

Some books come together very swiftly and easily, others require a little more patience. *Conflicts*, launched at the 2010 Eastercon, was of the latter sort. It took longer than anticipated to find stories of the right quality and type to produce the volume I'd envisaged. The result more than justified the effort involved, and the book's popularity both pre-launch and subsequently proved very gratifying. Of course, it was then announced that the 2011 Eastercon would be themed on military SF, and I almost wished that *Conflicts* had taken a little longer. It would have been the ideal book to launch there. That set me thinking. 'Conflict' lies at the heart of almost every narrative in one form or another. It's a very broad theme, which a single volume could only begin to explore. Why not do another?

I wanted this new volume to have an obvious kinship to the first but also to have its own identity; I wasn't after a 'Son of Conflicts'. So I decided to include a few of the same authors but mainly look for different voices to provide new interpretations of the theme. I also approached Andy Bigwood, who had created such a brilliant piece of cover art for the first book, and asked if he could do a new piece featuring the dart ships from that cover but in a radically different composition. Naturally, he came up trumps.

I would have been happy to ask any of the *Conflicts* authors to take part, but started with that master of military mayhem, **Andy Remic**. His sensitive nature and subdued writing style made him a natural choice... okay, who am I kidding? His enthusiasm for action and violence, his whole-hearted rev-it-to-the max approach to writing made him a must. "Yakker Snak" took me a little by surprise. Quite untypical, quite unusual, quite wonderful.

The second author I approached was **Eric Brown**. I knew his story in *Conflicts* to be one of several he's written featuring the same characters, and it struck me as fitting that this new volume should feature another. Eric agreed, and "The Soul of the Machine" proved to be everything I'd hoped for.

Right, that was the link firmly established; now for those new voices...

Putting together an anthology has its joys and frustrations. Sometimes authors you really hope to include are already overcommitted and can't take part; others who agree to submit fail to do so for all manner of perfectly valid reasons, and still others send you a piece which simply isn't suitable. All these played a part in the development of *Further Conflicts*. Thankfully, fate/coincidence/luck also stepped in more than once to lend a hand, putting me in the right place at the right time to connect with exactly the right author. As a result, the book came together far more swiftly and smoothly than its predecessor.

I've been wanting to get in touch with **Stephen Palmer** for a while now, having loved his two novels for Orbit, *Memory Seed* and *Glass*. In fact, while putting *Conflicts* together I'd obtained his email address from a friend with the intention of contacting him for a story, but other things distracted me and I never did. Then, in 2010, Stephen suddenly cropped up on a forum I frequent and we started talking, which led to my asking the inevitable question, "Do you write short stories at all...?" At NewCon 5 in October 2010, I had the honour of reading from Stephen's latest novel,

Urbis Morpheus and even from such a brief extract was instantly hooked.

Dan Abnett is an author I immediately thought of when deciding to produce *Further Conflicts*, but Dan was somebody I hadn't met; for some reason our paths had simply never crossed. Until, that is, I received an email from Lee Harris at Angry Robot asking whether the BSFA might be interested in interviewing Dan at one of their monthly meetings. Of course we were. Naturally, that put me in touch with Dan, and I was able to ask that all-important short story question. "The Wake" was one of the first stories I received for the book, and what a stonker it is, providing the perfect opener.

The last story I accepted for the anthology was from South African author **Lauren Beukes**. I had the pleasure of spending some time with Lauren during her brief visit to London in the Summer of 2010 to promote her new novel *Zoo City*. I'd read her first, *Moxyland* (Angry Robot) and been suitably impressed. Lauren was delighted to accept my invitation to submit, but warned me that, due to her many commitments – TV, novel, journalism, family – it might be a while in coming. Fortunately, "Unaccounted" proved well-worth the wait.

While organising the Newcon 5 convention, I received a membership form and cheque from one **Philip Palmer**. After a few email exchanges it emerged that this was indeed the same Philip Palmer who has written a number of deliciously retro space opera novels for Orbit in recent years (*Debatable Space*, *Red Claw* et al). Needless to say, I wasn't about to let such an opportunity pass me by...

I was still in the early stages of putting the anthology together when I bumped into **Tony Ballantyne** at alt.fiction in Derby. Having known Tony for several years and read and enjoyed both his short fiction and novels (and indeed published the excellent "Underbrain" in the 2008 anthology *Subterfuge*) I didn't hesitate in asking him for a submission. After reading "The War Artist", I was delighted that I had.

9

Kim Lakin-Smith is one of those authors who are bubbling under, set to explode on the scene at any moment. I'm fortunate enough to count Kim as a good friend, and, while chatting one day, it emerged that she'd just finished work on a novel and was taking a breather before the Next Big Project. Perfect time to write a short story, then, I suggested. "The Harvest" is Kim at her very best: nasty, dark, violent, but with a ray of hope running throughout. Great stuff.

Steve Longworth is already contributing a story to another NewCon Press anthology, *Fables from the Fountain*, so I definitely wasn't going to include him in this one, oh no… Until he workshopped "Extraordinary Rendition" at the writers group, the swine!

I've known **Colin Harvey** for a while, but his excellent 2009 novel *Winter Song* was what really brought his work to my attention. He was a natural choice to approach for the book, and his story, "Occupation" provides a sensitive counterpoint.

It's always gratifying when an author approaches *you* with a story, and this is precisely what happened with **Gareth L Powell**, who emailed to say that he'd written a follow-up to his *Conflicts* story. As I'd published the first piece, he was offering me first refusal on this one. Initially, that's what I did: refuse. With two authors already included from the first book, I didn't want to over-emphasise the link. However, a few weeks later I had second thoughts and asked Gareth if the piece was still available. Thank goodness I did. "The New Ships" is a terrific story.

I already had a piece from **Adam Roberts** lined-up for the book, a left-over from another project which looked to have been abandoned. However, at the last minute, that project was resurrected (without my involvement this time around, I'm relieved to say) which meant that Adam's piece was already committed. So I asked him if he had anything else that might be suitable for the 'conflict' theme. Almost apologetically, Adam offered me "The Ice Submarine", explaining that this was something he wrote a while ago but had recently been working on again. He needn't have apologised. It's an excellent piece, which dovetails perfectly with the anthology's theme.

Tim C Taylor has been working around the small presses for a while now. The first time I encountered his work was in #3 of the late lamented *Forgotten Worlds* magazine in 2006, the same issue that featured one of my own early stories. He then joined the Northampton SF Writers Group and has workshopped some cracking stuff. I had no hesitation in asking him to submit for *Further Conflict* and he duly wrote "Welcome Home, Janissary", one of his best pieces yet; strong enough to provide the collection's final word.

Thirteen stories, thirteen very different interpretations of the same theme. I hope you enjoy them.

Ian Whates
March 2011

The Wake

Dan Abnett

We were going to miss Mendozer.

He'd been with us, what, four tours? Five, Klubs reckons. Five. Well anyway, we were going to miss him. Mendozer was like a tin target. You know the kind? You knock them down, but the motor pops them up again, time after time.

Mendozer had a tin target quality about him. You get blokes like that. I don't mean immortal, indestructible fireproof angels of death like Boring, 'cause blokes like Boring, they're a whole other deal entirely. No, Mendozer's type, they're just reliable, like they're always going to be around, and if something knocks them down they'll soon be right back up again, thank you, banging away, making a joke.

Like a tin target on the practice deck. Bang! Down he goes. Then up he pops again.

When Mendozer got knocked down and didn't pop back up, we grabbed him and got him to the extract. Moke and me, we hoiked him under the armpits and ran with him, dragging his legs. Moke was yelling medic, but I was pretty confident that Mendozer was dogfood already. None of us actually saw what got him, due to the fact that it had all gone a bit cack-yourself-and-keep-shooting nutty at the time, but it looked like he'd run onto a pitchfork. There was wet everywhere. The stuff was all over us, soaking our sleeves and hips.

The Surge did his best. Credit for that. Tried everything. Split Mendozer's body jacket off, cracked the sternum, tried to patch the internal punctures, tried to get the slack heart to restart. We ended up soaking wet up to our armpits, kneeling either side of Mendozer in a blood slick the size of a fish pond, with dozens of spent injector vials and wadding tear-off strips floating around in it.

End of. Somebody find him a box.

The Surge put him in the fridge. We stayed on site four more days, expending our remaining munitions at anything that came inside the floodlit perimeter. It was not the light-hearted fun and frolics we'd been hoping for.

There was a technical problem with our extract, so we had to layover at Relay Station Delta for a week. All of us knew Relay Delta, because we stopped there every time on the way in to Scary Land, and none of us cared for it. Dark, pokey, rank, no light except artificial, no food except recyc. It was about as roomy and inviting as Mendozer's casket.

The trick was to recognise the up-side. A week's layover meant a week added to resupply turnaround, and a week extra before we'd get deployed back to Scary Land. That was fine by us, even if it meant seven days of breathing farts in the dark at Relay Delta.

We were all pretty sick of Scary Land, to tell you the truth. We were all pretty sick of banging away at the Scaries. We'd lost sixteen on seven tours, including Mendozer, and that was light compared to some platoons. The Middlemen, best of the best and all that, but banging away at the Scaries was beginning to feel like banging our heads against the proverbial. We've tangled with all sorts over the years, no word of a lie, but there was something relentless about the Scaries. Something cack yourself. Something shadow-under-the-bed spooky. I swear even Boring was beginning to get creeped out by them.

"Bosko," he says to me, "Scary Land is starting to make me miss Suck Central."

Which was saying something, specially coming from Juke

14

Boring, shit-kicking fireproof god of war. Suck Central, as the name suggests, had not been a family bucket of fun and frolics either.

Anyway, there's us, Relay Delta, a bit of downtime. So we're all in the Rec, just dossing around, and in comes Boring carrying a large carton pack, and behind him comes the Surge trundling a shiny plastic casket on a gurney from the ward. It rattles its castors as it comes in over the door trim. It takes us all of no seconds flat to realise this is Mendozer's bloody box. Everyone gets up. Everyone says a few choice words, the same choice word in most instances.

Boring, he points with his chin and directs Surge to park Mendozer in the middle of the Rec. The Surge does so, and heels the brake-lock on the gurney's wheelbase. Boring walks over to a side table, indicates by a narrowing of his eyes that Klubs should instantly remove the hand of clock patience spread out on it, and then dumps the carton. It clinks. Glass.

"We're holding a wake," he announces.

He opens the carton. It had been a stores pack for cans of rice pudding in a previous life. His big hands scoop out sets of chunky shot glasses, a digit in each, five at a time. Cripes only knows where he managed to scare up real glass glasses.

Then came the best bit. Twenty four bottles of the good stuff. Litre bottles, actual glass. Boring twists the top off the first one, and I can't remember how long it's been since I heard the fresh metal collar of a screw cap strip open like that.

He starts filling the glasses. Generous measures. It takes more than one bottle. We're all wary. Juke Boring has a history of playing cruel tricks in the name of character building experience. The stuff he was pouring might just have been cold tea. We're all braced for a metaphorical smack round the ear and a lecture on taking things at face value.

But this isn't a trick. You can't fake the smell of fifteen year old malt.

"Where'd you get this stuff?" asks Neats, the platoon

sergeant.

"Station commander owed me a million favours," Boring says. "Now he owes me a million minus one."

He picks up a glass. He doesn't hand the others out, but there's a wordless instruction for us all to go help ourselves. We take a glass each, and form a loose circle around the gurney. Twenty-eight men: twenty-four, plus Boring, Neats, the Surge, and Mendozer in his box.

Boring raises his glass.

"Here's to Mendozer," he says. "Middleman from start to finish. Skull it."

"Skull!" we all say, and chug back our glasses. We clonk the empties down on the lid of Mendozer's box, and Boring nods to Neats to refill them.

As Neats gets busy, Moke asks the question we're all thinking.

"We don't usually do this," he says. "Why are we doing this?"

"Because we should," says Boring. "Shows respect. Isn't usually enough time, or there's no place to do it. Thought it was a custom we should get into."

The glasses are full again. We hoist them.

"Middlemen, best of the best," says Neats.

"Skull!" we say. Refill.

I was told the platoon's nickname is the Middlemen because we get right in the middle of things. Klubs says it's because we're always stuck in the middle of bloody nowhere. In this particular instance, with a dead bloke in a box in a pressurised bunker that smells like bad wind.

The concept of the wake is unfamiliar to some of our number, so Fewry explains.

"It's a mourning custom," he says. "A watch kept over the departed."

"Why?" someone asks.

"In case they're not dead," says Klubs. "In case they wake

up."

"That's not right," says the Surge, who's the most educated of the Middlemen fraternity.

"It isn't?" asks Klubs. "I thought that's why it was called that."

The Surge shakes his head.

"That's just a myth," he says. "One of those old wives' tales."

"But I heard," says Klubs, never one to let a thing go, "that they used to dig up old coffins and find fingernail scratches on the insides. 'Cause people didn't have proper medic stuff back then, and sometimes they thought some poor sod was dead when they wasn't, and they'd bury them and then they'd wake up looking at the lid. So they'd hold one of these things to keep an eye on the body for a while and make sure it wasn't going to wake up before they bunged it in the ground."

"I understand," says the Surge. He has a patient tone sometimes. "I understand what you mean. It's just the word comes from a different root."

"Oh," says Klubs.

We neck a few more ("Death to all Scaries!", "Mother Earth!", "2nd Infantry, defenders of the World!"), and in between we remember a few stories about Mendozer. You could count on him. He was an okay shot with the Steiner, but really gifted with the grenade gun. He didn't snore much. He had a couple of decent jokes. There was that one really funny time with the girl from stores and the ping-pong bat.

The mood relaxes a bit. Each of us takes a moment to individually tilt a glass to the box sitting there on the chrome gurney, and say a last few words of a personal nature. A few of us sit back. The cards come out. Moke and some others dig out the sticks and the ash tray puck, and start playing corridor hockey on the pitch marked out on the tiled hallway leading through to medical. There's a lot of shouting and body-slamming into doors. Boring watches them, almost amused. The pitch outlines are wearing away. It's been there as long as any of us can remember. No one knows who painted them.

The Surge pulls out a second deck, and starts to do some of his famous card tricks. Nimble fingers. Fewry goes off to get some bacon strips, crackers and pickles from stores.

Every now and them, someone hoists up his glass and calls out a toast, and everyone stops what they're doing, even the hockey players, and answers.

Usually, it's a simple "Mendozer!" and we all answer "skull!"

If I'm honest, I'm not sure how long we were kicking back before someone noticed. Couple of hours, minimum. I know that Neats told me to go get another bottle out of the carton for top-ups, and I saw we'd skulled half of them already. The party had broken down a bit, and spread out through the rooms around the Rec.

Moke suddenly says, "What's he doing there? That's not respectful."

No one pays Moke that much attention, but I look up. Mendozer's box is no longer in the centre of the Rec. It's been wheeled aside, and it's standing under the big blast ports, three or four metres away from where the Surge parked it.

No mystery. I mean, it's obvious as soon as you look at it. The gurney's spring loaded brake-lock has pinged off and it's rolled. Maybe someone brushed against it.

Except they haven't, and it hasn't. The brake-lock hasn't disengaged to such an extent, in fact, Moke is actually having trouble unfastening it so he can roll the gurney back into the middle of the room where it's supposed to be.

I go over. Bend down. Help him. The Surge heeled that brake good. The pin needs oil. It takes a moment of effort and a few choice words to unfix it.

Moke and me, we go to roll the box back into pride of place.

"Wait," I says. He can feel it too. He looks at me. It's a bad look. I immediately wish I'd sat out the last couple of toasts, because the drink has got me paranoid. Maybe I'm being clumsy. Maybe I'm a little happy-handed and everything seems skewy.

The box feels too light. The gurney's rolling far too freely. There's no weight in it.

"'sup?" says Boring. He's right there at my shoulder all of a sudden. Around us, people are still playing cards and telling jokes. Out in the hall, the corridor hockey tournament is reaching its climax.

I look at him, say nothing. It's in the eyes. Boring puts one hand flat on the top of Mendozer's box and just moves it from side to side. He can feel it too. You can see it. The whole trolley fish-tails slightly under the stir of his palm. Nothing like enough weight. It'd have to be empty to behave like that.

Boring looks at me, quick, then back at the casket. Someone's left an empty glass standing on top, and it's left a ring of condensation on the shiny plastic. Boring picks up the glass and hands it to Moke. Moke has got eyes big as saucers by now.

Boring runs a finger along the edge of the lid. There are catches, but they're floppy plastic, nothing secure. He flicks them.

Then he opens the lid.

I don't want to look, but I look. It's not that I want to see Mendozer dead in a box, but I would find it reassuring at least.

We see the inside of the bottom of the box. Casket's empty. No Mendozer, nothing.

Boring shuts the lid.

"This isn't funny," I whisper.

He points to his stony expression, a familiar gesture intended to emphasise the fact he isn't cracking up.

"Did someone take the poor bastard out as a joke?" I asked.

It seems unlikely.

"Maybe the Surge pulled the wrong box out of the fridge?" Moke suggests. His voice is as low as ours.

That seems unlikely too.

"Wouldn't the Surge have noticed the box was light when he brought it through?" I ask.

19

Boring doesn't answer me. He looks around the Rec, winks at Neats. Neats makes an excuse about needing a slash to gently extract himself from his card school. Boring looks back at me.

"Bosko," he says. "Go fetch a Steiner. Meet me in medical."

"Okay," I say.

"Take Moke with you."

"Okay."

I don't know what to think. I get that creepy cack-yourself feeling you normally only get when Scaries are around. My hands are shaking, no word of a lie. Moke looks how I feel. We slip out the back way, avoiding the hockey insanity in the hall, and head down the link tunnel to Dock Two.

The lights there are down to power conserve. Half of me wants all the alcohol in my system flushed out so I can clean my headspace. The other half wants another skull to steady me.

All our platoon kit and hardware is stacked up in Dock Two where the extract discharged it. Most of the carrier packs are heavy duty mil grade, but some look disarmingly like Mendozer's box. Just smaller. Like they were made for parts, not whole bodies.

Nice thought to dwell on.

Moke watches the door, twitching from foot to foot, while I locate one of the gun crates in the pile of kit. I slide it out, punch in the authority code, and crack the lid. Half-a-dozen platoon weapons are racked in the cradle inside. There's a smell of gun oil. All Steiner GAW-Tens. I pull one, like Boring told me to. I pull one, and four clips.

The Steiner Groundtroop Assault Weapon Ten A.2 is our signature dish. Some platoons these days favour the Loman BR, and that's a fine bit of business, but it's big, and really long when it's wearing a flash sleeve, and it's not a great fit in a tight space where you might need to turn at short notice. The Middlemen have been using GAWs since bloody always, Eights back during the last war, then every model upgrade ever since through to the current Ten A.2s. The Ten is compact but chunky. It loads low friction drive band HV, in either AP or hollowpoint, and it's got full selective options. I take hollowpoint out of the crate, not AP. We're in a pressurised atmospheric environment. Penetration control is going to be an issue.

I'm clacking the first clip into the receiver as I re-join Moke.

"Screw this bollocks," he says to me. "This is a joke. This is someone's idea of a bloody joke. When I find out who, I'm going to de-dick him."

No argument from me.

"Unless it's Boring," he adds.

I nod. I let Moke hang on to that possibility, because it's more comforting than the alternatives.

But I saw the look in Boring's eyes.

This isn't his prank.

Boring's in medical with Neats. They've got the walk-in fridge open. It smells of ammonia and detergent wash. The light in the fridge is harsh and unflattering, sterile UV. Moke and I wander in. I wonder if it's like a normal fridge and the light only comes on when the door's open. I don't volunteer to stay inside to find out. There's no handle on the inside.

Boring and the Sergeant are sliding caskets off the rack and opening them. Just from the way the caskets move on the rollers, you can tell there's nothing in them.

"Checking the Surge got the right one?" I ask.

Neats nods.

Boring slams the last box back into place with an angry whip of his wrist, and it bangs against its cavity.

"Nothing," he says.

Behind us, we can hear the whoops and crashes of the hockey still in play.

"Makes no sense," says Neats.

"Somebody like to explain this?" a voice interrupts.

We turn. It's the Surge. He looks pissed off that we're

trespassing on his domain.

Boring explains. He uses the fewest possible words. He explains how we thought the Surge had pulled the wrong box, and that we came in here to find the right one. He explains they're all empty.

Now the Surge looks twice as pissed off.

"That can't be," he says.

"Tell us about it," says Moke.

The Surge pushes past us into the fridge.

"No," he says, "I don't know what's happened to Mendozer. That's a thing in itself."

"And?" asks Neats.

The Surge is checking the ends of the caskets for label slips.

"Nine Platoon lost a guy in a cargo accident on their way through last week. They left him here."

"What are you saying?" asks Boring.

"I'm saying Mendozer or no Mendozer, these shouldn't all be empty."

He locates the label he's looking for and pulls the box out. There's nothing in it, but it's not clean inside. There's like a residue, wet, like glue. There's a smell too, when the lid opens. Decomp. You can smell it despite the extractor fans and the detergent.

"The bloke from Nine should be in this one," says the Surge.

"What are you saying?" Moke asks. He's starting to get that whine in his voice. "What are you saying, exactly? We've lost two stiffs now?"

"Someone's taken a joke way too far," says the Surge. "Cadavers don't just get up and walk away."

He looks at us. He sees the look we're giving him. He realises it was a really bad choice of words.

We go back out into medical. Boring sends Neats and Moke to round up everyone else and get them into the Rec. If this is a joke, he's going to scare an admission out of the perpetrator.

The Surge touches my arm. I see what he's pointing to.

"Lieutenant?" I say.

Boring comes over. There are spots of wet on the floor.

"I mopped up in here," says the Surge.

The spots dapple the tiles. They're brown, not red, like gravy. There's no indication of spray or arterial force. Something just dripped.

Boring heads towards the bio-store that joins medical. The door's ajar. There are graft banks of vat tissue in here, flesh slabs, dermis sheets and organ spares kept in vitro jars. We can smell the wet as we approach the door. Wet and decomp, spoiled meat.

We hear something.

I catch Boring's eye and offer him the Steiner. He signs me to keep it, to keep it and cover him. I swallow. I toggle to single shot, ease off the safety, and rest my right index finger on the trigger guard. The stock's tight in the crook of my shoulder, the barrel down but ready to swing up. I feel naked without a body jacket. I'd have given real money for a full suit of ballistic laminate. The Surge drops back behind us. I edge in beside Boring. He picks up a tube-steel work chair by the seat back, one handed, and uses the legs to push the door open. Like a lion tamer, I think.

There's something in the bio-store. It's down the end, in the shadows. The tops have been pulled off some of the vitro jars, and slabs have been taken out. There's fluid on the floor. One of the jars has tipped, and stuff is drooling out like clear syrup. I can see a pink, ready-to-implant lung lying on the tiles, like a fish that's fallen out of a net onto the deck.

The thing in the shadows is gnawing at a flesh slab. It sees us. It rises.

The fact that it isn't Mendozer is hardly a consolation prize. It's just steak. A man-shaped lump of steak, raw and bloody, tenderised with a hammer. It has eyes and teeth, but they're none too secure, and it's wearing the soaked remains of a 2nd Infantry jump suit. It takes a step towards us. It makes a gurgling sound. I can see white bone sticking out through its outer layer of mangled meat in places.

"Bang it," says Boring. "Put it down."

Not an order he needs to repeat. I bring the nose of the Steiner up, slip my finger off the guard onto the trigger, and put one right into the centre of its body mass. In the close confines of the bio-store, the discharge sounds like an empty skip being hit with a metal post. Booming, ringing, resounding.

The thing falters. It doesn't drop.

I punch off two more, then another pair. The post hits the skip again: boom-boom, boom-boom. I see each round hit, see each round make the thing stagger. I hear the vitro jars on the shelves behind it shatter and burst.

Boring snatches the Steiner off me. In my fuddle, despite my best intentions, I've slotted AP rounds. The hyper velocity slugs are punching right through the advancing mass, not even stopping to shake hands and say hello.

Boring ejects the clip. I yank one of the spares from my pocket, this time checking it's got an HP stencil on it. Boring slams it home, charges the gun, and bangs off on semi.

The hollowpoints deform and expand as they hit, preventing over-penetration, while simultaneously creating maximum tissue damage. They gift their entire kinetic force to the target. The thing kind of splatters. It shreds from the waist up in a dense cloud of wet and vaporised tissue and bone chips.

Now it drops.

We approach. There's wet everywhere, splashed up all surfaces. Flecks of gristle are stuck to the wall, the ceiling, the jars, even the light shade.

The Surge grabs a lamp and a stainless steel probe. He squats down and pokes the mess.

"What the hell is it?" I ask, hoarse.

The Surge holds up the probe in the beam of his lamp. There's a set of tags hanging off it.

"Hangstrum, private first class, Nine Platoon."

"The one killed in the accident?"

"The pattern of injuries is consistent with crush damage from a cargo mishap," says the Surge. He looks at Boring. "Not counting the mincing," he adds.

"Any idea why he was walking around like it was a normal thing to do?" asks Boring.

"Maybe he wasn't dead," I say, grasping at straws. Reassuring straws. "Maybe Nine should've held a wake to make sure he was—"

"He was dead," says the Surge. "I read the path. I even checked in the box when we first came on station."

"But his body was in the fridge with Mendozer's," says Boring. It's not so much a question.

"Yes," the Surge says.

Oh, it'll all come out later. It always does. The stuff we don't know about the Scaries. The stuff we're still learning about how they tick, why they tick, their biological cycle, what they do down there in the blind-as-midnight darkness of Scary Land. We're still learning about how they kill us, how their bioweapons work, how they evolve as they learn more about our anatomy from killing us.

The techs don't even know for sure yet whether it's part of their regular life cycle, or just something they developed specially for us. It wasn't claws the Scaries killed Mendozer with, it was ovipositors. Parasitic micro-larvae, jacking the blood cells of his cooling corpse, joyriding around his system, multiplying, leeching out into the other dead meat in the fridge, hungry for organic building blocks to absorb.

Even now, we don't know what they'd do to living tissue. We don't take the chance to find out. Incinerators are S.O.P. Incinerators, or disintegration charges. The Surge keeps grumbling about airborne particles and microspores, about tissue vapour and impact spatter contamination. But Boring tells him to zip it. We've got bleach and incinerators and sterile UV, and that's all, so it'll have to be enough.

25

We find Mendozer back in the Rec. He'd been shuffling around the halls of Relay Delta aimlessly, lost, late for his own wake. Everyone stops and stares at him, baffled, drunk. Fewry actually raises a hockey stick like a club to see him off, like you'd chase away a stray dog.

Mendozer's blank-eyed. Glazed over. His mouth is slack, and his chin and chest are bruised black and yellow where the Surge tried to save him and then stapled him back up.

He makes a sound I'll never forget. Boring doesn't hesitate, even though it's Mendozer and it's got Mendozer's face. He hits him with the rest of the HP clip.

Boring says something, later on, when we've washed the Rec down with bleach, dumped the remains in the furnace, opened the rest of the bottles.

He says the wake was Command's idea. When he signalled them that we were bringing back a casualty, they advised him to watch it to see what happened.

Like it wasn't the first time. Like they were trying to establish a pattern. Like they were conducting an experiment to see what happened to the things that the Scaries killed. An experiment with us as lab rabbits. Middlemen, Middlemen, same as bloody usual. Fun, not to mention frolics.

We were going to miss Mendozer. Of course we were. I'm just glad Boring decided not to. Emptied the rest of the clip making sure he didn't. I'll drink to that.

I wish that extract would hurry up and get here.

Unaccounted

Lauren Beukes

The ittaca is wedged into the uneven corner of cell 81C, as if it is trying to osmose right through the walls and out of here. It is starting to dessiccate around the edges, the plump sulphur-coloured frills of its membrane turning shrivelled and grey. Maybe it's over, Staff Sergeant Chip Holloway thinks, looking in through the organic lattice of the viewing grate. The thought clenches in his gut.

He has been having problems with his gut lately. He blames it on the relentless crackle of the blister bombs topside. The impact reverberates through the building, even here, three floors down. You'd think, eventually, you would get used to such things.

The Co-operative Intelligence Resource Manual does not cover this exact situation. The CIRM advises a recovery period for the delegate, a show of mutual respect to re-establish trust and better yet to instil gratitude. But the CIRM also advises that if a delegate is critical, it is critical to press on.

Terminal is not an ideal result. Terminal can be attributed to lack of due diligence.

The corridor stinks of urine. Not from the ittaca, which is anaerobic and recycles its waste through its body again and again, reabsorbing nutrients. Strip-mining food. It excretes sharp chlorine farts that puff from the arrangement of spongy tubes like organ pipes fanning down its dorsal side. Just one of the chemical weapons to watch out for in the ittaca's natural biological armament according to *The Xenowarfare Handbook:*

Reaching Out To Viable Lifeforms.

There is a splatter of piss on the door. He will need to have a word with K Squadron. He knows they're just frustrated. That camaraderie sometimes takes itself out in casual acts of hooliganism. And still. The Co-Operative Intelligence Resource Manual does not cover what to do when respect for your authority is fraying like the ripped membrane frills of an ittaca's gastropod foot.

When they took occupation of the prison, there were ittaca med-scanners installed in all the cells and bacterial-powered screens mounted outside, monitoring vital signs: heart-rate, brain activity, adrenal spikes in the endocrine system that might indicate a prisoner about to erupt into violence. The first thing the military did was dismantle them.

Security risk, command said. He never saw a formal directive. Good for morale, General Labuschagne said, when he queried it. C'mon Holloway. Was he honestly saying his people didn't deserve a little celebration? After everything they'd been through? It still made him feel uneasy. A waste of resources, he told himself.

They'd torn the screens off the walls, whooping and hollering, then piled up the ittacan tech in the open courtyard under the shadow of the guard tower – back when it was still standing – and set it alight.

He turned a mostly blind-eye to the mulch moonshine being not-so-covertly distributed between the reserves because maybe the general had a point. A special occasion. But he circled the groups, making sure no one drank too much of the mildly psychotropic guano distillate and made a note to find out who was brewing it. He'd have to have a word with them.

It all went wrong, of course. The light from the bonfire or maybe the music seemed to enrage the insurgents, drawing down a fresh assault by the blisters. Chip was the last one through the doors. Dragging Reserve Lieutenant Woyzeck with him, reeling drunk, despite his best efforts, and swearing at him to let her go. Asshat. Shithead. Partypooper.

His eyebrows were seared off by the heat of a strike, even as the explosion scoured the reinforced coralcrete with venomous pus and shrapnel. Fucking Kazis, he heard, as someone slammed the door. He'd tried to discourage them from using the term as disrespectful to both the ittaca and those reserves of Japanese heritage. But the blisters are aerial suicide bombers and what are you going to do?

Fucking lucky, Chip, Ensign Tatum said, leaving out the 'sergeant', leaving out the 'sir' because Holloway encouraged his people to call him by his first name. And was that grudging admiration in Tatum's voice?

Chip found an unexploded blister in the courtyard once, deflated on one side and gagging on its own blood from the shrapnel tearing up its insides. Blisters swallow improvised weaponry whole, choking down nails and sharpened scrap metal and bits of coral through their gill slits, like an athlete carbo-loading before a game. Some of the reserves were using the blister as a football. He chased them off with a warning. But he couldn't bring himself to shoot it.

He can't blame them. There isn't exactly much in the way of recreational facilities for the reserves. Mainly they take pot-shots at the rats. Which are not rats, but something like them. Bald skittering things the size of Rottweilers with too many legs. They dig up body parts from shallow graves from the former regime and drag them around, scraping off the dried membrane with nubs like teeth, cracking the mantle spines to get to the marrow.

Let it not be said that the ittaca did not cast the first stone. Let it not be said that this was ever a good place to be.

Inside the cell, a spasm flutters through the ittaca's membrane, setting the spines along its mantle clattering. A xylophone made from insect's legs. Alive then.

The ittaca doesn't bleed exactly. It extrudes a clear viscous liquid. Tacky, like sap. The first time, it took him 48 minutes and a full bottle of military issue stainEZ (guaranteed to take care of even the most stubborn bio-matter tarnish with just one drop!) to get the stickiness out of his greens. The third time he wore an improvised poncho made out of a foil body bag. He wasn't prepared for a second time.

He made a note of it in his weekly report. 1x body bag. He is careful to account for almost everything.

- 407 Military Reserve Soldiers (human) stationed at Strandford Military Base formerly known as Nyoka Prison Satellite Facility. (Temporary posting). Broken down as follows: 241 Male. 113 Female. 53 NGS (non-gender-spec).
- 0 Indigenous translators. (Complement of 7 were dismissed on charges of info leaks.)
- 123 ittaca delegates (alive) kept separate in 123 cells.
- 4 ittaca delegates (deceased) in morgue-lab.
- 18 blister delegates (deceased) in morgue-lab.
- 6037 blister delegates (deceased) processed through central crematorium
- 550 TK-R surface-to-surface RPGs. Effective coralcrete penetration: 0.2%.
- 25 MGL-900s, HE grenades. Effective coralcrete penetration: 100%
- 200 MXR-63 multifunction assault rifles plus parts + 80 000 x 45mm rounds
- 50 000 x 30mm U-238 rounds, incendiary, armour-piercing + 5 x chainfed autocannons + mountings. Shelved. Useless. Who would have predicted that ittaca would be able to metabolise uranium?
- 263 268 carb-blasters (nutritional value as per military recommendations.) Sufficient for 213 days of rations for full staff complement. They have been here for 189 days

already. This does not fit the military definition of "temporary posting".

- 700 re-breathers, including ample issue for visitors. And there are ample visitors. No rankings. No name tags. If it weren't for the re-breathers taken off their hooks, set back to recharge, they might be ghosts.
- 23 field decontamination tents. 12 carbon atmosphere recyclers; includes 3 overflow tanks and 250 biohazard disposal bags. 2 tents unaccounted for.
- 24 x 12-tray silver sulfadiazine 1% topical cream packs for treatment of chemical burns. 1 tray missing. He blames the ghosts.
- 1050 field dressing packs plus standard meds.
- 800 Standard saline packs plus first aid supply kits. All date-stamps have expired. Bandages are bandages. Aspirin is aspirin, General Labuschagne said when he raised his concerns.
- 499 body bags aka meat sacks aka take me home daddy.

He came here on the highest commendation. In the provinces, planet-side, he was a core cultural liaison with the ittaca in the villages. Strategically critical, they said. Hearts and minds. This was before everything went to shit. Sorry. Before relations devolved with the indigenous population and assertive action became necessary.

He learned the basics of the language with its clicks and liquid gurgles using a translator pod. But it turned out a lot of it is in the nuance of how you arrange your mantle spines. He was popular with the young potentials, who would trail behind him on his rounds, popping and clicking, anthropological in their interest. He still feels a flicker of shame that he ever thought of them as grubs.

They detonated the central guard tower in the courtyard. Too much of a target, command said. It didn't make a difference.

31

The blisters kept launching themselves off the balconies of the apartment mounds surrounding the prison on a single propeller wing, spinning downwards like maple seeds, making that godawful crackling screaming sound through their gills. Isn't static supposed to bethe sound of the Big Bang?

Before the siege intensified, before they'd been forced to retreat three floors underground, he used to walk the ramparts, taking in the view of the coralcrete apartments growing up in unsteady spirals, following chemical markers laid by ittaca architects. Even their slums are beautiful, he'd commented once to the sentry at the door. He'd been met with a blank stare.

The reserves found the ittacan architecture disorienting. The warren of grown tunnels intersecting at strange angles. They ended up sleeping in the cells. Six to a room. Not exactly army protocol. Not exactly good for discipline. Soldiers cliqued up. They did things behind closed doors, regulation t-shirts stuffed into the viewing grates. Unauthorised sex. And other things.

What's the big deal. Chill out. We're just blowing off steam. Probably Tatum and the others didn't say any of these things. Probably they just stared at him and grinned those chimpanzee grins, all bared teeth and clenched jaws and contempt.

He included this in his report. He is careful to be accountable. He is careful to use neutral language. He is careful not to use the word maggots.

Members of Squadron K (night duty) reprimanded for inappropriate behaviour towards ittaca prisoners in cell block three. Video evidence, taken by the relevant members involved, is attached.

He deletes that last part. Retypes it. Deletes it again. Leaves it at videos were taken. Does not attach them. He is aware that this is a security risk. He is aware that he isn't qualified to know what is inappropriate anymore. Let's war.

He scrubs the videos. But he cannot shake the images. Or the sound of Tatum's voice – the laughing that accompanied it – as he rounded the corner, on his way to dish out rations.

Maggots. Fucking maggots. Suck on this. Fuck you. Fuck.

There are items that he cannot account for. Things that were not on the facility inventory lists when he took over command of the prison, but have mysteriously appeared. Bayonet tasers. Electrodes. High-density carbon-saws for butchering meat. A pillow case twisted around a broken chunk of coralcrete.

There are visitors. Irregular. Like ghosts. Did he already mention this? He's pretty sure they're MI. But they could just as easily be private contractors. Military development partners with an interest in developing new resources.

The reserves call them suits, but it's more the attitude than their attire. They wear sleek, expensive body-fitting hazmats. They don't carry identification or rank. They refuse to answer when he questions them. Should his people be wearing protective gear too? Is this okayed by command? Why hasn't he received notification? Where is their clearance? Can he see some identification?

Don't ask, don't tell, one of the suits says to him, smiling behind her rebreather like it is all one big joke. Then she takes him into the ittaca's cell. This was two days after his report. Which received no response. Officially.

You need to understand, is what the suit said. But what he thinks is: complicit.

It was just a lark, *Chip*, Ensign Tatum said, surly at being called into the cell that doubles as his office down here.

What Chip Holloway does to the ittaca in cell 81C with the suit is not.

Not the first or the second or the third time.

He wishes the ittaca would fucking die already. He wishes the blisters would break through three floors and the whole damn moon and blow them all to smithereens. But mainly he wishes he could sleep and sleep and sleep. The exhaustion nags in his bones like arthritis.

You ready? the suit says, appearing at his elbow. She flips open the viewing window. Looks like we don't have much time. Better stoke up the crematorium, baby. Oh. I brought you something. She reaches into the side of her toolkit and shoves a folded piece of plastic tarp at him. Surgical scrubs. Better than a rejigged body bag, she says.

She slides her chem-print keychain into the lock. The door grates open. In the corner the ittaca stirs, its spines clattering feebly. It resembles a clot of mustard. (A lump of custard. A pile of pus-turd he hears Ensign Tatum's voice sing-song in his head.)

Don't worry, she says, seeing his face – which has started to become something grey and sagging that he doesn't recognise in the mirror. Like he is starting to desiccate too.

She kneels down and snaps open her toolkit. Starts sorting through various unaccounted items, humming a tune he recognises from the radio, sweet and catchy. Don't worry. she repeats, her back to him, laying out things with serrated edges and conducting pads and blunt wrenching teeth. You can't dehumanise something that isn't human.

The New Ships

Gareth L Powell

London Paddington: The first thing Ann Szkatula did after stepping off the train from Heathrow was cross to the left luggage lockers and retrieve the gun stashed there by her new employers. It was a compact Smith and Wesson made of stainless steel and lightweight polymer, and it came with two additional clips of ammunition. She knew she didn't have much time, so she slipped the weapon into her pocket and closed the locker door.

Fresh off the plane from Switzerland, she still wore the thick army surplus coat and heavy boots she'd pulled on that morning. She sniffed the air. It was good to be back in London. The concourse of Paddington station smelled of diesel fumes and idling cabs; pigeons flapped under the glazed, wrought-iron roof. She started walking. Despite the boots, her feet felt springy, ready for anything.

The last eight weeks had been spent at a clinic near Zurich, where the staff had cleaned and toned her body while she drowsed in an artificial coma. Now Ann felt rested, and fitter than she had in years.

She passed a newsstand and it pinged her Lens, overlaying her vision with the day's top stories: the Chinese test firing their new orbital defence platform; a global upsurge in the production of nuclear weapons; the authorities in Prague reopening the city's subterranean fallout shelters. Irritated, she cut the feed with a twitch of her cheek.

Out on the street it was night, somewhere around ten

35

o'clock, and raining. The streetlights washed everything orange.

The house she wanted stood halfway along one of the small roads behind Westbourne Terrace, a few minutes' walk away. When she reached it, Ann saw it was a four-storey terraced Georgian building divided into flats. It had dirty white stonework and chipped iron railings. Without pausing, she splashed up its wet front steps. There was an intercom system by the door. She pressed the buzzer for the top flat, holding it down for several seconds.

The line crackled.

"Hello?"

She glanced up and down the street.

"It's me."

The door buzzed and she pushed it open. Inside, the hall carpet smelled damp. She crossed to the peeling wooden stairs, and clumped her way up four flights. At the top she came to another door. This was the attic flat. As she approached, the door opened a crack and a face peered cautiously around the frame.

"Annabelle?"

It was the voice from the intercom, and it belonged to a nervous-looking guy in his late twenties, with round glasses and a wiry hipster beard.

"Hello Max."

Max was a cousin on her mother's side. They hadn't seen each other in years. He stood back to let her across the threshold.

Inside, the flat consisted of a single room, with a bed beneath the window, a kitchen area against the opposite wall, and a bathroom door at the far end. The low, sloping ceiling made the place feel smaller than it really was.

Max hovered by the kitchen.

"I'll put the kettle on."

Ann ran a hand across her dripping hair, pushing it back from her forehead.

"We haven't got a lot of time."

The room smelled of mould and unwashed sheets. It was lit

by a solitary bulb hanging from a bare wire. The window ran with condensation. Apart from the bed, there was nowhere to sit.

Max opened the fridge.

"If you want a coffee it'll have to be black I'm afraid. I'm out of milk."

Ann watched him fill a plastic kettle from the cold water tap. His hands were shaking. He wore an unbuttoned plaid shirt over a white t-shirt, frayed jeans, and a pair of scuffed work boots.

"I wasn't sure you'd come." He scratched his beard. "Will you help me, Annabelle? Can you?"

Ann shook her head.

"You know I can't. You know who I work for."

Max hunched his shoulders. He looked disappointed. He set the kettle to boil and retrieved a pair of mismatched mugs from a shelf above the sink before spooning coffee granules into them. Watching him, Ann searched his face for traces of the boy she half-remembered from her childhood.

"I'm not here to help you, Max," she said. "I'm here to bring you in." She pulled the new gun halfway out of her pocket, just enough to let him see it. He froze and his eyes went wide.

With her other hand, she lifted the netbook from his bed.

"Are the files on here?"

"Y-yes."

"You didn't delete them?"

He shook his head.

"You're a dumbass." She closed the little computer and tucked it under her arm. "Now, do you have any weapons?"

Max pulled a multi-tool from his back pocket. It was a set of pliers with various blades and saws built into the handle. Hesitantly, he held it out.

"This is all I've got. Why? What do we need weapons for?"

She didn't answer. She pushed the gun back into her coat pocket and scooped a set of car keys from the kitchen counter.

"Are these for your car?"

"Yes, it's parked outside."

"Show me."

She let him lead her back down to the street. Cars were parked on both sides of the road.

"Which is it?"

Max pointed to a brown Ford. Ann pressed the key fob and its doors unlocked.

"Get in," she said.

"Where are we going?"

"Just get in."

Max slid onto the passenger seat and she closed the door on him, then walked around and got in behind the wheel.

"Why'd you do it, Max?" she asked, as she slotted the key into the ignition. "What were you playing at?"

Max rubbed a hand across his mouth.

He said, "Do you know what 'squatting' is?"

"Some sort of hacking?"

"More or less."

She turned the key and the engine started. They were still alone on the street. She pushed the car into gear and pulled out onto the road.

Max said, "After the explosion, when they evacuated the towns and cities around the Severn Estuary, thousands of businesses were left without premises or employees. Most went bust."

Ann put the car into first and they rolled off in the direction of the A40. She vividly remembered the panic and chaos of the explosion's aftermath. She'd been eighteen at the time. From forty miles away, she'd seen the flash, and thought it was lightning until she saw the mushroom cloud.

Max said, "'Squatters' are guys like me. We're electronic archaeologists. We hack into the websites and virtualities left behind by those failed companies. We mine information from abandoned servers. You'd be surprised how many are still running remotely, ticking along, waiting for their service agreements to expire."

He paused, shuffled his feet on the floor.

"All that stuff's just lying around, and some of it is valuable. And you know what they say: 'The street finds its own uses for things'."

Ann snorted.

"Oh, shut up. The 'street' can kiss my ass. What do you know about life on the 'street'? You're nearly thirty for god's sake. The kids on the 'street' are half your age. They'd eat you alive."

She shifted gear, jamming the stick into third. Max looked down at his hands, lower lip stuck out like a sulky teenager.

"Just tell me what happened," she said.

He turned his face to the window. "I got into something I thought was an abandoned corporate chat room, only it wasn't. It was still active."

"What did you see?"

He took a deep breath.

"How much do you know about the explosion, and what caused it?"

Ann came to a corner. She had a route plan loaded into her Lens, superimposing glowing arrows on her vision. They floated in front of the car like hallucinations, showing her the route to take.

"I've seen the wreckage of the crashed ship," she said. "I was there a few months back."

Max looked up, eyes wide.

"You actually went into the fallout zone?"

Ann flicked a hand. "It's been twenty years and the rain's washed most off the contaminated dust off the roads. As long as you stay on the tarmac and out of the buildings, the radiation levels aren't too bad."

She slowed for the lights at the junction with Edgware Road.

"I took a group in there," she said. "They wanted a motorcycle tour of Bristol, to race their bikes up and down the deserted streets. We ran into some trouble, but I sorted it out."

Max frowned. "That was you? I heard about that. There was something on the news a few months back." He scratched his beard. "I heard someone got killed."

Ann drummed her fingers on the wheel.

"As I said, I sorted it."

She glanced in the rear view mirror. With luck, she could wrap this up quickly and have them both away and out of here without attracting unwanted attention.

"You actually saw the crashed ship?"

"I've seen what's left, yes."

She glanced impatiently at the time display on her Lens. Every minute they spent in the capital increased the chances they'd be discovered.

"Then you know it was alien?"

She gave him a look. "Everybody knows that. Now, how about you answer my question? What happened?"

His cheeks were flushed.

"I cracked my way into a virtual meeting room. It was some kind of secret NATO conference. People from all over were there - politicians, military - sharing files and talking about the crash. They said it wasn't an accident; that there was a second ship, and that the two ships were fighting each other."

The lights changed. Ann released the clutch and the car rolled forward. As she worked the pedals, the gun in her coat pocket bumped against her thigh.

"It's true," she said.

Max let out a long breath. "So there really is a war, out there in space?"

"That's what we think. We don't know anything for sure, we've only had glimpses."

They passed a row of shops, closed for the night.

"But you're preparing? NATO, I mean."

"We all are. The Russians have their missiles, the Chinese are building their orbital defence platform."

"But you're the ones building the new ships?"

"Yes. We're back-engineering them from fragments recovered at the crash site."

He folded his arms. "That's terrible."

"I think it's a good idea."

Max curled his lip. "Do you know what they're doing to the *pilots*? I saw the files. Jesus."

"Those files are the reason you're in trouble."

He turned on her. "Those poor bastards are having their limbs amputated and alien control systems spliced directly into their brains. And after all that, they only live a few days before cracking up."

"And this was being discussed at the meeting you gate-crashed?"

Max nodded. "They were saying how disappointed they were by the project's lack of success. Disappointed? It's barbaric. It's butchery."

His fists clenched in his lap.

Ann said, "I know."

"How can you know?" he shouted. "How can you know all that and still work for them?"

"I volunteered."

That shut him up. Ann took them onto the Westway flyover, heading out of the city. There wasn't much traffic.

"My eyes were opened after that debacle in Bristol," she said quietly. "I saw the kind of shit that's heading our way and I decided I had to get involved."

Max swallowed. He squirmed in his seat. He didn't seem to know what to do with himself.

"So, Bristol was bad?"

Ann snorted. "I got mixed up in a plot to illegally recover an alien artefact from the crash site, and I had to kill someone to get out again. In the process, I saw what alien technology can do in the wrong hands."

In the orange street light, Max looked down at his fists. He was biting his lip.

41

Ann squeezed the wheel. "One scout craft got shot down and irradiated everything from Cardiff to Bath," she said. "One poxy scout craft. What happens if the war comes our way again? We don't know what the sides are, or who's fighting. What happens if one of them decides Earth's a strategic resource, or worse, a target?"

Max was quieter now, taken aback. "But if their technology's so far ahead of ours, how can we hope to fight them?"

"You know how."

Max made a face. "The new ships?"

"Bingo."

"But those pilots, it's slaughter."

Ann banged her palm on the rim of the steering wheel. "It's necessary! We have to make those ships work."

"So, the ends justify the means?"

"In this case, yes they do." She banged the wheel again, hammering home each syllable. "We're talking about the survival of the human race."

They passed through Acton and Perivale. The A40 became the M40, and they crossed the glowing orange ribbon of the M25.

"What happens now?" Max said. "Are you going to kill me?"

Ann took a deep breath. "That depends. Although we're working with those other countries, we haven't shared with them the technology we recovered from the crashed ship, which makes you and your downloaded files a serious security risk."

Max twisted in his seat and stared at her.

"The Americans take this kind of thing very seriously," she continued. "God alone knows what the Chinese are capable of."

"And you?"

She gripped the wheel and flexed her shoulders. She was keeping to a steady 70 mph, staying inconspicuous.

"I'm not going to kill you," she said. "You're an idiot, but you're also my cousin."

"S-so, what are we going to do?"

She checked the mirror again. There were cars behind them

but no sign they were being tailed.

"There's only one way out," she said. "I can get you onto a technical team, working on the project. We need bright young minds with the kind of skills you've got."

Max looked pained.

"Isn't there another way?"

"No."

The wipers clunked back and forth across the windscreen. They were out in open countryside now. Ahead lay Beaconsfield and High Wycombe, and a small airstrip on the outskirts of Oxford. If they could reach it, there would be a plane waiting.

If.

Searchlights crested a hill to their right. Helicopters. Two of them, hugging the treetops, spiralling in like sharks; their flanks painted with the eye-twisting black and white stripes of dazzle camouflage – geometric patterns designed to conceal their exact shape and size.

"Crap."

Ann slowed as the choppers descended. They were approaching a bridge. One of the aircraft took up position behind the car, blocking traffic. The other came down on the far side of the bridge. Both hovered a few feet above the tarmac. Their crazy paint jobs made it hard for the pattern recognition software in her Lens to get a definite visual lock on either of them. On the opposite carriageway, cars swerved and skidded to a halt. Horns sounded.

Max looked around. "What do we do?"

Ann knew what was coming next. She hit the brakes. "Close your eyes," she said.

No sooner had the words left her mouth than the lead helicopter angled its searchlight into the car. Blinded, Max cried out, but Ann already had her door open. Her Lens had polarized, throwing a black dot over the light. As the car slowed, she twisted the wheel and rolled out.

She took the impact on her shoulder, thankful for the

43

thickness of her coat. She had the gun in her hand. She rolled over twice and came up firing. She knew the helicopter's cockpit would be bullet-proof, so she aimed for the open hatch.

The first two shots killed the searchlight. To her left, she heard the stolen car's wing scrape the crash barrier at the foot of the bridge support. To her right, she saw curious motorists duck back into their vehicles. She kept firing, pumping bullets into the black-clad troops hanging in the helicopter's door.

When the trigger clicked empty, she sprinted for the car. Her legs were in peak condition, and she felt a surge of gratitude to her employers for the tune up at the Swiss clinic. Answering shots came from both helicopters. Automatic weapons clattered. Bullets zipped past her. She hit the car and slid across the bonnet, landing in a heap on the far side of the crash barrier. Bullets spanged off the old Ford's bodywork. A window shattered.

"Get out of there, Max."

"The door's stuck!"

"Use the window."

She fumbled a second magazine into her gun and got to her knees. She sent a couple of shots in the direction of each chopper. Masked troops were spilling out of both machines. She hit at least one of them, and the others dropped to the ground. Max's head and shoulders appeared through the car window. She grabbed the collar of his plaid shirt and pulled, and they both fell sprawling into the gravel between the crash barrier and the concrete bridge support.

"Keep down," she hissed.

She blinked up her Lens's IM function and sent a pre-prepared SOS to an anonymous orbital inbox.

Max had cut his hands on broken glass. His palms were bleeding.

"They're shooting at us!"

"Help's coming."

She fired a couple more shots. The soldiers were working their way to cover behind the barrier on the central reservation

between the carriageways. The car sagged as their answering fire
took out its tyres and shattered the remaining windows.

Max had his arms wrapped over his head. Blood dripped
from the tips of his fingers.

"They want you alive," Ann said.

He looked up, eyebrows raised. His glasses were scratched.
"They do?"

"That's why they're sat over there, trying to pick me off. If
they wanted to kill you, they'd have used grenades by now."

A fresh burst of fire rattled the car's frame. Chips flew from
the concrete stanchion supporting the bridge. Max curled himself
tighter.

"Are you sure?"

Ann shrugged. She leaned down, pointed her gun into the
gap under the car, and fired a volley at ankle height. On the other
side of the road, one of their attackers cried out, and the bullets
ceased.

"I've only got one more ammo clip," she said. "When that's
gone, there'll be nothing to stop them walking over here to get
us."

"You said help was coming?"

Ann checked the IM box in her Lens: there had been no
reply to her message.

"It is. At least, I hope it is. We've just got to hold on until
the cavalry arrives."

She fired the gun over the hood of the car, aiming carefully,
trying to make each shot count. When it was empty, she ejected
the spent magazine and clicked a fresh one into place. It was dry
under the bridge. On either side, the black and white helicopters
hovered in the drifting rain, the downdraught from their rotors
whipping up spray from the wet road.

Max said, "Why are they doing this? Who are they?"

Ann squinted into the darkness.

"I don't think they're Chinese. They could be Russian, or
Eastern European."

"I thought you said you were all working together?"

Ann laughed. "Nations only cooperate while they see an advantage in doing so."

There was a movement on the far side of the carriageway. The black-clad soldiers were inching forward, trying to outflank her. She sent a couple of shots into the closest, to encourage the rest to keep their heads down.

She said, "They don't want anyone getting too powerful and threatening their sovereignty. They don't want to submit to a world government."

Max rubbed his face. His fingers left bloody smudges on his cheek.

"So it's an arms race," he said. "Just like the Cold War."

Ann nodded. "Only this time we're all pretending we're on the same side."

Automatic fire rattled against the crash barrier. Ann rose to her knees and tried to shoot back. As she put her head level with the hood of the car, she saw Max's netbook on the car seat. She stretched over to grab it. As she lifted it out, bullets shredded the metal frame around her. Something bit her left cheek and she dropped back with a yelp of pain.

"Annabelle!" Max slithered over to her. "Are you all right? What happened?"

Her cheek stung. She raised her fingers to it and they came away bloody.

"Have I been shot?" she said.

Max screwed up his face. "I don't think so. But there's something..." He looked away.

Ann felt around the wound. Her fingertips brushed something sharp: a fragment of steel from the car. She tried to get hold of it but it was slippery with blood, and it hurt like hell.

"Max," she said. "Have you got your multi-tool?"

His hand went to his pocket.

"I've got it here."

"I need you to pull this out."

He hesitated, biting his lip as if trying to stop himself from being ill.

"Now, please."

From where she lay, she could see under the barrier and car to the huddled figures on the other side of the road. As Max leaned over her with the pliers, she gripped the pistol, ready to shoot at the first sign of movement.

Her eyes watered as Max tugged at the sliver of shrapnel. His cut hands were red with blood.

"It's stuck tight," he said. "I think it's in the bone."

Ann gritted her teeth. "Pull harder then," she said. She could feel warm blood running into her ear.

Max took a firm grip on the handle of his multi-tool and yanked. Ann screamed. Her hands clenched and the gun fired.

When she could see again, she found Max sitting before her with a nasty chunk of barbed metal clasped in the pliers' jaws. Now it was out, she needed to staunch the bleeding. She reached into her pocket and pulled out a handkerchief, which she wadded up and pressed to her face.

Beyond the car, black shapes flickered in the darkness.

"Looks like we're trapped," she said. It hurt to speak.

Max glanced over his shoulder. "Give me the gun."

"No way." Ann elbowed herself up into a sitting position. Over the noise of the helicopters, she could hear the sound of running boots.

"Get behind me," she said. She raised the gun and took a peep through the shattered windows of the car: the soldiers were closing.

To slow them down, she fired the last of her ammunition one-handed, and dropped to the dusty ground, wincing at the pain in her cheek.

Then she turned around and rested her back against the crash barrier. The pistol dangled from her fingertips.

"I guess this is it, then," she said. She flicked a glance at Max. "Listen, I-"

47

Her words were cut off by a sonic boom.

Something hit one of the choppers. Smoke billowed from its engine. It rose into the air and drifted towards the bridge.

Ann grabbed Max and pushed him to the floor.

"Get down!"

She heard the helicopter hit the parapet. It struck the span and recoiled, wobbling crazily as the pilot fought to regain control. Then it hit the ground on the far side of the motorway and its tail broke off. The main rotors dug into the soft earth bank and snapped, whipping the cockpit into the concrete bridge support, smashing it like an egg.

Moments later, a mirrored teardrop fell from the clouds. It slammed to a halt centimetres above the road, blocking all three lanes of the carriageway. Distorted reflections rippled on its curved surfaces.

The advancing troops froze, suddenly exposed and vulnerable in the centre of the carriageway.

"Get up," Ann said. She grabbed the netbook and hauled Max to his feet. They ran along the inside of the crash barrier, towards the ship. There were shouts from the soldiers, and she braced herself for shooting. No shots came. Instead, there was a flash of red light from the teardrop's tip, and when she looked back, the soldiers were lying in the central lane, charred and dead.

"Holy shit," Max said.

She pushed him forward. A hatch opened in the rippling hull and they bundled inside.

They lay panting, side-by-side on the cold deck of the airlock.

From inside, the hull wall appeared transparent. They could see everything: the bridge over the motorway; the dead soldiers; the waiting traffic; and the second helicopter rising into the air in an effort to escape.

Another red beam stabbed from the teardrop and the helicopter burst into pieces. Flaming debris spattered the road.

Ann dragged Max through the inner airlock door, into the

ship's cabin. It was circular. There were acceleration couches ringing the wall. A glass, liquid-filled pillar stood in the centre. Floating inside was the shaven head, torso, and abdomen of a young boy. A thick bundle of wires protruded from the base of his skull, linking him into the ship's instruments. Black rubber sleeves hid the stumps of his amputated limbs, the nerves spliced into the navigation systems. Whatever the liquid was, he appeared to be breathing it.

"Please, take a seat," he said, his watery voice bubbling from a speaker set into the base of the column.

Max gawped. The kid was maybe seventeen years old. There were spots around his mouth. He wasn't a professional pilot; he looked like kind of a geek.

"This is John," Ann said, still pressing the handkerchief to her torn face. "He's one of our best."

Through the transparent hull, blue lights flashed beyond the headlights of the stalled traffic: the emergency services were coming. She pulled Max over to the acceleration couches and they strapped in.

"Okay John," she said, "why don't you take us up?"

In the glass column, the boy grinned at her. He had braces on his teeth. He said, "Ladies and gentlemen, please fasten your seatbelts and return your trays to the upright position."

He closed his eyes and the drop-shaped ship punched into the sky without a sound. The ground fell away so fast Max cried out. Below them, the flaming wreck of the helicopter dwindled to a spark. The orange streetlights of Oxford and High Wycombe shrank until they resembled the embers of scattered campfires. Then they were through the cloud layer and rising toward a clear sky filled with stars.

Max looked down at his bloody hands. He said, "Jesus, what a mess."

Beside him, Ann dabbed her cheek. It still hurt like hell.

"I've gone to a lot of trouble to get you out, Max. I could have left you down there."

Max pushed up his glasses and rubbed his eyes. He looked at the amputee floating in the glass column and shuddered.

"He's just a kid."

Ann followed his gaze. "He used to be a hacker, like you. He's got a real feel for systems, an intuition that normal test pilots lack."

She turned her face to him. "As I said, we always need bright young minds."

Max looked at her in horror. "You want to put *me* in one of those tanks?"

Ann shrugged. "Think of it as your chance to volunteer."

The Harvest

Kim Lakin-Smith

Ridgeway School squatted in its nest of run-off chalk and clay. Gas light shone from tall windows fitted with slats of pig iron. Shadows moved behind lime-washed glass, small and flitting. Shadows of children. Young voices filtered out, dissolving on the misty air.

High up on one side of the bell tower, the steam clock struck nine. The bell stayed silent, long rusted to its hinges. Instead, a hand bell rang out through the vaulted classrooms, narrow corridors and echoing hall. When the clanging ceased, the school answered back with a low moan – wind beating at the rafters – the dry thwump-thwump of the furnace bellows in the boiler room, and the rattle of the radiators as they gave off their filmy heat.

Inside the small reception office, Bluze Christchurch was generating a letter to the parents on her typewriter ball. The concave keyboard didn't allow for a view of the document being created, but Bluze attacked the keys with confidence. She gave the last character a decisive punch. Sliding the typewriter away on its thin metal tracks, she held up the page. The reconstituted paper was the same off-white as Ridgeway School's exterior.

She read aloud: "…Need volunteers to patch the library roof, apply lime-wash sealant and re-bracket with spare pig iron."

"Spare pig iron?" The woman who appeared at the doorway snorted. Tucked up in rolls of her own fat, May Moon was chief dinner lady and pig slaughterer. She kept blood in the creases at her elbows. Her hat was a ward matron's – crisp, white and authoritarian.

"Never know unless you ask." Bluze took a fresh sheet off the stack between the wood pulping hand-mixer and the twin metal plates of a papermaking press. Unscrewing the typewriter's ink feed cap, she reached for a large stoneware bottle that was stained bluish-black. She uncorked the bottle and topped up the ink reservoir.

May watched from the doorway. "Want to put on gloves before you mess with that poison. You never know what it's made from. Could be Devil's Rain, could be effluence." She spread out the vowels of this last word, pleased with her use of it.

"I make it myself. Every morning I mix two solutions, iron salts and tannic acids." Bluze stabbed the cork back into the bottle. "Nails and vinegar, and an extraction of oak galls." She glanced up and smiled. "Don't want to develop a case of Sticky Skin, do I? We've enough mayhem dealing with eighty kids, let alone inviting the sickness in."

The other woman stared back. Her lip curled. "Got to go scrub up... with filtered water." Retreating to the hallway, she continued to stare in. "We got need for eggs. Hens have gone grey at the legs and are only good for eating. I told Mr Gower, leave birds wallowing like pigs in their own mire and they're gonna go grey-legged."

It didn't surprise Bluze to hear that the headmaster was uninterested in May's drenched farmyard. Ridgeway's inner courtyard might well produce the meat for meals and the dung cakes to fuel the boiler, but it was also responsible for the underlying stench of mildewed feathers and animal shit that permeated the school.

Not that Bluze had any interest in stoking the feud between the two factions. She nodded. "I'll add a request for eggs."

May eyed the typewriter with suspicion. "Uh-huh." She slumped off down the corridor.

Out on the Ridgeway, the wind punished the last of the beech trees and broadleaves, branches straining against its bite. Rain soaked down from a roiling sky. Either side of the ancient path, the hills were beaten back to a chalk undercrust. A wash of white swept down and out across the plains.

It started thirty years earlier. 2009, fifteen million worth of waste treatment plant opened in Westbury. The site was dedicated to the transfer, bulking up, acid neutralisation and solidification of waste. The stewing pot included pharmaceutical, photographic, printing, painting, laboratory chemicals, acids, alkalis, solvents, chlorinated hydrocarbons, cyanide compounds and elemental chemical waste. The resultant fly ash was intended for controlled disposal in Bishop's Cleeve and Stoke Orchard, Gloucestershire. The railcar incident at 20.18BMT on 22nd February saw an unseasonable north-easterly wind carry 40 tonnes of fly ash into the atmosphere over south-east England, though it drifted further.

For a country ravaged by political divide, the fall of acid rain – or Devil's Rain as it became known colloquially – was just another environmental issue to wrangle over. For the families affected by its fall and a resultant sickness called Sticky Skin, the incident proved devastating. Wiltshire became the 'Whited Out' county. Home to ghosts, ancient burials, and the Harvesters.

The Harvesters were men, or had been before the sickness curdled their looks and minds and they took to mixing mechanical bolt-ons with the living flesh they stole from others. Over their shoulders they carried giant keep-nets. In the folds of long leather kilts they kept weapons – serrated blades and keratin-shelled Sone guns. Warrior-like in their black armour, they moved noiselessly over the pale land.

Pig iron furnaces littered the hills like demon eyes. Inbetween, the housing pods were scattered. Slathered with a plaster of lime-kiln dust mixed with clay from the north-west hills, the barrows resisted the rain. But they were vulnerable as snails' shells to the footfall of the Harvesters.

Except, the dry leathered bodies of the old and the furnace workers were not to the invaders' taste. Their eyes were on closer quarry – the large lime-choked building with a bell tower.

The boy pressed his face into the monitor mask located alongside the meshed hatch. Words filtered out into the passage, the voice tinny and distorted.

"Thank you, Sam. I'm pressing the buzzer to let you in."

He pulled away from the chilled metal. Weak daylight flooded his corneas. The thin rasp of the buzzer sounded. He grasped the handle of the heavy dividing door – reinforced on the inside with wavy sheets of pig iron and thick wooden buttresses – and entered the main lobby of the school.

"Late again, Sam?" The secretary, Ms Christchurch, put her head around the door of her office. Ms Christchurch had a wide smile that showed her gums, bright red hair that fell lankly around her shoulders, and a tendency to seem smaller than the rest of the teachers and staff at Ridgeway.

He nodded. "My mother got a frickentickle in her throat. Couldn't walk me here and I'd already missed the Sledge."

Ms Christchurch smiled. Her eyes flitted between the boy and the handgun she was polishing. "Never known you catch the school bus, Sam. As for your mother, you ought to get her some elm syrup. Has she ever seen you to school?"

Sam scratched his hairline, chasing a louse. "Sometime maybe." He undid the heavy layers of blanket and sealskin that had protected him from the acid rain and shook them off like a dog. Then he slumped off down the corridor in the direction of his classroom, dragging the heavy layers of outerwear behind him.

The room was silent but for the knocks and sighs of steaming water in the radiators. Each child sat spine-straight and alert. Overhead, a large gas lamp gave off its insubstantial glow. Rain attacked the high windows like tiny beating fists.

"Burrow down. Lock up. Don't make a sound," repeated the

class in unison.

"Again," said the headmaster, Mr Gower. A dry scab of a man.

"Burrow down. Lock up…"

"Sam Devises!" Mr Gower looked over his half-moon glasses.

The children broke off.

Sam stared down the barrel of a blackboard eraser.

"I suppose you have no need to fear the Harvesters." Mr Gower reared. "I suppose they won't have use for your skin, your fat, your organs."

Sam stared back. The headmaster sucked in his cheeks. He retracted the eraser and presented the boy with a folder.

"Since you were last to class and so clearly well versed in what to do should the bastards break in, you can take the register to Ms Christchurch."

The front door to Ridgeway School softly unclicked. Wind swept into the passage like a biblical flood, scooping up all that lay in its path: dried mud, skeletal leaves, the odour of not-quite-clean. The door drew to.

Bluze did not trust the sound. This was how they came, too quietly, where the children and parents brrr'd against the cold or coughed or squabbled.

The mesh at the hatch was woven on a slant which enabled her to see out but prevented those outside from looking in. She depressed a slim iron lever to one side of her desk. A set of kick steps smoothly unfolded. She climbed them and stood on the desk, feet ledged between the paper-stack and the large irons of the press. Her fingers moved as lightly over the munitions rig as they had over the typewriter ball. She selected a pair of ear defenders: tiny, tight-fitting shells secured by a thin black harness that fed across the forehead and looped in tight around the back of the head. The pockets of the utility vest she wore were already packed with cartridges and spark dust. She snatched up a couple of sawn-offs, packed in the fat magazines, crossed her arms behind her head and packed the ammo down into her back harness. The hand gun she'd polished earlier went into a hip holster. A bowie knife slotted in at the side seam of the utility vest. A brace of thin black sparklers clicked into the sprung brackets to form an 'X' over her chest.

Pinning up her knee-length skirt at either hip in a well-practised series of folds and garter snaps, she kicked on steel toecaps around her blue buckled biker boots and leapt off the table in a backwards somersault.

She yanked out the voice funnel alongside the window hatch.

"Face to the mask," she barked.

Ten seconds later there had been no response from the other side of the mesh. A Harvester would trigger the mask's magnetism, the quantity of metal additives to their flesh signalling them as the flesh-warriors they were.

Bluze checked the grip of her ear defenders. They were snug. Blood roared inside her head like a hurricane. She eased up to the grid and peeped through. At first she saw nothing but the empty corridor. Then a huge shadow blocked the greater part of her view. She got an impression of other figures, but, before she could focus in, she felt a sharp tug on her arm.

She spun around and brought her handgun up under the chin of the boy, Sam. The kid didn't blink, just offered his class register. Bluze put a finger to her lips. Placing the folder in its correct tray on the desk, she slid open a drawer and retrieved a spare pair of ear defenders.

"Put these on," she mouthed. The Harvesters were clearly opting to save their Sone weapons until they were closer to their prey, else the boy would be twitching on the ground, mouth frothing.

Sam put the ear defenders on. He'd the look of a kid who had lived so long with fear that he'd developed a thick skin against it.

She pointed at a large red dial on the wall.

The kid nodded and she lifted him up by the waist. She watched him struggle to unhook the wind handle, felt the soft expulsion of air from his chest as he grunted and revolved the alarm dial. Bluze knew the signal would filter out silently through the building while triggering a stopcock on the gas feed to each lamp to plunge the school into semi-darkness. Valves in the radiators would open, releasing a steady blast of hot steam to fill each classroom with its own early morning mist. Harvesters were used to the acid rainfall outside, but the sickness cramped their joints in the steamy heat.

As for the children, they would be donning their ear plugs, crawling into the individual panic rooms of their lock-ups, and bolting the door to each metre-sized cube on the inside. Then silence would fall and the waiting would begin.

She didn't have time to get the boy safely back to class. He'd have to take his chance in the tiny reception office.

"Harvesters," she mouthed and pointed to the mesh. The kid followed her finger. "You stay here." She mimed the instruction with absurd emphasis.

No reaction appeared to mean agreement as far as the seven year old was concerned. Bluze peered through the mesh again – just as a Harvester brought his face to the magnetic mask and broke it in two with a head-butt. Seconds later, shockwaves off a crushed semtex strip knocked Bluze sideways. She clutched the boy to her; he felt stiff in her embrace. She thrust him away.

"Stay here," she mouthed.

Bluze slid up to the door and opened it. The corridor was dusty from the blast, and empty. No doubt, the Harvesters had retreated as far away as possible while the blast punched in the dividing door. She ducked out into the dust, pulling the door to behind her.

Reaching over her shoulders, she drew the sawn-offs, pressed her back against the wall and glanced left then right. Her stoppered ears threatened to play havoc with her balance. But better to deal with that potential disability than fall victim to the Sone gun and end up on her back.

She saw the shapes of the Harvesters forming through the dust cloud. Running down the corridor to where it hooked a sharp right, she leapt onto a rickety chair and up on top of a locker cabinet. Biker boots planted firmly on the sheet steel, she swung the automatic 12 gauge sawn-offs up in unison.

The Harvesters materialised. Seven of them, by her quick head count. Half living-scarecrow, half reanimated, the men pressed towards her. She peeled off a dozen shots, striking an arm, a shoulder blade, a cheekbone. The red flashes as the AA shot landed told her that she had hit metal mostly. But one brute took a canon-punch to the face; the patched flesh tearing back to reveal bone and welded metal. Bluze fired another couple of shots in the direction of that one. The head ricocheted back at a distorted neck angle.

But the others were on her now. Six devils who'd cut the flesh from others to re-patch their acid-scorched skulls and upper backs. They were broad, made so by the metal grafted under and on top of their human bones. Their height was just as sinister; they rose up and retracted on long, spindle limbs like human spiders.

Two drew their serrated blades and lunged for her. Bluze raced to the end of the lockers, thrusting off with one foot at the last second. She leaped upwards. A ceiling tile popped as she slammed a fist into it. Grasping the iron framework either side, she levered herself up inside the false ceiling.

Her breath came in tight, agonising bursts. A blade shot up into the ceiling space; she bucked backwards, only to roll sideways when a second point broke through and swiftly withdrew.

Their interest in her was short-lived. Bluze knew the Harvesters had come for the children, lured by the possibility of those young bodies with their fresh living cells and bone growth. Adults were an irritant, best ignored or despatched with no more care than a child tearing off a butterfly's wings.

The Harvesters headed for the first classroom. Bluze knew she would need to get closer yet retain her higher ground in order to take them out.

Sam stood in the office. He slipped off the ear protectors. They were uncomfortable, plus they brought to mind dark crevices where a child might sleep unnoticed. He discarded them.

Standing in the room, he noticed mist seeping under the door. A small window in the door had escaped the lime-wash. Through it, he saw an atmosphere of steam and dust that reminded him of fog out on the hills and the spill of rain.

He considered trying to reach the handle of the alarm again. It had been fun to turn the dial around and around. He'd pictured the children scrabbling past their desks like mice desperate to escape an overflowing drain, and how the teachers had donned ear protectors and run away to the staff room, leaving the young boxed up and alone. This was the first time he'd experienced a harvest free of the constraints of his own one-metre cube.

He gripped the door handle and stepped out into the corridor. Either side of the narrow passageway, radiators piped a continual flow of steam. They fizzed slightly under the effort, water knock-knocking inside their tin ribs.

Sam turned and walked down the corridor towards the first classroom. His view was obscured by the false mist and he drew up sharply. A Harvester occupied the space ahead, pinned steel craning out from beneath a long leather kilt. The not-quite-man started to shrink down; Sam felt the space between them growing smaller.

Now he saw there was no head to the thing, only flopping neck threads and arms that clawed just short of him.

Sam crouched down and lay flat on the floor. Drops of burning water splashed onto him from the ceiling. Condensing steam. He inched slowly forward, beneath the reach of the swaying headless carcass.

Bluze moved across the framework of the false ceiling in a crab-like motion. The classrooms had the original vaulted ceilings, her only option being to scoop out the two tiles directly next to the doorway, hook her legs over the metal bars and propel her body down. She prayed to all that was holy that she survived to swing back up.

Stowing the sawn-offs at her back, she uncrossed the two black sparklers from their harness at her chest. Tucking them into one palm, she slid the opposite hand into a pocket of her utility vest and nipped out two precious packets. Spark dust was expensive but effective, possessing the same magnetic signifiers as the monitor mask. She fed the packets into the batons, used two fingers to press in the load springs and flipped the ignition switch. A tiny spark appeared at the tip of each baton. She held them carefully away from her body, took a deep breath and dropped.

Legs hooked over the frame, she swung upside-down at the open doorway and fired the sparklers with a splatter-gun approach. Harvesters recoiled from their efforts to prised open the boltholes where the children hid. Hands clutched at their Frankenstein's monster faces. Spark dust. A cloud-mass of nanites that grouped together to form centimetre-long metal grubs that attached themselves to the Harvesters' metal nips and tucks, then found the soft connecting flesh and began to burrow in. If the Harvesters were swift, they could peel the grubs off and squash them underfoot like swollen leeches.

Two of the invaders drove through the pain to attack her. The first bled from one eye. She saw grubs inching in at a plate stitched beneath the eye socket, and felt a wave of revulsion. The distraction gave the man the chance to attack. He drove his blade into her shoulder and dragged it free. Bluze gasped, lost her leg hold and crashed down onto the floor.

She flipped onto her hands, spine bowing, and landed, hopping back a couple of steps. The two Harvesters bucked against the agonies of the spark dust, but carried on coming. The slash of their blades had brute strength but lacked skill. She ducked, drew her bowie knife out the seam of her utility vest and volleyed. Tucking in tight under the first brute's underarm, she scored the blade along the tender flesh. Immediately, she faced the second monster. Again she used the knife. The spark dust grubs acted as a dye, indicating the weak spots. She bowed back to avoid the tremendous swing of the Harvester's blade, stood up straight and slid her knife in quickly at the neck sinews. The grubs crept in at the open flesh. She abandoned the two Harvesters to those drilling mites. They were walking dead men.

Through the steam, she saw one of the monsters work his serrated blade into the door seal of the first of the miniature panic rooms. The spark dust must have disintegrated; it was a temporal weapon that dissolved two minutes after impact. She considered loading her two remaining packets into the sparklers. Better to save them and take the creature out by hand, she decided. She started to stride towards him, bowie knife dancing like a silver fish in that sea of half-light. Her breath caught as a colossus stepped across her path.

The Harvester was a witch's poppet stitched from different shades of skin. Leather strips crisscrossed the length of each arm, mummifying them. In place of hair, long black feathers were grafted to his skull. Half of the face had melted back to the bone. Small riveted steel sheets covered the remainder of the face, like scales.

He had a Sone Gun trained on her. She looked down. A tiny red dot danced over her chest.

Bluze felt a crush of nausea as the sonic waves hit. She fell off to the side, her hands clawing until she found and collapsed against the wall. The sound blast was repelled by her ear protectors, but the noise still managed to assault her at a cellular level. Her head swam. Shapes loomed.

Get back up, Bluze demanded of herself. *Make your legs carry you before the monsters use their blades.* She felt them closing in. Flesh and metal warriors with minds like ice. She had to get control back. She had to fight to save herself.

Bluze strained to see past the billowing white. The shapes were gone. Her mind quietened. Steam drifted.

She pressed her palms against the moist wall and stood up. It terrified her to think of the Harvesters having moved on to the classroom belonging to Ridgeway's five to seven year olds. She remembered Sam. A strange child. Stiff as an armful of frozen washing when she'd lifted him up. She hoped he endured back in her office.

The bulky figure that materialised through the mist had Bluze reach over her shoulders for the sawn-offs. She froze mid-act as the figure took on the vaguely feminine aspect of the dinner lady, Mrs Moon. The woman carried a meat cleaver in one hand, a Harvester's head suspended by the hair in the other. Bluze was used to seeing the woman waddling through school, some decapitated animal clutched to her breast like a ragdoll. The sight of Mrs Moon in possession of a human head seemed perversely acceptable.

The woman performed a grand mime of taking off a pair of imaginary ear protectors. Bluze caught on. Begrudgingly she held one headphone out from an ear.

"Mrs Moon?"

"Bastard Harvester tried to muck in with my beasts," said the woman with bright-eyed excitement. "Maybe he fancied plucking himself a new pair of eyebrows or cooking up stew. Either way, he's dead now." Mrs Moon grinned ghoulishly. Shaking the head at Bluze, she added, "You can take them ear plates off. The nasties and their Sone guns are out of range. Saw the lot shuffle off to Mr Gower's classroom."

Despite the dinner lady's reassurance, Bluze desperately wanted to keep her ear defenders in place. But closing off her hearing was resulting in an increasing sense of claustrophobia. Plus, it was easier to stalk the enemy when she was in possession of all five senses.

"I've got to catch them up," she said.

Mrs Moon tossed the Harvester's head off into the cloudy atmosphere. She placed a hand on Bluze's undamaged shoulder, fingers gripping in.

"Funny how it's left to a bit like you to save the babies. We ain't about to see Mr Gower risking his neck out here." She released Bluze and scrubbed her hand around her fleshy chin. "Our headmaster's too scared the Harvesters will tear his pretty face. Truth of it, as you and I have witnessed, is the nasties'll let grownups alone if there's young 'uns to be had." She leant in conspiratorially. Her breath stank of straw and vinegar. "But you and I, we ain't going to let it unravel like that."

The boy walked through the steam and approached the staffroom door. He held up a fist and knocked. The door opened a crack, a great many safety chains pulling taut.

Mr Gower peered out. His eyes were nervous as a cat's, switching every which way. They settled on Sam and tightened.

"Sam Radley. Why are you out of your lock up? The alarm to give the all clear hasn't sounded yet."

"Harvesters are here," said the kid plainly.

"I'd gathered." The headmaster's mouth queered.

Sam kept on staring up at the man. "Ms Christchurch is fighting them on her own, Mr Gower."

"As is her job as secretary and school security." The headmaster's voice matched Sam's for inexpressiveness.

A second face peered over the headmaster's shoulder. Miss Keggle, the school nurse. Her features melted into a mask of fear.

"Shut the child out, Robert!" she exclaimed. "We don't want Harvesters blundering near here by accident."

"I suggest you tuck yourself away somewhere, Sam, if you don't want to end up in a Harvester's keep net."

The door to the staffroom closed, leaving Sam alone in the dark corridor.

Bluze eased in alongside the door to the classroom housing Ridgeway's youngest. Mrs Moon shuffled in behind her. With her ear defenders back in place, Bluze couldn't tell what was occurring inside the room. Mrs Moon, though, had refused to wear the standard ear plugs provided for all staff and pupils. "Just let those bastards try to put me down with a bit o' noise," she'd told Bluze minutes earlier. Folding her arms over her chest, breasts bundled up like egg sacks, she'd added, "Reckon I can holler louder than any of them flesh freaks or their Sone guns." Bluze hadn't seen the point in arguing with the woman. Instead she stood alongside her outside the classroom and prayed Mrs Moon would prove more help than hindrance.

She felt a rap to her bleeding shoulder. Glancing back, she saw the dinner lady pretend to rub her eyes with her fists, a mock crying motion.

The children! Bluze fought against her natural terror, balled the emotion in the pit of her stomach and used it to fuel her attack. Tucking her last spark dust packets into the twin batons, she stepped across the doorway, raised her arms and fired. The powder sprayed into the mist with the quick release of a puffball fungus.

Throwing the emptied batons aside, Bluze strode into the room. Several of the children's' lockups had been prised open and the Sone guns fired to render the youngsters passive. The kids twitched, as if they shared one nervous system inside the large keep-net. If they cried or whimpered, Bluze was glad she could not hear it.

While the largest marauder continued his vile harvest, the others beat off the spark dust grubs to redirect their attention to the newcomers. Bluze stood her ground and let the first two come for her. Mrs Moon was keener to get into it and charged head-on at a third, meat cleaver raised. The dinner lady fought with a slice-and-dice motion, powering into the Harvester with bullish grit. Bluze, meanwhile, had drawn her sawn-offs. She wondered why the Harvesters facing her didn't draw their Sone guns. Then she noticed the convulsing children held in each brute's grasp.

Bluze tried to aim. The combination of children as a shield and the steaming environment meant she couldn't get a clear shot. At least not immediately. While the Harvesters staggered towards her, dragging the children along as easily as sacks of feathers, Bluze made a quick assessment of the lockups, teacher's desk, small tables and two dozen wooden chairs. Her gaze lifted to the unlit gas lamp overhead, a huge bowl of dank green glass.

She rammed the sawn-offs into the back harness and ran between the two Harvesters. Both launched their serrated blades out at her in unison. She dodged the blows; the blades clashed off one another, steel sparking. The wooden chairs became stepping stones; she skipped across those and onto the desk, where her footfall sent papers flying. She kicked off and up onto the first set of lockups – and couldn't help imagining the children cooped up inside. The Harvesters were on her tail, their human shields tucked inside the crook of one arm, leaving the other free to wield a serrated blade. The sharp steel sliced into the lockups as she dodged, flashes lighting up the darkness. She propelled herself off the far edge of the lockup cabinet, hands grasping for the silhouetted shape overhead. She got a grip with one hand, the other clutching wildly at thin air. A brief instant of floundering then her hand found its grip on the gas light. Bluze pulled herself up, each breath a painful squeeze and tug. The huge bowl threatened to tip under her weight; its fastening held tight and she fought her way up to stand, legs straddling the curve of heavy opaque glass.

She retrieved the sawn-offs. Below, the Harvesters pinned the young hostages across their organ-rich bodies. But Bluze had her clear shots now. She aimed in-between the plated metal at the vulnerable skulls and fired. The guns kicked back. She sucked in air against the pain from her stabbed shoulder. The Harvesters would have felt the blaze of pain as well, if only for an instant as their skulls burst. The hostages broke free from the slackened grip as the Harvesters' bodies slumped.

Across the room, Bluze made out a clash of Titans, Mrs Moon versus her opponent. The dinner lady had the upper hand as she brought her meat cleaver down twice in quick succession, taking off a hunk of the creature's forearm then a slice of face. But just as it seemed Mrs Moon would win herself another head, the Harvester delivered a lethal stab with his serrated blade. Mrs Moon took the length of it through the chest. Bluze was glad of the distance between them. She was spared the old maid's look of shock at the death blow, how the eyes would fix wide, drained of excitement and horribly pitiful, how the mouth would pop-pop for air and at last be still.

She could offer Mrs Moon one consolation. Bluze took out the Harvester with a single shot to the throat.

Sam walked back from the staffroom, trailing a hand along the steam-soaked wall. He didn't understand why the teachers canned themselves away in the staffroom. Adults had bodies which could achieve so much. Then again, they were just as easily broken, he concluded, turning into his classroom to be met with the sight of slain Harvesters and the crumpled body of Mrs Moon.

He focused on Ms Christchurch, standing on top of the vast gas lamp that was suspended from the ceiling.

"Hello," he said.

Opposite was a huge birdman of a Harvester. The man stared at the child and put down his keep net, already half full of children. Producing his Sone Gun, the Harvester trained it on the boy while Ms Christchurch worked hard to perforate the brute's armour with shots from her sawn-offs.

The Harvester fired the Sone gun. In spite of her ear protectors, Ms Christchurch appeared mildly stunned and fell from the gas lamp, landing on the desk in a sprawl of limbs. Immediately, she was fighting to stand again.

Sam winced. He stayed upright though and pointed a finger at the crenulated Sone gun. "They don't work properly on me."

The Harvester discarded the gun and produced a pair of colossal serrated blades. He whipped them in front of his body like a silver Catherine Wheel.

"Goodbye," said Sam, and he turned and ran out of the classroom.

Behind him, the Harvester forgot his existing catch and focused on the live mouse of a boy who'd darted away. Tucking the blades in tight to his elbows, he ran out the doorway on steel-pinned limbs.

What did the kid think he was doing offering himself as live bait? Bluze threw aside her emptied sawn-offs and strode determinedly out of the classroom.

The Harvester had discarded his Sone gun. She removed her ear protectors and broke into a jog. Hearing the steel clug of metalmorphosed limbs further along the corridor, she sped up, running past a blur of lockers, water fountains and stairwells.

She stopped suddenly. A wheeze of sprung steel alerted her to the opening of the heavy boiler room door. Her heart got tight. She approached the door, inched it open and slid through the crack.

Inside, the pyramids of dung bricks had been demolished where the child had presumably scrabbled over while the Harvester's twin blades gorged out hunks of the stuff. Ahead, the huge algal water tank was running dangerously low; the school's steamy atmosphere was beginning to dissipate, which would allow the Harvester to move even more easily. The tank was hooked up to the furnace and colossal bellows by a great many pipes. Rigged with levers, hose, and a stitched skin of bolt plates, the furnace exuded a rich red glow.

The boy stood silhouetted before a large glass window in the furnace door. Meanwhile, the Harvester became less human-seeming than arachnid. He craned up on two fat limbs of scaffolded metal. Each limb split into four. Squatting over the centre of the room, limbs craning out in all directions, the invader wove the serrated blades above his head, an action that reminded Bluze of silk being spun from spinnerets. The blades were brought to bear on the child like huge fangs.

Bluze opted for higher ground. She charged into the room's bloody glow. Suppressing her instinctual revulsion at contact with the thing, she clamped her hands around the nearest metal limb and climbed. The Harvester bucked in an effort to shake her off. But she continued to climb, slicing her palms on the sharp, bolted rods.

Sam stood below, a small morsel with ever-staring eyes. The Harvester clattered forward, the folds and feathers in his skin scraping up against the hot boiler. Bluze gasped as her own thigh made contact with the roasting plate. She drew her handgun, positioned it against the soft meat beneath the intruder's chin and fired.

The Sledge drew up to the main entrance, a ravaged hole of dust and brick after the grenade blast. Children began to climb aboard the idling school bus, a mechanical warthog with spines of pig iron sticking out at every angle and fat bull bars.

Bluze had already started working on the punctured door, retooling the lock mechanism. She waved off the children, a monkey wrench in one hand, a fistful of fresh bolts in the other. "See you tomorrow, Lloyd," she called, and, "Walk don't run, Meg." Wincing, she put a hand to her shoulder where she had stitched her skin. The burn at her thigh pulsed angrily. "Don't forget to hand the letter to your parents," she called after the rabble, adding, "And ask for any spare eggs!"

"Ms Christchurch." Mr Gower appeared alongside her, blocking out the weak afternoon sun.

"Afternoon, headmaster."

"Congratulations on fending off the raid." The man sniffed and pushed his half-moon glasses up the bridge of his nose. "With Mrs Moon departed, we'll need someone else to tend the farmyard. The teachers voted and allocated you the job. We have our hands full looking after the children."

Bluze would have responded, perhaps with a brief nod, a generous smile or a monkey wrench smashed into the headmaster's ungracious face. But the man had already stalked back inside.

The Sledge pulled away, honking goodbye. Bluze watched the bus recede into the misty landscape.

She became aware of the boy at her side.

"Did you teach yourself to lip-read, Sam?" she asked, staring down.

He nodded.

Bluze nodded too. The boy was deaf. It explained why the Sone gun had barely registered with him.

"What happened to your parents?"

"They got the Sticky Skin. I ran away."

"And you've been living...?"

"In the woods behind the school." The boy wrinkled his nose. For the first time, Bluze saw a hint of real human emotion. "It's frightening at night," he said.

Bluze put the wrench down on the floor just inside the blast hole. She eased up the folds of oil skin and cloth around her face. It was beginning to drizzle.

Reaching down, she adjusted the boy's outerwear to protect him. He peeped at her from inside his hood. Bluze tried not to think about the hours the child had endured out in the freezing woods, or how the Devil's Rain may have already started to eat its way into his skin.

She extended a hand and the boy took it.

"You'd best come home with me," she said.

They walked down the chalk path, away from Ridgeway School.

The War Artist

Tony Ballantyne

My name is Brian Garlick and I carry an easel into battle.

Well, in reality I carry a sketch book and several cameras, but I like to give people a picture of me they can understand.

The sergeant doesn't understand me, though. He's been staring since we boarded the flier in Marseilles. Amongst the nervous conversation of the troops, their high-pitched laughter like spumes of spray on a restless sea, he is a half-submerged rock. He's focussing on me with dark eyes and staring, staring, staring. As the voices fade to leave no sound but the whistle of the wind and the creak of the pink high-visibility straps binding the equipment bundles, he's still staring, and I know he's going to undermine me. I've seen that look before, though less often than you might expect. Most soldiers are interested in what I do, but there are always those who seem to take my presence as an insult to their profession. Here it comes...

"I don't get it," he says. "Why do we need a war artist?"

The other soldiers are watching. Eyes wide, their breath fast and shallow, but they've just found something to distract them from the coming fight. Well, I have my audience; it's time to make my pitch to try and get them on my side for the duration of the coming action.

"That's a good question," I reply. I smile, and I start to paint a picture. A picture of the experienced old hand, the unruffled professional.

"Someone once said a good artist paints what can't be

71

painted. Well, that's what a war artist is supposed to do."

"You paint what can't be painted," says the Sergeant. It's to his credit he doesn't make the obvious joke. For the moment he's intrigued, and I take advantage of the fact.

"They said Breughel could paint the thunder," I say. "You can paint lightning, sure, but can you make the viewer *hear* the thunder? Can you make them *feel* that rumble, deep in their stomach? That's the job of a war artist, to paint what can't be painted. You can photograph the battle, you can show the blood and the explosions, but does that picture tell the full story? I try to capture the excitement, the fear, the terror." I look around the rows of pinched faces, eyes shiny. "I try to show the heroism."

I've composed my picture now, I surreptitiously snap it. That veneer of pride that overlays the hollow fear filling the flier as it travels through the skies.

The sergeant sneers, the mood evaporates.

"What do *you* know about all that?"

I see the bitter smiles of the other soldiers. So I paint another picture. I lean forward and speak in a low voice.

"I've been doing this for six years. I was in Tangiers after the first Denial of Service attack. I was in Barcelona when the entire Spanish banking system was wiped out; I was in Geneva when the Swiss government network locked. I know what we're flying into, I know what it's like to visit a State targeted by hackers."

There are some approving nods at this. Or is it just the swaying of the craft as we jump an air pocket? Either way, the sergeant isn't going to be convinced.

"Maybe you've seen some action," he concedes. "Maybe you've been shot at. That doesn't make you one of us. You take off the fatigues and you're just another civilian. You won't get jostled in the street back home, or refused service in shops. You won't have people calling you a butcher, when all you've tried to do is defend their country."

This gets the troops right back on his side. I see the memory of the taunts and the insults written on their faces. Too many people were against us getting involved in the Eurasian war, numbers that have only grown since the fighting started. There's a cold look in the troops' eyes. But I can calm them, I know what to say.

"That's why the government sent me here. A war artist communicates the emotions their patron chooses. That's why war artists are nearly always to be found acting in an official capacity. I'm here to tell *your* side of the story, to counteract those images you see on the web."

That's the truth, too. Well, almost the truth. It's enough to calm them down. They're on my side. Nearly all of them, anyway. The sergeant is still not convinced, but I don't think he ever will be.

"I don't like it," he says. "You've said it yourself, what you're painting isn't real war..."

All that's academic now as the warning lights start to flash: orange sheets of fire engulfing the flier's interior. I photograph the scene, dark bodies lost in the background, faces like flame in the foreground, serious, stern, brave faces, awaiting the coming battle. That's the image I will create, anyway.

"Get ready!" calls the sergeant.

There's a sick feeling in my stomach as we drop towards the battle and I wonder, how can I show that?

A shriek of engines, a surge of deceleration and a jolt and we're down and the rear ramp is falling...

We land in a city somewhere in southern Europe. Part of what used to be Italy, I guess. Red bricks, white plaster, green tiles. I hear gunfire, but it's some distance away. I smell smoke, I hear the sound of feet on the metal ramp, the rising howl of the flier's engines as it prepares to lift off again. I see buildings, a narrow road leading uphill to a blue sky and a yellow sun. I smell something amidst the smoke, something that seems incongruous in this battle scene. Something that reminds me of parties and dinners and dates with women. It takes me a moment in all the confusion of movement to realise what it is.

Red wine. It's running down the street. Not a euphemism, there's a lorry at the top of the hill, on its side, the front smashed where it's run into a wall, the driver's arm drooping from the open window, the silver clasp of his watch popped open so it hangs like a bracelet... Jewels of broken glass are scattered on the road, diamonds from the windshield, rubies from the truck's lights and emeralds from the broken bottles that are spilling red blood down the street. It's such a striking image that, instinctively, I begin snapping.

The soldiers are flattening themselves against the vine-clad walls that border the street, the chameleon material of their suits changing to dusty white, their guns humming as they autoscan the surrounding area. Their half-seen figures are edging their way up and down the hill, changing colour, becoming the red of doors and the dusty dark of windows. They're sizing up the area, doing their job, just like me, cameras in my hand, in my helmet, at my belt. Sizing up the scene.

The peacefulness of the street is at odds with the tension we feel, and I need to capture that. The lazy smell of the midday heat mixed with wine. Lemons hanging waxy from the trees leaning over the white walls, paint peeling from window frames. A soldier pauses to touch the petals trailing from a hanging basket and I photograph that.

As if in response to my action, someone opens fire from up the street and there is a whipsnap of movement all around. The sergeant shouts something into a communicator, the flier whines into the air, guns rattling, I see thin wisps of cloud emerge from the doorway of a house up the hill. Someone fired upon us, and now the flier's returned the compliment. Incendiaries, I guess, seeing the orange-white sheets that ripple and flicker up the plaster walls of the building.

I snap the picture, but it's not what I'm after: it's too insubstantial. If I were to paint this, the explosion would be much bigger and blooming and orange. It would burst upon the viewer:

a heroic response to a cowardly attack.

Then I see the children, and the image I'm forming collapses. Children and women are tumbling from the house. The sound of the flier, the crackle of the flames, they paint a picture in my mind that doesn't involve children. But the truth is unfolding. There were civilians in there! The camera captures their terrified, wide-eyed stares, but it can't capture that weeping, keening noise they make. It can't capture the lurching realisation that someone just made a huge mistake.

I see the look on the sergeant's face, that sheer animal joy, and I turn the camera away. That's not what I'm after, but my hand turns back of its own accord. If I had time, I'd try and sketch it right here and now. There is something about the feelings of the moment, getting them down in pencil.

The sergeant sees me looking at him, and he laughs. "So? Innocents get hurt. That's what happens in war."

I make to answer him, but he's concentrating on his console. The green light of the computer screen illuminates his face.

"That's St Mark's church at the top of the hill," he says. "There's a square beyond it with a town hall facing it. We occupy those two buildings, we have the high ground."

He runs his finger across the screen.

"Big rooms in there, wide corridors. A good place to make our base."

A woman screams. She's pleading for something.   I see a child; I see a lot of blood. A medic is running up, and I photograph that. The gallant liberators, aiding the poor civilians. That's the problem with a simple snap. Taken out of context, it can mean anything.

But that's why I'm here. To choose the context.

We make it to the top of the hill without further incident. The cries of pain are receding from my ears and memory. I focus on the scene at hand.

A wide square, littered with the torn canvas and broken

bodies of umbrellas that once shaded café patrons. Upturned tables and chairs. Panic spreads fast when people find their mobile phones and computers have stopped working. They've seen the news from other countries; they know that the rioting is not far behind. Across the square, a classic picture: the signs of money and authority, targeted by the mobs. Two banks, their plate glass fronts smashed open, their interiors peeled inside out in streamers of plastic and trampled circuitry.

The town hall is even worse. It looks like a hollow shell; the anger of the mob has torn the guts out of this place, eviscerated it.

This is what happens when a Denial of Service attack hits, wiping out every last byte of data attached to a country, smoothing the memory stores to an endless sequence of 1's.

Everything: pay, bank accounts, mortgages, wiped out completely. The rule of law breaks down, and armies are sent in to help restore order.

That was the official line, anyway.

"Funny," says the woman at my side. "We seem to be more intent on securing militarily advantageous positions than in helping the population."

"Shut up, Friis," snaps the Sergeant.

"Just making an observation, Sergeant." The woman winks at me.

"Tell you what, Friis, you like making observations so much, why don't you head in there and check it out? "

"Sure," she says, and she looks at me with clear blue eyes. "You coming, painter boy?"

"Call me Brian."

"Aren't you afraid he might get hurt?" laughs the Sergeant.

"I'll look after him."

I pat my pockets, checking my cameras, and follow her through the doorway, the glass crunching beneath my feet.

A large entrance hall, the floor strewn with broken chairs. The rioters haven't been able to get at the ceiling though, and I snap the colourful frescoes that look down upon us. The soldier notices none of this; she's scanning the room, calm and professional. She speaks without looking at me.

"I'm Agnetha."

"Pleased to meet you."

She has such a delightful accent. Vaguely Scandinavian.

I've heard it before.

I see strands of blonde hair curling from beneath her helmet. Her face is slightly smudged, which makes her look incredibly sexy.

We move from room to room. Everything is in disarray – this place has been stripped and gutted. There's paper and glass everywhere. Everything that could be broken has been broken.

"Always the same," says Agnetha. "The data goes, and people panic. They have no money to buy food, they can't use the phone. They think only of themselves, looting what they can and then barricading themselves into their houses. They steal from themselves, and then we come in and take their country from them."

"I thought we were here to help!"

She laughs at that, and we continue our reconnaissance.

Eventually, it's done. Agnetha speaks into her radio.

"This place is clear."

I recognise the Sergeant's voice. "Good. We'll move in at once. There are reports of guerrilla activity down at the *Via Baciadonne*."

"*Baciadonne*." Agnetha smiles at me. "That means *kisses women*."

She's clever as well as pretty. I like that.

The area is quickly secured, which is good because outside the random sound of gunfire is becoming more frequent. I feel the excitement of the approaching battle building in my stomach. The flier comes buzzing up over the roofs, turning this way and that, and I watch the soldiers as they go through the building, filling it with equipment bundled in pink tape.

We find a room with two doors that open out onto a balcony with a view over the city beyond. Agnetha opens the doors to get a better field of fire, then leans against the wall opposite, her rifle slung across her knees. She smiles coquettishly at me.

"Why aren't you taking my picture?" she asks.

I point the camera at her and hear it click.

"Are you going to use that?"

"I don't know."

"Keeping it for your private collection?"

She stretches her legs and yawns.

"You don't mind me being attached to your group, then," I say, "not like your sergeant."

She wrinkles her nose.

"He doesn't speak for all of us. I don't agree with everything the government says, either. We're sent out here with insufficient equipment and even less back up, and when we get home we're forgotten about at best. I think it's good that we have people like you here."

She frowns. "So tell me, what *are* you going to paint?"

"Actually, I don't just paint. I use computers, software, all those things. It's all about the final image."

"I understand that. But what *are* you going to paint?"

I can't keep evading the issue. For all my fine words about reflecting the war as it really is, the Sergeant had it right. I'll paint whatever Command wants me to. I like to paint a picture of myself as a bit of a rogue, but, at heart, I know the establishment has me, body and soul.

"I don't know yet. That's why I'm here. I need to experience this place, and then I can try and convey some emotion."

"What emotion?"

"I don't know that, either."

There's a crackle of gunfire, sharp silver, like tins rattling on the floor. I ignore it.

"You're very pretty," I say.

"Thank you." She lowers her eyes in acknowledgement. I like that. She doesn't pretend she isn't pretty; she takes the compliment on its own terms.

"How did you end up in the army?" I ask.

She yawns and stretches.

"I worked in insurance," she says, and that seems all wrong. So drab and everyday. She should have been a model, or a mountaineer, or an artist or something.

"I lost my job when Jutland got hit by the DoS attack. Everything was lost, policies, claims, payroll. The hackers had been feeding us the same worm for months: the backups were totally screwed."

"I'm sorry," I say, and I am. Really sorry. So that's why her accent sounded so familiar. Fortunately, she doesn't seem to notice my reaction.

"Other people had it worse." She shrugs. "We had a garden; we had plenty of canned goods in the house. My mother had the bath filled with water, all the pans and the dishes. We managed okay until your army moved in to restore order."

She seems remarkably unperturbed by the affair.

"So you joined us out of gratitude?" I suggest.

She laughs.

"No, I joined you for security. This way I get to eat and I'm pretty sure that my salary won't be wiped out at the touch of a button. If your army's servers aren't secure, then whose are?"

"Fair enough."

"No, it's not fair. It's just life. Your army wiped out Jutland's data. Just like it did this country's."

I try to look shocked.

"You think that we are responsible for the trouble here?"

"It's an old trick. Create civil unrest and then send in your troops to sort out the problem. You've swallowed up half of Europe that way."

"I don't think it's that well planned," I said, honestly. "I just think that everyone takes whatever opportunity they can when a

DoS hits."

As if to underline the point, the staccato rattle of gunfire sounds in the distance.

"Aren't you worried that I will report you?" I ask. "Have you charged with sedition?"

She rises easily to her feet and walks towards me.

"No. I trust you. You have nice eyes."

She's laughing at me.

"Come here," she says. I lean down and she kisses me on the lips. Gently, she pushes my face away. "You're a very handsome man. Maybe later on we can talk properly."

"I'd like that."

She looks back out of the window, checking the area. Little white puffs of cloud drift across the blue sky.

"So, what are you going to paint?" she asks. "The heroic rescuers, making the country safe once more?"

"You're being sarcastic."

"No," she says, and she pushes a strand of blonde hair back up into her helmet. "No. We all do what we must to get by. Tell me, what will you paint?"

"I honestly don't know yet. I'll know it when I see it." I look down into the square, searching for inspiration. "Look at your flier."

She comes to my side. We look at the concrete- grey craft, a brutalist piece of architecture set amongst the elegant buildings of this city.

"Suppose I were to paint that?" I say. "I have plenty of photos, but I need a context, a setting. I could have it swooping down on the enemy! The smoke, the explosions, the bullets whizzing past."

"That's what the army would like…"

"Maybe. How about I paint it with you all seated around the back? That could send a message to the people back home: that even soldiers are human, they sit and chat and relax. Or should I evoke sympathy? Draw the flier all shot up. The mechanics around it, trying to fix it up. One of you being led from the scene, blood seeping from the bandages."

She nods. She understands. Then her radio crackles, and I hear the Sergeant's voice.

"Friis! Get down to the Flier! We need help bringing equipment inside."

"Coming!"

"I'll tag along," I say.

The whine of the Flier is a constant theme; the engines are never turned off. We join the bustle of soldiers around the rear ramp, all busy unloading the pink-bound boxes and carrying them into the surrounding buildings.

"What is all that?" I wonder aloud.

"Servers, terminals, NAS boxes," says Agnetha. "I saw this in Jutland. We're establishing a new government in this place."

"Keep it down, Friis," says the sergeant, but without heat. I notice that no one seems to be denying the charge. The head of the soldier behind him suddenly spouts red blood. I'm photographing the scene before I realise what's happening.

"Sniper!"

Everyone is dropping, looking this way and that.

"Up there," shouts someone.

The Sergeant is looking at his console, the green light of the screen illuminating his face.

"That's the Palazzo Egizio. The Via Fossano runs behind it…"

He's thinking.

"Friis, Delgado, Kenton. Head to the far end of the street. See if you can get into that white building there…"

I raise my head to get a better look, and I feel someone push me back down. At the same time there are more shots and I hear a scream. I feel a thud of fear inside me.

Agnetha has been shot.

Shot protecting me.

She's coughing up blood.

"Agnetha," I begin…

"Get back," yells the Sergeant. "You've caused enough trouble as it is…"

Agnetha's trying to speak, but there is too much blood. She holds out her hand and I reach for it, but the sergeant knocks it away.

"Let the medic deal with it," he says. "Let someone who should be here deal with it," he adds, nastily.

The other soldiers have located the sniper now, and I'm left to watch as a man kneels next to Agnetha and takes hold of her arm. She looks at me with those brilliant blue eyes, and I don't see her. For a brief moment I see another picture. Blues and greens. Two soldiers: a man and a woman, standing in front of a flier just like the one behind us. They're surrounded by cheering, smiling civilians. A young child comes forward, carrying a bunch of flowers. A thank you from the grateful liberated.

The picture I painted of Jutland.

I push it from my mind, and I see those brilliant blue eyes are already clouding over.

"We all do what we have to do," I whisper. But is that so true? She joined the army so her family could eat. I'm here simply to build a reputation as an artist.

The medic injects her with something. She closes her eyes. The medic shakes his head. I know what that means. The sergeant looks at me.

"I'm sorry," I say.

"So?" he says. "How's that going to help?" He turns away. The others are already doing the same. Dismissing me.

I take hold of Agnetha's hand, feel the pulse fading.

The picture.

I wonder if Agnetha would approve of what I had done? I suspect not. She was too much of a realist.

I included the flier after all. But not taking off, not swooping down from the skies.

No, this was a different picture.

The point of view is from just outside the cockpit, looking in at the pilot of the craft. And here is where we move beyond the subject matter to the artistic vision, because the person flying the craft is not the pilot, but the sergeant.

His face is there, centred on the picture. He's looking out at the viewer, looking beyond the cockpit.

What can he see? The dead children in the square, sheltered by the bodies of their dead parents? We don't know. But that doesn't matter, because there is a clue in the picture. A clue to the truth. One that I saw all the time, but never noticed. It's written across the sergeant's face. Literally.

A reflection in green from the light of the monitor screen, a tracery of roads and buildings, all picked out in pale green letters. Look closely at his cheek and you can just make out the words *St Mark's Church*. All those names that were supposedly wiped for good by the DoS attack, and yet there they were, still resident in the Sergeant's computer. And none of us found that odd at the time. We could have fed that country's data back to it all along, but we chose not to.

They say a picture paints a thousand words.

For once, those words will be mostly speaking the truth.

Brwydr Am Ryddid

Stephen Palmer

Information Nugget 43v98
Subject: The Hogger Leads Inn
Content: an inn in the Old Quarter of Shrewsbury

"Your nugget is nonsense – the Hogger Leads Inn is in St Collen's Quarter."

Although nobody in Shrewsbury has ever spoken to me, nor even noticed I exist, I am the only one who can relate this tale since I alone know every relevant detail. Innkeeper Nirian missed the early events. Jane was fascinated by her tambourines and did not notice how the incident ended. Delia and Perria were busy playing their flutes. Only I was aware of everything from start to finish.

"For goodness sake. This paragraph contains untruth. Already!"

It was a cold evening a few weeks after the Day Of Canol Gaeaf and my joints were creaking fit to wake the dead. But winter already showed signs of coming to an end: blustery days, nights bright from the town-glow reflecting off low cloud. Less snow, more sleet. I noticed a few snowdrops in the back garden.

It all began with an argument between Melody, a priestess of the Shrine of Cambria, and her partner Harold, a man who had been plucked from the kitchens at the Shrine of Rhiannon and become – after a fashion – a free man. Melody had rented a room in which she could enjoy a passionate affair without interference from her colleagues and peers. Every night I would hear the couple panting and groaning.

On the last day there was a blazing row. I can remember every word.

"That's impossible; it's been proven."

Harold had not realised that the fourteenth day of the affair would bring his return to the kitchens. He had assumed that Melody would continue to protect him against his former owners, the priestesses of Rhiannon. Melody, who had just turned fourteen, was so naive she had not realised she might have to provide shelter and support for the man she had plucked from slavery. Harold was shocked when he realised he would be cast adrift in the town without means of survival. "You mean you will simply let me go?" he asked.

"Of course," Melody retorted in her high-pitched, almost wheedling voice. "I've got to get back to the Shrine of Cambria."

"But—"

"There's only another three years before I'm too old for them. No time to hang about."

"But how will I eat?"

"Don't care. You should be happy I got you out of the kitchens."

Harold bellowed, "At least they fed me there!"

"Don't *shout*. Go away, leave me alone. I've got to pay Nirian for renting this room, I don't suppose you'll be able to help me with *that*." And, pulling her coat over her shoulders, she made for the door.

She was only a girl.

Harold tried to get work, but Nirian knew where he had come from, she knew his character – immature, opportunistic -- and she wanted nothing to do with him.

I saw him only once more, when he brought the hound. It was that same evening. I can see his face now. Angry. Revenge twisting his features, brow furrowed from the intense concentration required to carry such a dangerous beast. Of course there was astonishment when he entered the common room, threw a wicker basket to the floor and shouted, "This is for you, Melody! This is for everybody here!"

He ran off faster than a beggar after a crust of bread.

"Oh, yes? Following the Month Of Scourge no hounds have lived on the streets in Shrewbury."

That is not true. Two months after the scourging a pair of hounds, one male and one female, were found in a hidden cellar beneath Dogpole. Apparently they were killed. I acquired that from the same source as I acquired the original tale.

That hound! At first it did not leave its basket, so nobody knew what lurked inside. There was chortling from the regulars, wags muttering and suchlike. But then the hound leaped through the basket door and onto an empty chair, its back curved, barking fit to wake the nonliving. For two and one third seconds there was silence; then a scream changed everything. This was a beast whose envenomed slobber would kill everyone in the room, whose teeth were deadly. Panic spread. People ran everywhere, bumping into one another, into chairs and tables; chess pieces and boards scattered to the floor.

Now, I know much about hounds. Popular opinion claims all hounds are deadly: this is the logic behind scourging. In fact only one in three will attack in the street: the rest hide down holes. Our hound was one of the latter. It jumped off the chair, eyes big and round, then howled once and skittered through the doorway leading to the main staircase. It vanished.

Then there was silence. Nirian walked in from the back

kitchen and said, "What in the name of the Rhiannon is going on here?"

There was nobody left who could provide an answer. But forty seconds later Oleana crept into the room brandishing a laser pistol. She said, "Get your gun. Hound loose!"

Nirian swore in the Welsh tongue and pulled a long-nose revolver from behind the bar.

Welsh, of course, is no longer spoken in Shrewsbury – I leave the sentence unedited.

"Yes, it is. Shrewsbury is part of the Cymru Protectorate."

The Cymru Protectorate is not yet recognised as a legitimate land.

"Oh yes it is."

Here, then, was the dilemma upon which my tale focuses. A hound with the potential to kill everybody present was at large, hidden in some nameless hole. Four paws with five claws each. Possibly the creature had been genetically enhanced; as yet I did not know. There would have to be a hound hunt.

Nirian first took a head count. There were four permanent staff, including herself. Add seven performers who paid for their accommodation and food by attracting custom, plus Delia and Perria, the flautist twins. And that night there were seven paying guests – I know. The total number of people was nineteen and all were present. I can remember Nirian's sigh of relief when she realised the hound had not attacked anybody. Everyone stood huddled together in the common room – nineteen weapons pointing out, like the spines of a sea-urchin.

A nasty state of affairs, but at least the panic was over.

"This is what we'll do," Nirian whispered. "We'll go from room to room, maybe three of us, open all the windows and hope the hound jumps out. If we don't see it... I'll have to assume the thing is still hiding somewhere."

Oleana looked the most nervous. "Then what?" she asked.

Nirian grimaced. "Then I'll decide what to do."

The search proved fruitless. Cold air blew in through the windows and everybody was annoyed. Three hours passed and again they were clustered together in the common room, with not one of them aware that the hound had stuffed itself like a dirty flannel into a cupboard on the top floor.

It was midnight, but how could they sleep?

Nirian's face had changed from pale to bone white. This was a nightmare she did not need, like the threat of a sarin cloud, deadly on a westerly wind. She said, "There's only one thing we can do. Set a hound to catch a hound."

There was a general response of, "What are you talking about?"

Nirian explained. "We'll have to get somebody in—"

"Wait," Oleana interrupted, "you can't bring anybody here from the Shrine of Canis."

There was agreement all round on this. People sat squirming, so uncomfortable was the notion.

Nirian was adamant however. "If it's not scared of us, then the hound *might* jump out of a window. But I can't risk not knowing. I've got to get someone in to tell me it's definitely gone."

"Fumigate the place," Delia suggested.

"What with? Your stinking breath?"

Jane the percussionist said, "Make lots of noise, then when it appears, shoot it."

Nirian was scornful. "And what if we scare it so much it just finds a deeper hole? Then crawls out a day later and bites you in the face? One dead Jane."

Megan the folk-dancer nodded. "We have to be sure. A hidden hound makes this place uninhabitable – we can't leave the windows open for ever."

"Exactly," said Nirian. "Think of the talk. The inn with the hound in it."

Much cursing ensued at this point, but I knew that Nirian was right and everybody would come around to her way of thinking before long. Of course, I saw nothing of Nirian's journey to the Shrine of Canis, of her discussions with the people there, and I have no idea what payment she made for the service of the man who followed her home.

This man was called Edward. I can see now the expressions on the faces of the people in the common room as he followed Nirian inside: disgust, terror. Edward wore a cloak of hound hair sewn with silver threads, the symbols of his religion hanging on chains around his neck: hound teeth in silver, a dangling paw. Without a word he sat on a chair, cradling his head in his arms, bent over, silent, until he began howling like some banshee of the Weme Marsh. Then, sudden as an off-switch, he stopped. There was a momentary echo. Edward and I knew that it had issued from the hidden hound, but nobody else did.

He hesitated before giving his diagnosis. "There is indeed a hound in the Hogger Leads Inn, hiding at the top of the building. It has been genetically altered by one at my Shrine."

Nirian babbled, "Remove it, remove it!"

"Very well. You must all stay here."

Edward left the common room and ascended the stairs. From a pocket he pulled out a portable communicator of the type used by street people. (I mean, beggars. Sorry.) I heard every word that he spoke into it. "The hound is still inside the inn. Do you want me to carry on?"

It was difficult to locate the frequency of the carrier wave but I managed, three-fifths of a second later, to hear, "... I do, inform me when the union is complete. I'm standing outside."

"Very well."

Edward found the hound without difficulty, whistling and calling, until the creature emerged from its hole and began licking his hand. Edward picked it up and took it to the nearest network port. With a single swipe of the nails on his right hand he cut the hound's throat. Then he twisted off its head and touched the bloody central unit to the port matrix. When I realised what he was doing I tried to close down the port, but it was too late. The union of hound and network had been made. Edward ran down the first flight of stairs then made to a south-facing window, where he tapped the glass and waved an all-clear sign with one hand.

Outside, I heard Harold sniggering.

It was only then that I realised what was happening. Bringing the hound in its basket had been the first part of Harold's devious plan; what he had really wanted to introduce was a priest of Canis.

Far worsewas to come. Now I feared for the safety of Nirian, her staff and guests, and even for my own future.

"Huh! Sheer melodrama."

Information Nugget sdh3
Subject: Harold
Content: a male aged twenty-eight, sold at age sixteen to the Shrine of Rhiannon, evaluated by High Priestess Tamara and sent to the Kitchens for the delight of defender-class women. Abandoned son of the Shrine of Canis. H 6'1", W 12-5

"This also is nonsense – Harold was thirty-five and suffered from cancer. He weighed nine stone six."

You did not know him. You have only recently arrived here from the west.

The noise of hounds howling can be horrific. I know from history computers that hounds were once the pets of human beings, that many were pleased by the presence of hounds in their homes. But not in Shrewsbury... not now. Hound howls strike terror into everyone in Amwythig.

Before he departed, Edward showed Nirian the body of the hound and told her, "Here's your problem." There was silence, then the thud of Edward closing the outer door.

Oleana said, "That's odd. I've never heard of a Canis worshipper killing one of their own."

Nirian shrugged. "Who cares? The Hogger Leads Inn is safe."

Those few people in the common room relaxed, Delia and Perria setting up a microphone, Nirian pouring a nightcap tot of whiskey. An hour later nineteen people lay asleep.

They awoke to howling. I can remember exactly what the servant Morgan ap Nirian said. "Blue blood will spill. We're surrounded."

And they were.

Overnight, a dozen hounds had migrated from Milk Street, settling in a circle, so that from every window – from the common room, the back kitchen, the side chambers, even from the garret under the roof – the shape of a hound could be seen, black upon grey, sheltering as best they could against the sleet. I can recall every human curse, every vile epithet, but such language is inappropriate to my tale and I will forbear from setting the reactions down. Suffice it to say that fear, even terror were abroad. Such a scene had never before been witnessed outside of the Shrine of Canis.

"That clearly can't be the case if the words of the tale as related so far are true. If, as I suspect, some words are false, then such a scene had been witnessed before. Incidentally, Morgan is not related to Ninian – you didn't correct that did you? Yet another mistake…"

Are you relating this tale or am I? And who found it, me or you?

"Huh! I have more outputs than you realise."

It was Oleana who once again took the first step towards understanding. "It's like wolves seeking one of their kin," she remarked.

Jane nodded. "They sound like wolves," she said. "Howling, howling…"

Judging from the expression on Oleana's face, she was cogitating. "But there's no hound here," she said. "That priest took it away."

Nirian muttered something that even I did not hear, then added, "Probably the stench of that foul Edward. The hounds will depart tonight for the Abbey ruins."

And yet, unbeknownst to all, Harold's plan was proceeding. All six guests took their leave. Come evening there was a pile of cash on the bar, everybody paying up in full, everybody gone. Nineteen were reduced to thirteen. No hound departed the gardens. A siege mentality began to form.

A meeting was held in the common room. Nirian began by saying, "There's no hound inside this inn, we've nothing to worry about, it's just the canine aura of that priest."

How different was the truth: the aura of a hound, haunted networks. Of course the hounds outside could sense this aura.

"Haunted networks, you say? And were there seven guests or six?"

At length Oleana said, "What exactly *was* the hound Harold brought here?"

She was quick, Oleana, some quirk of her background or her thought process leading her down the correct path, though she did not know what I knew, that Edward had acted for the greater good of Canis. But Oleana did know that a hound would attract other hounds of its immediate family to the Hogger Leads Inn. That this was a virtual hound made no difference to the canine kin.

"What are you talking about?" Nirian asked.

"I think you're wrong," Oleana replied. "I don't think these hounds will go. That man Harold... how did he get hold of a hound? Why dump it inside the common room?"

"To kill us," came the answer from various people.

Oleana nodded. "Maybe," she murmured. "Or maybe there is something more."

Nirian tapped the table with her tankard. "If those hounds don't leave soon," she said, "the Hogger Leads is dead and gone. Without guests I'm nothing, even in these times of Welsh Supremacy."

Oleana looked at her. "That is true, isn't it," she said.

Nirian had in one sentence enunciated my fear. If people departed, what would I do? Communities and technologies are interdependent, each reduced, even destroyed without the other. I wanted to survive. I wanted Harold's plan foiled. But I could do nothing. I was helpless.

They *had* to get rid of that network hound.

But how? How, when they did not even know it existed? And they had but days to act. Soon the rumour of the Hogger Leads Inn would not be one of warmth and light and folk music, but one of hounds and terror. I knew I would not survive such a rumour.

That night nobody slept well. I heard every occupied bed squeak as the person upon it tossed and turned, or dreamed dreadful dreams.

It was the following morning when Oleana initiated her plan. I saw nothing of her walk through the alleys of Amwythig, of her search in Market Square. I saw nothing of the package she purchased, until she returned to her room.

Oleana was a thief, she was a magpie. She had to be: stone deaf, she had stolen two slug-like computerised ears. Blind in one eye, she had also acquired a sensor eyepatch. Her room was paradise: soft rugs, a large couch, multi-coloured cotton on the walls. She survived by trading illegally. Technology mostly, though she also dealt in small animals.

This background allowed her to access the more sophisticated parts of Market Square. In her room she unwrapped the package to reveal a black lump, which she connected to other technological oddments strewn across her table until, after one and three-quarter hours, she had constructed a device. At first I did not recognise it, but when I saw the type of port interface she had chosen – the mate of the matrix on the port used by Edward to begin the canine haunting – I knew it must be a simulation module.

At last I saw what desperate ploy would be attempted to chase away the virtual hound.

Information Nugget zxn435n
Subject: Old Quarter Simulation Module BX3-T
Content: devised by Cerys to complement the software architecture of her partner Bryn. Details, a stand-alone module with morphic ability, mimicking any network environment so that the defence systems of said network are not alerted, at the same time allowing the user to manipulate said network to the desired end, most often through the use of camouflage.

"I know that to be true."

You think you are so clever. But you do not exist, Scourger. You only believe you do.

Oleana, I think, knew what she was doing. She had considered the evidence and drawn her conclusion. The simulation module would be used to struggle with the virtual hound. So the day passed, then evening, then it was night, and one by one people went to bed. No hounds had tried to enter through door or window, but still they howled, frightening off anybody brave or foolhardy enough to tread the street outside. When all was silent Oleana crept up to the port through which the virtual hound had leaped, connecting her machine, switching on the monitor, then sitting cross-legged with the device on her lap. In her hands she held two joysticks. *Beep.* The connection was made: device to network.

It seemed to me that a new wing had been added, but it looked normal, and I wasn't sure for how long it had been present. I have a long memory. I can recall inn designs from way back. I wasn't worried by this new bit of architecture.

Using the twin joysticks, Oleana navigated her representative (which she had chosen because it had the fastest weapons) down the stairs to the common room. With little traffic coming in from external sources, the simulation was smooth, the action fast. Oleana was familiar with her machine. She used IR-mode to scan the chairs for heat signs of the virtual hound. I remember seeing displays pop up on her monitor warning her of loose objects and so forth.

At this point I became aware of damp shapes slinking in between the curtains of downstairs windows.

While Oleana sought the virtual hound I looked out into the gardens, to see a unique sight. All twelve hounds stood poised as if to pounce, tails swishing, eyes and ears locked on some presence inside the common room. Yet they did not move. Knowing they were enhanced I scanned frequencies, detecting their gestalt influence three and a half seconds later. I knew then that Oleana faced not one but thirteen virtual hounds.

Tiny forms were bounding along corridors and across rooms to get to the common room.

Of course, there was nothing I could do to help, I could not even warn Oleana. She had taken this task upon herself. If her representative was killed, the hounds would stay and my future was bleak.

Now the common room was full of silent menace. Thirteen canine shapes faced a single person who could not hope to kill all of them before the hounds bit their throat out. The situation was a standoff. The weapon muzzle trembled. Thirteen hound tails swung from side to side, slow, deliberate, as if to deny me the possibility of action.

And then I had an idea. My perfect memory could import any scene it desired. In microseconds I caused a simulation of Edward re-enter the virtual common room then pause by the door, so that every virtual hound turned to look at its totem. Oleana took a deep breath, straightened her back and gripped tight the joystick controls. In one fluid movement she fired and swung the muzzle across the line of hounds. Her monitor showed the result: every one burst into flames.

The hounds vanished. I leaned back against the bar and blew across the smoking muzzle of the weapon. A green sign flashed upon one wall of the new wing: *simulation complete.*

Success. The attention of the hounds had been diverted long enough for Oleana to make one attack and destroy them all. Together, we had won. I looked out into the garden to see the hounds slinking away. The gestalt entity was shattered, the virtual hound no longer attracting them. I was safe… until the English should come again.

The English will never return to claim back what they once held. And if they try, we shall oppose them. The dragon shall oppose them with every last drop of blue blood.

"Croeso y Cymru."

O'n i'n aros mewn gwesty gerllaw'r Afon Hafren ar y pryd.

"Ceir cyfoeth o atyniadau gerllaw."

Ha ha ha ha ha ha!

"Do you seriously think people are going to believe the version you've just related?"

Occupation

Colin Harvey

Doctor Hue was on the beach teaching José to read when the Nzaghi craft crashed in the bay off Puerto Rosario.

They'd sought peace and quiet in the bay next to the village, one of a chain of scallop-shaped inlets stretching down the coast to Tarragona. The February afternoon was cloudy, the still air redolent with pine, sage and the tarragon that gave the region its name. Birds chirped and insects buzzed.

"Bueno, José. ¡Qué es esto?" Hue underlined another word. The boy mouthed the word, wrestling with its meaning. José was the brightest child in the village, but he struggled with even simple words. While most of the older villagers could read, the skills weren't being passed on. Without Hue's teaching, José's generation would have faced a long slide toward barbarism. *Perhaps that's what the Nzaghi want*, Hue thought, *they watch while we fall from grace.*

A roar from the North rent the afternoon: a small flyer, perhaps a single seater from whose side smoke and flames boiled. It lurched crazily sideways through the air, as the pilot fought for control. Then it disappeared behind the headland. Hue stood statue-still until galvanised by the explosion that followed seconds late.

He rushed over the rocks of the headland, almost breaking his ankle several times. Even so José passed him, and was dancing with impatience when Hue finally caught up.

The flyer had sunk. The only trace was a pall of smoke hanging over the water. Hue was about to trudge away when José plucked his arm. "Mira!" José pointed. *Look!*

They waded into the surf to retrieve the bobbing Nzaghi. Hue felt a moment's anxiety when the shore dropped away beneath his feet, then he swam strongly out into the brown scum, cheered on by the shrieking boy, trying not to swallow any of the polluted water.

Hue had intended to save the alien; the idea of losing a patient – any patient – bothered him. But when he reached the body, a sudden rage seized him and he pushed the helmet under the water, in revenge for Tranh and the billions of others the creatures had murdered.

"Doctor!" José's voice cut through Hue's rage. The boy was wading out further and further. "¿Es muerto?" *Is it dead?*

Hue waved José back and grabbed the alien's body under the arms and pulled. He was helped by the alien's flotation suit, but had to stop for a breather every few metres, and when he felt sand beneath him, he collapsed in a fit of coughing.

He regained his feet, slowly hauling the body up the beach beyond the tide-line. The alien was taller than him, but surprisingly light, and Hue moved it quickly, Jose dancing attendance all the while.

"José!" Hue urged. "Help me get its suit off! Quickly!"

Between them they removed the suit, and Hue rolled the alien onto its side. He had never been near an Nzaghi, and was painfully aware of his ignorance. He could only hope its lungs were in the same place as a human's, as he pumped the chest. This seemed to work. The alien coughed, retching water. It doubled up, still coughing, and he leaned back, watching.

The Nzaghi looked like an upright panther without the tail, its skin colour a mixture of blues, purples and greys: Hue had heard the blotches were a means of identification, and could change as part of their language, though he had no idea if this were true. The creature wore a vocoder round its neck, a box about fifteen centimetres by five by two deep, growing into the flesh beneath its throat.

"¿Habla español?" Hue asked. The creature said nothing. "English?" Hue persisted, then switched to Vietnamese, tried his French, and even prised a little Chinese from his memory.

The alien lay there blinking, eyelids closing from the sides. Its jaw was more pointed than a panther's, but the overall resemblance was remarkable. Hue sighed, and helped *it* to its feet. He had to think *it* as such: he had no idea whether this was male, female, or neuter. "Lean on me." Hue propped it up. "Get my things," he commanded José, "and bring them to my house."

The village was barely a kilometre away, but they made slow progress.

Hue was surprised that no one met them. The villagers must have heard the crash. There were a few olders too frail to work, and mothers nursing their children; they stared in bemusement as he shuffled the alien to his house. At this time of day most villagers gathered food. They fished from the rocks, risking broken limbs to cast drift nets; the aliens sank any boats that broke the interdiction. The young men dived to gather the molluscs beneath the water. A few tilled the fields inland or gathered nuts, berries and fungi from the scrubby forests. Hue's status made him probably the only able-bodied person exempt from the all-consuming need to gather food. The villagers accepted that his skills were needed elsewhere.

"They think me more than half mad, anyway." He said to the alien in Spanish, still unsure if it understood a word he said, not really caring: it was a relief to have someone new to talk to: maybe someone of his own education and intelligence. "Their uncertainty has probably kept me alive over the years. And the fact that at my age, I'd probably taste foul."

One of the women ran off, and Hue guessed El Jefe would arrive soon.

José waited for him. "You'd better go," Hue said, dropping the alien onto his bed. "I'll see you tomorrow."

José looked disappointed. Hue suspected he had been looking forward to the fun when El Jefe arrived. Hue didn't have long to wait. A pounding at the door announced Emilio, who barged in, a small mob pressing behind him.

"Encantado, Jefe," Hue greeted him formally. "Please ask them to leave." Hue was more anxious than he dared show, and needed to establish his authority.

The Jefe hesitated, and Hue called out: "Leave now. My home is not the Village Square!"

Emilio turned, and nodded. "El Médico is right: Outside."

They muttered, and some shook their heads, but they left.

One voice shouted, "You mad old bastard!"

Martin, Hue thought wearily, *who else?*

Emilio waited until they were alone. "Are you crazy?" he hissed. "They'll come looking for it. We've survived by minding our own business, not interfering where we shouldn't. You'll bring them down on us."

"I don't think so, Emilio," Hue answered calmly. "It's hurt. We've helped it. If anything, they should thank us."

"You know they don't think like us!"

"And you're not thinking at all." Hue added gently, "There's nothing to fear, as long as we don't harm it."

Emilio shook his head, unconvinced. "Why?" He asked plaintively, "Couldn't you have left well alone?"

"I'm a doctor —"

"I know. You've done so much."

"No," Hue answered firmly. "It's not my occupation. It's what I *am*." He paused: "I took an oath to save lives. You've said how much I've done for you. Now it's your turn." He nodded at the doorway. "Calm them. Convince them there's nothing to fear."

Emilio stood looking at him, as if he were a stranger. "I must convince them of something I don't believe myself. By God, this uses up all the goodwill you've ever earned."

The next morning as usual Hue checked the tumour in his groin. *Six months, maybe a year*, he thought. He'd survived longer than he'd ever dared hope, but he felt the shortness of time weighing heavier every day.

He made a simple breakfast, while talking constantly to the creature, perhaps the result of years spent on his own, or a touch of nerves: or simply the need to communicate, almost as great as the need to heal.

He talked of his childhood in Hanoi: of growing up in a cratered cityscape, streets still pockmarked by American bombs, having to use and re-use everything again until it wore out from exhaustion; of thirty-year-old Citroens packed like mini-buses, and buses packed like sardine cans; the smell of ginger and pak choi, garlic and chilli. He talked of school days, of medical school, and meeting Tranh.

When he'd performed his morning rituals, he visited his patients and noticed the first change: people behaved differently. They drew back, or watched him like hawks. A few scowled. He had lived amongst them for more than twenty years, and in one day he'd jeopardised their trust. He wasn't surprised, just a little hurt; though he knew that was foolish. They had always been a suspicious people, and the Occupation had done nothing to improve that.

"Where's your pet devil?" the bravest of the old women asked.

"At home," Hue answered. "Recovering."

The old woman snorted contemptuously. "You're a soft fool."

"Maybe," Hue said. "But if I weren't, Mabel, I'd have kept walking all those years ago. And you'd have no one to insult."

The woman cackled. "And you'd have been dead long ago." She softened briefly. "You're a good fool, but still a fool." Her face hardened again: "I hope you're not the death of us all."

In truth most of his doctoring was just common sense, a good manner, and the judicious use of herbs: in the Middle Ages any witch could have done as much. His real status was his surgery, the penicillin growing in a fermenter, a still brewing home-made anaesthetic, and his herb garden. He was currently irreplaceable.

Hue stumbled, and looked down at a foot. Looked sideways, and upwards, at the small black eyes set in a glowering face.

"Martin," Hue said. "Buenos días. Are you unwell?"

The youth shook his head, scratched the bumfluff on his chin. He only needed to shave once a fortnight, but wore his wisps of beard with pride. "José works today." Martin spat on the ground to punctuate the sentence, clenching, unclenching his great hams of fists.

"Emilio has agreed?" Hue kept his tone mild, lest he provoke a beating. Emilio had agreed Hue could teach one child. Children worked beside their parents, but Martin and José were orphaned. There were few births, and most were mutants. José was no exception: he had only one testicle and a pair of extra nipples below the regular ones. But the boy was brighter than most, and his youthful energy lit up Hue's day. If he and Tranh had had children, he would have liked one like José.

"José is *my* brother!" Martin scowled, and strode away. "*I* decide when he works!"

By mid-morning Hue's work was done. Facing an empty day, he went home.

The Nzaghi sat by the window, watching the village.

"You'd better close the shutters," Hue said. "They're nervous enough without thinking you spy on them."

Hue's examination the day before had revealed a few burns that he'd covered with cold compresses, and what were probably the after-effects of shock. Otherwise, the alien was miraculously unscathed. It had cut the sleeves and legs from the flotation jacket to make a tunic, and sat immobile, as if in a trance; only the watchful eyes moved. He had no idea what it ate, and it had refused all food.

Hue watched it, hoping to provoke a response. The creature

sat there. Eventually Hue gave up and went into his garden.

The next day followed the same pattern. Rain set in, though fortunately not acid-laden. He could cope with being wet; that reminded him of his youth. Rain was rare here. He did his rounds. Then home, to write his diary, and check on the surgery and the garden.

The rain stopped the day after that, and Hue worked in the garden. The alien watched him. Hue held each item up, naming it.

Watching him impassively, the alien leaned forward, tasting each item in turn. Once it spat something out, but mostly it swallowed. Only when it tried the Oregano did it indicate a desire for more. Hue had to stop it eating every Oregano leaf he had. Experimenting with his meagre larder confirmed the creature to be vegetarian, with a fondness for mushrooms and peppers.

Hue had noticed an increase in the amount of alien activity offshore since the crash. There were a few of the bee-like Qell, far rarer than the Nzaghi, and Hue watched their ponderous dancing with fascination. The aliens were always around, busy moving whales and dolphins to the orbital habitats, but this was different: Hue suspected they were searching for the Nzaghi's flyer.

Two days later, the Nzaghi joined him on his rounds. Ignoring his misgivings, Hue pointedly introduced it to Mabel. "This is El Silencioso," he said, making a point of its normality – a risk, but necessary. "It doesn't speak."

Mabel and others looked unhappy, but didn't openly object to its presence, though Hue was unsure whether that was fear of speaking in front of the alien.

It seemed to work, though: the next day José approached Hue shyly.

"Mama says I can resume my reading lessons, Señor médico," Mama was the boy's maiden aunt: their mother had died giving birth to José, and their father had been swept to his death fishing from the rocks. "She says only if I learn to read can

I be a doctor like you, Doctor Hue. I told Martin that that is what I want."

Hue felt a surge of joy. "You'll be a better doctor than me." He ruffled José's hair.

Over the next few days the alien walked with Hue on his rounds, but only in the mornings, and always near cover. Hue suspected the smoke that had belched from El Silencioso's flyer wasn't from an accident.

His suspicions were confirmed one morning when a larger craft hauled the wreckage from the sea and presumably carried it up to the Mother Fleet. Just before dusk another flyer approached the village, flanked by a flight of Qell.

Every evening the villagers lit pitch lamps in the central square. The lamps flickered, shadowdances casting a roseate glow on the white stone buildings. Tonight the flyer hovered over the square, whilst the Qell circled. Hue counted eight of them. They looked like metre-long bumble-bees with an extra pair of wings, and tiny paws at the front of the thorax. They buzzed like bees, but Hue felt an irritation that he suspected might be due to ultrasonics. The flyer landed, and from it climbed another Nzaghi, markedly different from El Silencioso.

This one was shorter, and Hue thought it was hunch-backed. Then he realised that a Qell rode astride its shoulders. He shuddered in disgust.

"Humann."

Hue was the only one left in the square. He bowed.

"We search for an Nzaghi." The alien's voice was toneless, though that could have been the vocoder. "A machine crashed. What did you see?"

Hue swallowed. "We saw it come down. Nothing came ashore." It was reckless, but he couldn't resist the dig: "If we could launch boats without you sinking them, we would've helped you search."

The alien turned away, surveying the square.

"It was venting smoke," Hue said. It turned back to him. "It was damaged. Perhaps deliberately."

"It iss illl," The Nzaghi said. "If it survived, it iss dangerous. You should not approach. We will search here."

Hue shrugged, showing no emotion. He prayed no one would tell the aliens, and that they would miss his house. It was a vain hope, he knew.

The aliens spent an hour checking the village. He kept expecting someone to shout, "It's at the doctor's." His house was last. He made to follow them, but another Nzaghi barred his way, while two searched his home. He held his breath, his heart beating a panicky tattoo.

To his astonishment they reappeared without El Silencioso, and left empty-handed.

Hue sat on a bench, his legs turned to jelly. It was a long time before he was able to stand. The villagers watched his walk home silently, from their doorways. Emilio passed, walking his daughter Victoria: a pretty seven-year old with vestigial arms.

"Our debts to you are cancelled, Hue," Emilio murmured. "You now owe us."

His house was neat and tidy. El Silencioso sat as if everything were normal.

"What the —" Hue checked himself. "You must have hidden beneath my bed. They can't have searched very well." He shook his head in bemusement. "We risked our lives tonight, and for what? A lunatic, they said."

"They were right." The alien's voice was like a bucket of bolts. "I opposed the consensus, which by definition, makes me insane."

Hue jumped. "What?"

"You do not understand the principle of —" the vocoder could not translate the word, turned it instead into a sizzling hiss. "I believe that their interpretation is not correct, and acted."

"What did you do?" Hue asked, so quietly he barely breathed it.

"I worked on one of the micro-worlds with a chimpanzee colony." The alien spoke slowly, as if weighing every word. "One day a youngster fell, its back broken. Our medicine is sophisticated. But there are things we cannot heal. Smashed spinal columns are beyond us. The creature was in agony. I ended that agony."

"You killed it." This was not a question.

"I killed it."

There was a long silence, before Hue said, "You *can* talk. Why now?"

"Now is appropriate." Its voice was harsher than the Nzaghi /Qell's vocoder.

"El Silencioso. Is that right – are you male? Female? Neuter?"

"Yes."

"Yes, what? You're male? Female?"

"Sometimes."

Hue shook his head. *Aliens.* He changed tack. "So you're a lunatic?"

"Like your species."

"Oh?" Hue's voice was velvet. "When you walked out of the UN, you called us a criminal species. Yet you bombed us into barbarism and killed many of the species you claimed to protect. Isn't that a lunatic act? Who set you up as combined judges, jury and executioners?"

"I am a criminal," The creature said. "But the habit of living is a hard one to give up."

"Oh yes," Hue agreed fervently. "We know that."

There was a long silence.

Hue spoke: "When I finished my post-doctorate in the States, I came to Spain. I was studying paediatrics at the Javier Gomez Institute in Seville, when these huge ships of yours just... appeared." He continued: "There were all the great hopes, the talk of exchanges of medicine, science; I thought we had the means to conquer disease and famine, anything!" He calmed himself. "Then there was talk, that things had gone wrong. That you just walked out of discussions. Whaling offended you. It offended a lot of humans, but *we* didn't bomb others back to the Stone Age because we disagreed with them."

"Nor did we," the alien replied. "We identified four near-sentient families at risk from you: Chimpanzees, Gorillas, Whales, Dolphins. When we took chimpanzees from their local habitat for their safety, your ground troops attacked us." It paused; Hue thought about interrupting, but he had learnt more in minutes than in years, so kept quiet. "We defended ourselves; your people made air attacks. The conflict spread like a fire. We used lasers against aircraft, but then a missile was launched. If it had penetrated our defences... So we struck back using low-rise explosives; but we hadn't calculated on how fragile your civilization was – how reliant on your electronic communications, and your cars and petrol you were. Your world fell like... what is your word in another of your languages? *Dominoes.*"

Hue had no idea what the word meant, but he got the alien's gist. "Still... half the continent vaporized, and thrown up into orbit," Hue breathed, the enormity of it sinking in. He remembered the double sunrise he'd seen even from down South, the distant thunder, the heat.

"Had it been much worse, none of you would have survived," the alien admitted.

"We did what we had to, to keep some of you alive... but no more."

"It was bad enough," Hue replied. He had been in Granada on a weekend break, stopping at a street bar for *tapas*; it was a pure fluke that he saw on the television screen the views of Tokyo, Beijing, New York; what could have been the same pictures from three different places. An almighty flash, and as the static on screen stabilized, the low-lying shockwaves radiating outwards from the blast site – but barely *upwards* at all. That was what had convinced him that these were indeed alien weapons – they seemed to disobey all that Hue knew of the laws of physics.

The buildings amputated a few floors above the ground, falling into the maelstrom of dust below.

"And we're supposed to be grateful?" Hue remembered the panic, the desperate night-time ride train through Spain, the hope that he might make it to Paris, from there back to his family in Hanoi. The crammed carriages, and forced disembarkation at Barcelona. "The midday skies darkened, temperatures plummeted. Millions died, from plague, from hunger, maybe even despair." The bodies washed ashore at Sitges beach. The pork taste, when the will to live overcame even that last taboo: the never-ending guilt of the survivor.

"We needed survivors to run factories to manufacture habitats. We helped as many as we could," The alien said. "It seemed fitting…" it paused "…that your species should work to atone for your actions. Not everyone believes this is right, or that those factories should pollute so heavily."

"Yet you do nothing now," Hue snapped. "You leave us to freeze, to die in our millions from starvation, plague, and exposure. As I could have left you. Think of that." He went to bed, unable to continue.

That night he dreamt of Tranh. The vivid nightmare stayed with him when he awoke. *Thank God, at least she was spared having to live through that*, he thought.

El Silencioso was already up when Hue rose.

"Why did you help me?" it asked.

Hue continued eating while he pondered.

"Why?" He wondered how much he could bear to say. "You see the picture?" He nodded at Tranh's faded portrait. "That's all I have to remind me of her. That and my Hippocratic Oath." He paused. "All doctors swear to save lives, to assist in any way they can. I betrayed my oath."

He paused again. Resumed. "I was a doctor; she was my nurse. It was all she ever wanted to be. We married. We were going to go to America, the land of milk and honey one English book called it. Even then, when America was a declining giant, all we had ever heard was how wonderful it was. Hollywood and Motown, Broadway and Coca-cola." Hue smiled, but it was more the grimace of a wounded animal.

"She became pregnant. But we feared they'd deny us entry. We couldn't afford that. There would be time later on for children, we said." He exhaled a long slow breath. "But for years the abortion rate had rocketed upwards, and only a month before the government had banned it. We were so close! So... *damned...* close. But no one dared touch us."

Hue paused, swallowed.

"We couldn't afford the clinic fees. So I performed the abortion. She begged me not to... but I told her, 'I am a doctor.' In my pride, I thought that I could do it... could do anything." He fell silent, remembering Tranh's tears, then her increasingly strident cries, the copper smell of blood from the womb. Then silence – before he could even call for help; broken only by his crying, rocking backwards and forwards, cradling the vessel now empty of her life.

Hue said none of this, simply: "It went wrong. She died. I fled in panic. I swore then I'd never allow harm to befall another, if I could help." He paused. He'd exhausted his tears long ago, but needed to collect himself.

"You could have told them where I was last night," El Silencioso said.

"I could have," Hue agreed. "But any form of resistance, no matter how passive – even hiding something they want, is fighting back."

He left then, to visit his patients.

They returned at the same time as the previous evening. Eight Qell. Six Nzaghi. And the creature that El Silencioso had explained was a symbiont, all led to the village by Hue.

That afternoon, El Silencioso had answered Hue's question: "The Qell communicate by dance and ultrasonics. We communicate by scent and fur-patterns. The symbiont provides the interface between the species. The connection is at the base of the cranium."

"Like a cyberjack," Hue commented.

"Exactly. Without symbionts, there is no communication between Nzaghi and Qell. The queen's tendril has evolved, to connect with a nerve, at the base of your neck, there." It showed him. "Not every Nzaghi is suitable. I'm not. Maybe you could be joined. You might even live."

"Why tell me all this now?" he had asked El Silencioso.

"You asked me."

"That was days ago."

"But still the question was asked. I owe you much, and answers may pay some debts." El Silencioso spoke increasingly fluently, *but sometimes still without meaning*, Hue decided.

Many questions remained unanswered. *And would remain so*, Hue thought, leading the patrol to his house. He'd walked over the headland and approached the nearest aliens.

"We need medicines and food," Hue explained sheepishly, wishing he felt better about his betrayal.

"I understand," El Silencioso said as they led it out, an Nzaghi flanking it on each side, fur dappling in furious exchanges. El Silencioso lunged, and pushed one of its guards, brandishing the gun it had taken earlier from under Hue's bed.

It bolted for freedom, and someone screamed as a shot rang out; one of the patrol slumped. Lasers lanced across the square in response.

El Silencioso fired again; the symbiont's larger head jerked back, then it flopped to the ground.

Lasers flashed again; El Silencioso staggered and dropped, the smell of searing flesh drifting in the evening breeze.

Hue ran to the fugitive first. He turned it over, though he knew it was dead.

"I'm sorry," Hue whispered, closing the alien's eyes. He turned toward the symbiont, pushing through its colleagues.

"This creature is dying," another Nzaghi said. "We must

connect the host to another."

"Are you volunteering?" Hue asked.

"We are unsuitable," the alien replied. "We will take too long to return. It will die."

"What if you connected it to me?" Hue surprised himself. *Does the need to heal run so very deep?*

"You?"

"Me." Hue added, "Theoretically, it's possible."

"You," it said, "are too old. And you are needed to perform the operation."

"You'll have to patch a comm-link to your ship, to talk me through the operation. We still need a host."

"That one," the Nzaghi said. The Qell circled José.

"Impossible!"

"If you refuse, we will destroy the village," the creature said.

"If we agree, can we have more drugs? More medicines?" *You can't do this!*

"We do not barter." The alien's voice was flat. "You must co-operate."

But if you don't, the whole village dies!

Emilio shook his head., "God forgive us."

"Oh, I hope so," Hue agreed. "José, will you help me be a doctor?" The boy nodded and Hue thought, *Call me Judas.*

"No!" Martin gripped his arm so tight Hue thought it might snap, but Hue managed to prise Martin's fingers loose. "You mustn't do this!"

"Then tell me how, Martin!" Hue hissed. "Tell me how I save these people!"

"We can fight them!"

"With what, *boy*? Sticks? Rocks? Against those things?"

Martin whispered, "You did this. You brought them here." His head dropped.

Hue thought, *I'm sorry I couldn't save your mother, Martin.* He turned to the alien: "Set up a comm-link. I'll need guidance."

"Agreed."

Hue held out the mask they brought, and José put it on. Hue's world narrowed to a tunnel containing only him, José and the Nzaghi. Instruments seemed to materialise from thin air. His hands became slick with his sweat and José's blood. Snick; sever the vestigial link between the Qell Queen, an ugly flaccid thing limply waving around for a new home. He felt his gorge rise, but forced it down. Cut, the incision either side of the medulla oblongata, *careful of the braceiocephalic artery, Hue, we don't want to damage him* and the waving tendril forcing its way in with his assistance, enzymes from the tendril bonding with the boy's vestibulocochlear nerves. Hopefully, the Qell can fire signals up the fibres to the brain. *And God help him, if the enzymes damage him, or the boy's immune system rejects the truly alien tissue.*

"I don't know if this is going to work," Hue said.

"It must," The Nzaghi said. "This is an honour for your species."

"Enough for you treat us like civilised beings?" Hue asked.

"Perhaps," the alien said. "It will be a start. If the boy lives he will be an ambassador."

"I'm sure he'll be thrilled," Hue closed the incision and stitched it.

"What he feels is irrelevant. It is –"

"– necessary. Yes, I think we understand. Now he must sleep."

His tunnel world opened, and Hue noticed the intent way the onlookers watched them.

"He can sleep while travelling with us," the alien said.

José's eyes opened. "Mar. Tin," he gasped. Hue thought what looked out was already not wholly human, but perhaps that was imagination.

"Here, little brother." Martin stroked José's forehead.

"Be...not...fear, for me."

The Nzaghi lifted José into the transport, and Martin wrapped his arms around his aunt's shoulders.

The flyer lifted off in near silence.

Hue's hands shook in reaction from having to hold them steady. He had thought that nothing could be worse than when Tranh died, than when he passed the corpses lying in ditches on his long walk south from Barcelona. He knew now that he had been wrong.

Hue bowed his head, unable to meet the villagers' eyes.

Martin spat at his feet, and turned his aunt around, so that their backs faced Hue.

Emilio cleared his throat: "Martin was right. You brought them here. From now on, you live apart."

One after the other, the villagers turned their backs on him.

"Six days," Hue spoke into the wind. "And I'm already half-crazy with boredom." *And loneliness.* He watched the ship that had hovered over the village all morning. It was like watching a mountain clamber into the sky when it eventually ascended. "They carry on as if nothing has happened," he murmured. He ate the bread they villagers left him at dawn. They wouldn't let him starve. They might need him yet.

He heard a noise, but didn't turn around.

"The aliens visited us," a familiar voice said. "They offered to take the children. For education, they said." He spat the words, "for a fresh start. I suppose you were right," his visitor said. "We won't beat them with sticks or rocks."

Hue turned around, surprised. "You shouldn't be here."

Martin stared at him, his expression unreadable – it might have been hate, or it might not. "Teach me to read," he said.

The Soul of the Machine

Eric Brown

We were a day out of Sinclair's Landfall when I left my cabin and climbed to the flight-deck.

Since lighting out from the pleasure planet I'd slept for twenty hours solid, leaving Ella in charge of *A Long Way From Home*. As I neared the hatch I could hear Ella and Karrie chattering away. I paused outside.

"Sounds tough..." Karrie was sympathising.

"My parents were very strict," Ella said.

"So you just upped sticks, took the first outbound ship, and ended up on Sinclair's Landfall?"

"I'd dreamed for years of getting away."

"So why the haste in leaving Landfall? Sounds like you were being chased."

Ella fell silent.

I stepped onto the flight-deck.

"Why don't you tell Karrie the truth, Ella?" I said. "We'll be spending a long time together from now on. I don't want lies coming between us."

I slipped into my sling between the women. The viewscreen showed the marbled expanse of void-space. Ella pierced me with her midnight eyes. She murmured, "I think the fewer people who know, the better."

"We're all in this together, Ella. Now tell Karrie the truth."

Karrie looked from me to Ella, bemused.

Ella leaned forward, looking around me, and stared at Karrie. "I am an AI construct, Karrie, designation MT-xia-73, running on an integrated self-aware paradigm. Technically I am the property of the Mitsubishi-Tata combine."

She lay back in the sling, her face serene, and gazed into the void.

Karrie was open-mouthed in astonishment. "So all that loveless childhood shtick... the strict parents?"

"My cover story."

Karrie turned to me. "She's an AI? A robot?"

"I am not, actually, a robot. I am a biologically nurtured entity constructed around a self-aware matrix core."

Karrie nodded. "That's good to know." In a whisper she said to me, "And you let this... this *thing* aboard the ship?"

I shrugged. "What else could I do? There were spider-drones after her. They'd've taken her back to a life of servitude."

Karrie just shook her head. She hissed, "One, it's not a 'she', it's an 'it'! Two, it's a goddamned machine, and that's what machines are built for – servitude."

"She's self-aware, Karrie. To me, that means she has rights. She can make choices. She wanted out. She wanted freedom. And I decided to help her get away."

"Ed, she's a soulless machine, a self-serving mechanism lacking in the slightest humanity."

"That's nonsense," I began.

"Jesus..." Karrie breathed. "Listen to me, Ed. If Miss Universe here had been a Lyran cephalopod, would you have helped it then?"

I stared through the screen. "Of course I would."

"Bullshit, Ed! She's sex on legs and when you met her your balls were bursting after six months banged up on this tin can – that's why you helped her." She barked a laugh. "And then you find out she's a machine!"

"Karrie!" I snapped.

She slipped from her sling and hurried to the hatch, muttering to herself.

When Karrie was gone, Ella turned to me and said, "I'm sorry if my presence has caused distress between the two of you, Ed."

"Karrie'll be fine. She gets hot-headed from time to time. She'll calm down soon enough."

She reached out and squeezed my hand.

A couple of hours later Ella left the flight-deck, saying she wanted to take a tour of the ship and familiarise herself with its features. She hadn't been gone long when Karrie climbed up and slipped into the sling beside mine.

"Calmed down?"

"I still think you're one goddammed fool, Ed. You realise Mitsubishi won't take kindly to having their property kidnapped like this?"

"I'm not exactly kidnapping, Karrie. She came of her own free will."

"And let's see how that defence'll stand up in a court of law." She looked across at me. "You're smitten, Ed. Admit it."

"Don't talk rubbish."

"You should see your eyes when you stare at her–"

"Karrie. Look... She reminds me of my kid sister, okay? She died when I was–"

"You told me." She shook her head. "But, Ed, she isn't real. She's no more a personality than... than the ship's smartware core. She just looks a lot prettier, that's all."

I shrugged. "What's real, Karrie? Ella seems real enough to me."

Footsteps sounded on the rungs of the ladder. Ella inserted her slim form through the hatch and padded across to her sling.

After a short silence, she turned to us and said, "I can be of immense benefit to you, Ed."

119

Beside me, Karrie snorted, "You bet!"

Ella continued. "Not only can I pilot this ship, and assist you, Karrie, with repairs – but my memory cache can be of benefit in locating the wrecks of starships."

I looked at her. "It can?"

Her Venezuelan features remained neutral, watching me. "For instance, I know the precise location of a cargo vessel abandoned in the Dzuba system five light years from our present position."

I blinked. "You sure? I've heard nothing–"

"It was never made public. The *Nakamura* was chartered by the Mitsubishi company to ferry classified products from one of its manufactories. When its ion drive exploded and the ship emerged into real-space near Dzuba, Mitsubishi decided to empty the wreck of sensitive materials and destroy what remained."

"So why haven't I heard about it on the grapevine?"

"Mitsubishi scorch-earthed the ship, but thought it wise not to publicise its whereabouts. I suspect they were hauling contraband, but I cannot be sure."

"When was this?"

"Five years ago."

"And you say you know where the wreck is situated?"

Ella nodded. "To the precise metre."

"Lay in co-ordinates to Dzuba," I said. I tried not to look too smug as I glanced at Karrie, but she was busying herself with the controls.

We were a few hours from Dzuba, and still in void-space, when Karrie looked up from her com-screen and murmured, "We're being followed, Ed."

"You sure about that?"

"Well, the same ship's been on our tail for the past hour."

Ella said, "Longer than that, Karrie. I noticed it a few hours after we phased into the void, a day ago."

"Great," I said. "Why didn't you mention it then?"

Ella stared at me with impassive eyes. "Your knowledge of the situation would have made no difference to the fact of our being followed."

"But I might have been able to do something about it."

She opened her mouth to contradict me, but thought better of it.

I said, "Karrie, can you get a visual of the ship?"

"Working on it..." She tapped her touch-pad. Seconds later the viewscreen before us flickered, and the vista of marmoreal grey was replaced by the close-up of a small, sleek ship.

Ella said, "It's the same vessel that tracked me to Sinclair's Landfall."

I looked across at her. "I thought we'd got rid of the spiders."

"We accounted for three of them on Sinclair's Landfall. The Watson Interceptor carries a complement of twelve." She stared at the screen. "Just nine to go."

I considered our options. "Right... How about we phase from the void and make for Dzuba? If we head around the sun at maximum speed and then phase back..."

Karrie said, "That's a Watson Interceptor, Ed. We'd never outrun it in a straight race."

"I have a suggestion," Ella said. "We phase from the void, as Ed says. But instead of rounding the sun, we take refuge in the Mitsubishi wreck."

"And they'd just follow us in there and flush us out."

Ella turned her wondrous gaze on me. "Ed, the wreck is vast. The ship was Titanic class. We could insert ourselves in the wreckage and they'd never find us."

"This is madness!" Karrie said.

"We have no other option," I said. "What do you suggest, we let them catch up and take Ella?"

Karrie stared at me. "You said it," she muttered to herself.

I nodded to Ella. "We'll phase from the void. As soon as we're out, lay in co-ordinates to the wreck."

"Good God," I said, "will you take a look at that..."

Dzuba burned in the right of the viewscreen like a naked furnace. Before the sun, centre screen, the wreck of the Mitsubishi ship hung like some demented sculptor's schematic representation of an explosion in a scrap yard. At its centre was a solid tangle of concertinaed chambers, bulkheads and decking, warped and blackened by the blow-out.

"Okay," Ella said, "I suggest we make for the core."

I nodded. "Do that." I glanced at Karrie. "Have the spiders emerged from void-space?"

She checked her com-screen. "Not yet, but I reckon they won't be long."

"Let's accelerate. If we can get to the wreck before they phase-out—"

I was silenced by the sudden thrust, pitching my sling backwards. I hung on as the ship careered through space towards the wreck, dodging peripheral shards and scraps of metal.

I glanced across at Ella. "You doing this?"

Tight-lipped, she nodded. "I am considerably faster than your smartcore drive."

"That's good to know," I said as a blackened engine nacelle tumbled past the viewscreen with metres to spare.

Five minutes later we slowed our slalom ride as Ella eased us past great chunks of debris that resembled metallic icebergs. We made for a relatively intact section of the ship which I guessed must have once been its cargo hold and storage decks. Wreckage hung all around us, eerie in its stillness.

"Still no sign of the other ship?"

Karrie shook her head. "We're in luck."

We slowed even more and inched between sections of buckled decking. The glare of the sun cut off suddenly. Ella activated searchlights, which picked out hanks of Medusa cabling and jagged superstructure. We were near the centre of the explosion.

We emerged into sunlight again, the glare dazzling.

"Okay..." Ella said, her tongue showing as she inched the ship onto a vast shelf that had once been a cargo deck. "If we hole up here, switch off the operating systems and hang silent..."

I nodded. "Do it."

We settled gently and Ella powered down the ship little by little. Soon we were running just enough energy to keep the viewscreen operating, showing the view back the way we had come.

A few minutes later Karrie said, "There is one big flaw in this scenario, you realise?"

"Which is?" I asked.

"So we sit tight, twiddling our thumbs. Hoping the spiders get bored and go home. Only, ah, they're machines, right? They don't get bored. They have mission goals, and they stick to them, whether they take days, years, or decades to achieve."

I looked across at Ella.

She said, "Karrie is right."

"So...?" I asked, a little exasperated.

"So... the spider-drones will wait."

"Which," Karrie pointed out with sweet malice in her tone, "is all very well for non-human entities like you, Ella. But for me and Ed here, meaties – isn't that what you call us? – we, like, need food and drink. That might run out after a year or so, no?"

"I have considered that eventuality, Karrie. That's why I'll be going out there to apprehend and destroy the spiders, when the opportunity arises."

Karrie looked across at Ella. "Back on Sinclair's Landfall," she said, "you were running from just three of the critters... Now you're talking about confronting a whole shipful of the bastards."

Ella regarded Karrie impassively. "Back then running was an option, Karrie. Now there's nowhere to run. I have to fight."

Fear fluttered in my chest. "Is this wise?"

"It's the only option."

"I don't want you to come to any harm."

"Your concern is unwarranted. I'm perfectly capable of ensuring my own safety."

Karrie interrupted, urgently, "When you two have quite finished – we have company."

I looked up. The viewscreen showed a narrowing vista of decking, terminating in a wedge of dark, star-flecked space. As we watched, the Watson Interceptor settled at the far end of the vanishing point, facing us.

I said in a whisper, "Have they seen us?"

"Pretty much looks that way," Karrie said. "So much for their never finding us."

I wondered, then, if Ella had meant the spiders to find us, all along. Perhaps she wanted the ensuing showdown?

She leapt from her sling and strode across the flight-deck.

"Ella?" I called after her.

"Let her go," Karrie said.

I slipped from my sling and followed Ella. "I'm suiting up and coming with you. You can't go out there alone."

She disappeared through the hatch and descended the ladder.

"Jesus, Ed. She's a damned machine. She'll be ten times more capable than you in any situation—"

I knew the sense of Karrie's worlds, but right then my heart was overriding my head. I slipped through the hatch.

"Christ!" Karrie yelled after me. "You're not going out there alone, dammit. I'm coming with you!"

Five minutes later Karrie and I were suited up. I broke out three rifles from stores and handed them out. Ella moved towards the exterior hatch.

I stopped her with a hand on her arm. "What about—" I began.

"I don't need a suit, Ed."

Behind me, Karrie snickered.

Ella said, "We'll move away from the ship, gain high ground.

When the spiders show themselves..."

We cycled through the airlock and stepped onto the buckled deck, to be greeted by a chiaroscuro panorama of black shadow and golden sun glare. The vista was disconcerting. The brain is soothed by order, neat lines and precise geometry, but the blow-out had rendered normality chaotic. What should have been the interior of a prime class cargo vessel was a blasted travesty of order, a haywire tangle of metal and machine parts. The spacer in me was troubled.

Ella gestured, and I made out a twist of metal rising like a spiral staircase to a section of horizontal decking: a perfect vantage point.

She took off, sprinting and leaping and covering a couple of hundred metres in about ten seconds. Karrie and I gave chase, using our thrusters to assist us over the uneven deck and up the jagged rise of metal. A minute later we crouched behind a scorched radiation baffle and stared back the way we had come.

My ship sat directly below us like a contented toad. Five hundred metres away, the Interceptor perched daintily akimbo on thin magnetic stanchions, twinkling in the sunlight.

As we watched, movement showed towards the rear of the Interceptor. A gaggle of spider-drones jetted from their ship and took cover behind scraps of metal.

My heart thudded.

"Did you see exactly how many left the ship?" I asked.

Ella's reply sounded tinny in my helmet. "I counted four. That leaves five in the ship. I'll take out the four, then tackle the Interceptor."

Down below, a spider broke cover and jetted towards my ship, its domed carapace twinkling in the sunlight. In a couple of eye-blinks it reached *A Long Way From Home*.

The spider landed on the side of my ship and clung on, one tentacle directed towards the viewscreen. I wondered if it was scanning for life...

I glanced at Ella, gesturing at my rifle. She shook her head.

"Don't want them to know where we are. We'll wait till the other three show themselves."

The first spider climbed across the skin of my ship. Karrie touched my arm, gesturing back towards the Interceptor. The other three spiders were breaking cover and jetting towards the first.

Ella said, "I'll take out one and two. You take number three. Karrie number four, okay? Fire when I fire."

Heart pounding even faster, I nodded. Karrie gave the thumbs up.

I arranged myself on the edge of the deck, gazing down at the floating spiders.

Ella lifted her rifle, aimed and fired. Two quick blasts took out the drone beside our ship and the leader of the follow-up party. I aimed at the third drone and squeezed off two rapid shots, surprised and elated as the spider exploded in a dazzling blast. Beside me, Karrie accounted for the spider bringing up the rear.

Suddenly, all was stillness down below. Adrenalin coursed through me, bringing involuntary laughter to my lips.

My elation was short-lived.

Ella touched my arm and pointed. Another five spider drones jetted from the Interceptor and headed towards us.

And now they knew where we were.

The leading spider raised a tentacle and fired. A line of flechettes hosed towards us, missing Karrie's head by half a metre and ricocheting off a metal spar next to my shoulder.

Ella pushed herself away. I rolled, grabbed Karrie and applied vertical thrust. We shot into the air, earning a round of fire. A second later we thumped against what had been a bulkhead and I cut the thrusters, applied horizontal thrust, and sped off after Ella.

We dodged through a crazy obstacle course of tortured starship, fleeing for our lives.

Karrie and I might not have made it by ourselves, but Ella came back for us. One second she was nowhere to be seen, and the next she landed before us, grabbed our hands and took off towards a floating corridor. We passed within, jetting between flame-scorched walls.

The corridor snaked for a hundred metres then turned at a right angle unplanned by the starship's designers. We eased through a tight gap and found ourselves in a small observation nacelle. Ella looked around, checking for another way out. She found one: a rent in the far wall of the bubble-shaped chamber.

I pulled myself towards the long, curving screen and gazed down on a sunlit scene of mangled starship, my heart thudding. Ella and Karrie floated beside me, staring out.

"There," Ella said, pointing. "There, there and there..."

I made out four small, sunlit specks jetting their way through the wreckage, moving relentlessly towards us.

Karrie said, "It's as if they know exactly where we are."

"Impossible," Ella replied. "They're merely going on last observations and extrapolating."

"So what do we do now?" Karrie asked.

"We circle back towards their ship. When we get there, we disable it and light out."

Ella's long, black hair floated, dishevelled, about her perfect features. I wanted to reach out and stroke her cheek.

Karrie said, "And how the hell do we do that – I mean, find where the ships are? I don't know about you, but I'm lost."

"I know exactly where the ships are located," Ella said.

I stared through the screen. Four spider-drones were leaping through the debris towards us.

"Where's number five?" I said.

"Maybe they left it guarding the ship," Karrie said.

"If so, then one spider will pose no threat," Ella said. "Okay, let's go."

She made for the slit in the nacelle, eased herself through, and disappeared. I followed, squeezing through the rent and turning to help Karrie.

We were standing on a narrow ledge, staring at a vertiginous drop past what had been the ship's reactor. Below, all that remained was a blackened cauldron, littered with charred wires and what might have been shattered skeletal fragments.

Above us, two slabs of thickened metal provided a hidey-hole like an equals sign. Ella took my hand and leapt.

We sailed through the intervening space, blinded as we came back into sunlight, and landed on the lower slab. I swam inside, eager to be away from the open end. Karrie caught up with us.

Ahead, Ella stopped.

Now we knew the whereabouts of the fifth spider.

The spider leapt, caught Ella before she could move, and retreated with her into the shadows.

Karrie was faster, and more accurate, than I could ever have been.

She fired her laser and hit one of the spider's standing tentacle. The spider tottered, giving Ella the opportunity to twist in its grip, raise her rifle and insert it into one of the drone's cranial ports. She pulled the trigger. The resulting detonation sent her tumbling backwards.

She fetched up in my arms. The front of her onepiece was scorched, showing burned flesh beneath. I glanced at the spider gyrating before us, limbs twitching. Karrie fired again and finished it off.

"Thanks," Ella said to Karrie. "I owe you one."

"No sweat." Karrie sounded dazed, as if she couldn't believe her own accuracy. I wondered if it had been a lucky strike – helped by the fact that she had not been overly bothered about hitting Ella at the same time.

"Okay," Ella said. "This way."

We followed her down a helter-skelter of twisted metal, emerging in a sunlit chamber minutes later. I recognised what must have been the dining hall decorated with assorted art-works, its walls slotted with horizontal observation screens.

I took Ella and Karrie's hands and jetted off across the void, fetching up against the far wall. We hung near a screen, gazing out.

Karrie pointed, and I nodded. A kilometre away, partially obscured by tortured spars and floating bulkheads, I made out the squat bulk of *A Long Way From Home*, and beyond it the Interceptor.

There was no sign of the pursuing spiders.

Ella turned, holding onto the frame of the screen, and stared through. She showed no reaction to the burn across her drumskin-tight abdomen. Floating there, she looked like a troubled teenager treading water, her expression pulled into a frown.

"What?" I said.

She pointed through the viewscreen, to a blocky, blackened chamber floating before the fiery ball of Dzuba.

"What about it?"

She ignored my question and pointed across the hall at a corridor. "This way."

Confused, but trusting her, I took Ella's hand, then Karrie's, and applied horizontal thrust. We jetted across the hall towards the corridor, then pulled ourselves through the swing doors.

Ella led the way along a series of corridors and passageways, twisted out of true by the blast. We were heading away from the ships.

Seconds later the corridor ended abruptly, giving on to open space. Twenty metres away was the chamber Ella had indicated through the screen, connected to a floating corridor.

We joined hands and jetted across the gap, then inserted ourselves into the umbilical and bobbed along the snaking corridor. Minutes later we came to a thick door marked: Limited Access. Authorised Personnel Only.

The sliding door was ripped diagonally. Ella eased herself through the gap. Exchanging a glance with Karrie, I followed.

We were in a long chamber, the entire left side of which had been torn away in the explosion. The chamber was open to the dazzling light of Dzuba, which illuminated a row of tanks along the length of the right-hand wall. I counted ten in all.

I approached the first tank, peered through the shattered glass, and grimaced at the contents.

The body was bloated, its nakedness swollen to gross proportions. He had been a young man, once. The expression on his face suggested he'd been conscious of his demise.

I looked along the row of tanks. Most of them had been punctured and depressurised in the blow-out. I saw a tank whose screen was still in one piece, and jetted towards it. I peered in, shielding my eyes, and made out the contorted form of another human being. Whatever powered the tanks was still in operation: a strip-light illuminated the corpse's tortured death mask.

Ella was examining the last tank. "What the hell was this?" I asked.

She stared at me, an odd expression in her eyes, and just shook her head.

I couldn't work it out. Cold sleep had been superseded decades ago, when the void was discovered. So why had the Mitsubishi-Tata combine been transporting corpsicles through space?

Ella pressed her face against the glass and peered into the tank.

"I always thought there was something strange about this ship," she said. "Why did Mitsubishi leave it becalmed, why the scorched-earth policy? They sent in operatives to destroy the evidence. This chamber was originally closer to the core of the ship, but blast pushed it all the way out here. The operatives obviously assumed it'd been destroyed in the blow-out."

"How do you know all this?" Karrie asked.

"I downloaded a classified file just before I absconded from the manufactory asteroid. The file contained encrypted information about the ship and its cargo."

I stared at her perfect face and indicated the tanked corpses.

"They were illegally transporting colonists, right? Or ferrying criminals or..."

She said nothing, just nudged past me and headed for the entrance. I had no option but to follow.

For the next fifteen minutes we skirted the outer edges of the explosion. To our left, the fiery giant of Dzuba burned. To our right, somewhere in the tangled sphere of wreckage, five spider-drones continued their remorseless search.

Ella came to a halt, clutching a girder, and signalled for us to join her. "The ships are down there," she said, pointing. We peered over a sheared bulkhead and saw the two ships, less than a kay away. "Follow me."

There was still no sign of the spiders, and that made me jumpy. The drones were perfectly camouflaged in this realm of sunlight and silvery shards: they could be anywhere.

Ella swarmed over the bulkhead and pushed herself from one piece of floating debris to the next, pausing between each push to scan ahead. Cautiously, we followed.

We were half a kay from the ships when we came across the next spider-drone.

Ella was leading the way, scaling an abbreviated sponson. Karrie went next, using her suit's jets, and I brought up the rear. We came to the top, paused and looked ahead. A battlefield of assorted debris separated us from the ships.

I actually saw the spider, perched on a blackened engine cowl five metres ahead and to our right. Its legs were retracted and it sat absolutely still, as innocent as a pepper pot. My gaze flicked over the drone, and only a fraction of a second later did I realise my mistake.

But by that time it was too late.

It waited until Ella was level with the spider, then struck like a mechanical cobra. A tentacle lashed out, snaring Ella. Karrie aimed her laser again, but this time she was too slow. The spider, clutching Ella, raised a second tentacle as quick as lightning and fired at Karrie.

I yelled out loud as a flechette struck her face-plate.

She tumbled head over heels, careering away from me, and I could only think that if a flechette had breached her face-plate...

I looked back at Ella. She hit her captor with a karate chop, snapping its weapon's tentacle, then raised her laser and – instead of firing again at point blank range – smashed the butt into the drone's optical sensor.

The drone released her, tentacles flailing, and she gave an expert karate kick. I watched the spider sail into space, impotently windmilling its limbs. Ella raised her laser, took aim and fired. The drone exploded, the beautiful bloom of its detonation quickly extinguished in the vacuum.

A second later she dived, hit me in the midriff and hauled me into the cover of an engine block just as line of flechettes stitched the air where I'd been standing. She pulled me after her, stopping only when we were a good hundred metres from where we'd been ambushed.

I looked around for Karrie. "Where – ?" I began.

Ella pointed. "Look..."

I peered through a briar patch of tangled circuitry to where she was pointing.

"Oh, Christ..." I whispered.

Fifty metres before us, the four remaining drones were hauling Karrie's unconscious form towards the ships. Unconscious, I hoped – not dead.

I attempted to reach her via the radio link, but she didn't reply.

I said, "What do they want with her?"

Ella thought about it. "A bargaining chip?"

"But that'd work only if Karrie were alive."

"She is. I am monitoring her suit's metabolic read-outs. Karrie was knocked unconscious by the blast, but her suit retained its integrity. She'll be okay."

I felt a wave of relief. "So... what do we do?"

I stared through the wreckage. The drones had reached their ship, bearing Karrie like a trophy, and laid her on the buckled decking. Karrie lay very still, floating a metre above the deck.

"Ed, make sure the spiders don't catch sight of you, okay?"

"What about you?"

"I have an idea."

"What?"

But a second later she was gone – vanishing behind a jackstraw mess of metal-work – back the way we had come.

I reckoned she was going to make a detour around the ships and somehow effect Karrie's rescue. She had said she owed Karrie one, after all.

I opened the radio link and told Ella to be careful, but she chose not to reply.

I raised my head and stared down at the quartet of drones. They floated above the deck, surrounding Karrie's bobbing form. They appeared to be discussing what to do next.

I willed Ella to appear and annihilate the bastards single-handedly...

I clung to the girder, floating in space, and I had never felt as helpless in all my long life.

Fifteen minutes passed, thirty...

One hour later I was beginning to think that the drones had caught Ella when I glimpsed movement a hundred metres ahead and to my left.

A slight, nimble figure moved through the wreckage towards the decking where the ships sat. My heart surged, then sank. I could hardly bring myself to watch the fire-fight that was bound to ensue.

Ella pushed herself from one chunk of floating debris to the next. As she kicked off, her momentum impelled the debris with motion, leaving an easily traceable pattern of wreckage swirling in her wake.

And if I could see it, then so could the drones.

The odd thing was, it seemed as if Ella wasn't that concerned about being seen. I wondered if this was part of her master-plan, some tactic beyond my merely human cognitive capabilities.

She picked her way through the wreckage towards the gathered drones, and minutes later appeared before them... and still I expected some last minute twist, some grand combative gesture that would render the spiders kaput.

She pushed herself from her last place of cover and landed on the deck with a quick genuflection, as if curtsying to her enemies.

And then she raised her hands into the air and gave herself up to their custody.

I called out her name, cursing her stupidity. I tried to get through to her on the radio.

Silence.

I watched as the drones surrounded her, pinioning her arms and legs with their flashing tentacles and jetting with her towards the Interceptor.

She disappeared into the ship and the hatch slid shut behind her.

My attention returned to the ramp of my ship, snagged by movement there. Karrie was stirring. Dazed, she raised a gloved hand to her shattered face-plate as she floated above the deck.

Then she applied thrust, directed herself towards the ship, and hit the entry sensor. A second later she disappeared inside.

"Karrie..." I tried to get through to her. Still no reply: I assumed the laser blast to her helmet had affected the receiver.

I cursed Ella for her capitulation, and at the same time felt a welling of strange pride.

Seconds later I saw sudden movement to my left. I turned, raising my laser, thinking for a terrible second that I had miscalculated and another spider had found me.

I blinked. Ella was floating across the gulf of space towards me.

Ella?

I caught her, feeling her slim form through my padded gloves. "Ella! What the...?"

She positioned her head before my face-plate and smiled in at me. Christ, but I wanted to kiss her.

"Ella?" I said incredulously. "You got away?"

She silenced me with a raised forefinger, pressing it against my face-plate. Her lips described a moue. "Shh," she said. "Those corpsicles back there, they weren't criminals or colonists, as you surmised. They were a series of state-of-the-art AIs, proto-types of the series that would become the MT-xia-73 designation."

I stared at her. "You?"

She nodded. "Me. But back then, five years ago, there was a Federation-wide proscription on the manufacture of semi-sentient, self-aware AIs. That didn't stop Mitsubishi from developing the series, though. This ship was hauling a dozen individuals from the manufactory to Sirius III, where they were to be field tested, when the blow-out happened."

I shook my head. "I don't understand," I said, but I was beginning to guess at what had happened.

Ella said, "Back in the cryo-hold I found a survivor. The only one. I decided I'd go back for her, once we'd sorted out the spiders... but then the bastards captured Karrie and I had an idea."

I shook my head in silent wonder.

"I resuscitated the AI," she went on. "She was blank, just meat and an inchoate operating system. So I downloaded a doctored copy of myself into her program core –"

I stopped her. "So the AI who gave herself up in return for Karrie's release... she's a version of you?"

Ella smiled. "A very limited version. She has a fraction of my memory capacity and mentation. But she is me inasmuch as she knows that she had to give herself up to the spiders in order not only to save Karrie, but to save me... *herself*, in effect."

She touched my shoulder, gestured. I turned and followed her gaze. On the plane of decking below, the spiders' ship rose slowly, turned on its axis, and burned away from the wreck of the *Nakamura*.

"The AI is sufficiently me," Ella went on, "to fool the spiders for a while. The drones will reach the manufactory in around seven days. We have a leeway of that long before Mitsubishi realise they were duped."

Laughing like a fool, I hugged her.

"Come on, Ed. Let's get back to the ship. Karrie will be wondering what's happened to us."

Karrie was in her sling on the flight-deck when we pulled ourselves through the hatch.

She stood, elation making her look twenty years younger, and moved across the deck. "Jesus, Ed... What happened? The spiders' ship just up and left!"

"It's a pretty complicated story," I said. "Ella, why don't you tell Karrie while I start tractor beaming some of this junk."

I slipped into my sling and ordered the smartcore to activate the beam. There were some mighty chunks of machinery out there that would fetch good money on the open market back on Altair III.

While I worked, I watched Ella as she recounted what had happened, and I smiled to myself.

When Ella had finished her story, Karrie nodded and said, "Thank you, Ella." She glanced across at me, sharply. "And what are you smiling at?"

I waved. "Oh, I was just thinking of the killing we'll make when we haul this junk back to Altair," I said. "Okay, tractor beam established?"

"Affirmative," Karrie murmured.

"Then let's get out of here."

"Phasing out," Ella said, smiling across at me.

I returned her smile, considering what she had done back

there. Karrie had called Ella a selfish, soulless machine, lacking in humanity, but I had no doubts at all. Okay, in rescuing Karrie she had also saved her own skin...

But if self-preservation isn't a human motivation, I thought to myself, then what is?

We phased into the void and headed to Altair III.

Extraordinary

Rendition

Steve Longworth

Huang watched impassively as the prisoner transport ship fired its landing rockets and descended silently to the lunar surface.

Ignoring a spectacular view of the Earth, he turned and walked unhurriedly from the observation deck to the arrivals hall where he stood and waited for his new charge to complete the necessary administrative processes.

This one was special.

An automatic door slid silently open. Two heavily-armoured security droids marched up to Huang and stopped in front of him. Manacled between them, dressed in bright orange prison fatigues, was a small, fit-looking, wiry man who managed to maintain an air of dignity despite struggling to cope with the transition from weightlessness to one-sixth earth gravity.

"Welcome to the Moon, Mister Li."

"An actual human being," said Li. "I was beginning to wonder if the whole place was automated."

"As you well know, there are still some things that people can do better than machines," Huang replied.

The prisoner looked around him, calmly taking in his surroundings. A faint tang of ozone itched the air.

"The Moon," said Li with a nod. "You know, a lot of very powerful people have been at pains to point out that this facility doesn't exist. The Party goes to enormous lengths to achieve its ends."

Huang consulted the sheet of smart plastic in his right hand. Words and images scrolled under his gaze. "You've escaped from some of our most secure prisons; you've made a real nuisance of yourself."

"The Party can't hold me."

"You are here at the will of the people."

"I'm here at the will of the Party; The People's Republic will thrive, but the Party's doomed," replied Li in a matter-of-fact tone.

Huang allowed himself a tight little smile. "Those are propositions we'll have plenty of time to discuss. Let me show you to your room."

As they left the arrivals hall, the transport ship launched for the return journey to Earth. The prisoner party walked in near silence through nondescript windowless corridors, the only sounds being the air circulators and the servomotors of the droids. They stopped in front of a door that opened when Huang placed his palm against the ident-panel. The small group stepped inside. At a gesture from Huang one of the droids released Li from its manacle and stepped out into the corridor, taking a position directly facing the door.

"Make yourself at home," said Huang, stepping back into the corridor himself. He touched the panel again. The door closed and became transparent, a sophisticated version of a one-way mirror. Inside, the second droid released its manacle and stepped backwards into a corner of the cell. Li rubbed his wrists and walked around his new accommodation, taking in the bed, the table, the chair, the small cupboard and the toilet. He stopped in front of the opaque door, raised his right hand and waved. On the other side of the door Huang smiled, turned, and walked back down the corridor.

They did not meet again for two weeks, a deliberate tactic and all part of the standard softening-up process. Huang realised it was pointless in this instance, but if unsuccessful he did not want to be vulnerable to criticism from disappointed superiors.

Huang stood outside Li's cell, watching through the one-way-mirror door. Li was performing a Tai Chi exercise routine. During the last fortnight the prisoner had spent much time meditating and exercising.

The lights never went off inside the cell; the temperature varied randomly, never allowing the body to acclimatise, and meals were served at irregular intervals. There were no books or other distractions. All these measures were designed to disorientate, but they were wasted on Li, and Huang knew it.

At a signal from the controls embedded in Huang's smartsheet the droid in Li's cell walked over to the exercising prisoner and manacled his hands behind his back. Li made a small startled movement as the droid abruptly sprang into action, but almost instantly recovered his poise.

Satisfied that Li was appropriately restrained, Huang opened the cell door and the droid from the corridor strode in carrying a simple upright chair, which was placed on one side of the small table. Huang sat. The other droid prodded Li to sit in the chair opposite. The men faced each other, less than a metre apart, but divided by a void large enough to swallow the solar system. Their eyes met; the inscrutable versus the impenetrable. Li spoke first.

"This is illegal. I have been kidnapped, subjected to extraordinary rendition, tortured and abused. I demand to be tried or released." He spoke calmly and without rancour.

"Tell me what I need to know and you can go," said Huang.

Li gave a thin smile.

"Of course," he replied. Then said nothing.

They sat there in silence for another five minutes, after which Huang rose and without another word left the cell. The droid followed him out, carrying the extra chair.

Three days later Huang returned. This time Li was asleep, and so the droid in his cell woke him, applied the manacles and brought him to the table. The men sat staring at each other in silence until Li asked, "Is this it?"

Huang remained silent.

"No waterboarding? No psychoprobe? No 'truth serum'?"

"What would you have done?" asked Huang.

"I wouldn't have let me escape, for a start," replied Li.

"You were good," said Huang.

"I was the best."

Huang nodded, slowly. He consulted the smartsheet. "Says here that during your previous sojourns with us on Earth you withstood every known form of interrogation. I guess that's not too surprising, seeing that you invented many of them."

"Oh, believe me, I was good, very good at your job, but even I wouldn't have cracked me. You're wasting your time. Every technique you intend to utilise has been anticipated. You'll kill me before you break me."

Huang didn't doubt this. The scrolling characters described how his predecessors had almost killed Li twice before, once while waterboarding him and once with the psychoprobe.

"We'll see," said Huang.

Their conversation continued, weeks turning into months.

When not questioning Li, Huang occupied himself with the interrogation of the other elite prisoners and the management of The People's Number One Deep Space Lunar Observatory, an establishment that doubled as a prominent projection of Chinese scientific prowess and a cover for the secret prison. The scientific aspect of the facility was mostly automated and required little hands-on input from its single human operative. The giant optical and infrared telescopes and cosmic ray detectors produced astounding images from the edge of the visible universe; the edge of time. Huang, with his firmly imbedded cultural sense of veneration for his ancestors, was impressed and deeply moved by the sight of the ancient cosmos. The astronomers from the

School of Aerospace at Tsinghua University told him that through the instruments he was seeing the Universe as it was thirteen billion years ago, 380,000 years after the Big Bang. It was impossible to see back any further in time, as prior to this the Universe was an opaque plasma of superheated fundamental particles. The Chinese cosmologists pooled their observations with the data from the American, European and Indo-Arabian lunar observatories to produce composite images of astonishing beauty and clarity. Under their patient, combined scrutiny, the whole universe would eventually surrender its structure and origin.

Meanwhile, Huang's interrogation of Li made no headway at all.

Their sessions sometimes lasted for days at a time, Huang bolstered by anti-fatigue endorphins. Then there would be long gaps when Li was left on his own for days or weeks while Huang studied the recordings of their interviews from the array of surveillance devices hidden in Li's room, compiling and submitting reports to his superiors, all the while searching for a way past Li's formidable defences.

Huang's superiors asked why he had decided against physical torture. He told them that this was not because torture offended his sensibilities, but because it was unreliable. In his experience, the subject would tell you whatever they thought you wanted to hear in order to make you stop.

Besides, he wasn't a sadist, he was a technician; and Li was his biggest technical challenge to date.

"Why the Moon?" asked Li.

They had been in intermittent, intimate conversation for over three months. During that time Huang felt they had started to build a grudgingly respectful relationship; two grand masters of their dark art, pitted against each other in a painfully slow combat.

Huang allowed himself a small, grim, internal moment of

satisfaction. He had analysed their interviews and read Li's file over and over, looking for a potential weakness, and he thought he'd identified one: curiosity. Not surprising, really, from the man who was formerly his organisation's most effective interrogator. Huang ignored the question. He would take it away with him, explore the implications, see if he could fashion a tool to get underneath Li's skin.

"Why did you do it?" asked Huang.

Li leaned back in his chair and nodded at the tabletop.

"You've read the file."

"Yes, but it's bullshit."

Li simply grunted.

"You had the ear of the Politburo. You had immense power. Your thoughts mattered. You were a Party man to your fingertips, Li. Then you suddenly developed a liberal conscience? You threw away everything for the sake of – what? I don't get it."

Li leaned forward again.

"I grew sick of it: the hypocrisy, the corruption, the criminal stupidity, the indifference; the monumental incompetence that perpetuated the mess I was supposed to help to clear up. It eventually dawned on me exactly what I was working so hard to protect: greedy, self-serving interests that would stop at nothing to maintain the status quo."

This was good. He was talking now, anger straining at the leash of his self-control.

"Go on…"

"Look at Nigeria, Ethiopia, Sri Lanka, to name but three. What did we do? We promised them help. We sent in experts to assess their industrial and domestic power needs and then we offered them loans to pay for the construction of the necessary infrastructure. 'Don't worry,' we said, 'once you have a modern economy up and running you will be able to pay us back in no time'. But we deliberately overestimated their needs then billed them for massively redundant oversupply. They had no chance of paying, even if their economy had worked as well as we forecast.

When they defaulted on their loans we demanded payment in kind; sites for military bases, mineral rights, their vote at the UN, exclusive contracts for our companies to build all their future infrastructure and rent it back to them at extortionate cost. We enslaved them. We didn't need to invade." Li closed his eyes and tilted up his head. "'The greatest conqueror is he who overcomes the enemy without a blow'."

Huang nodded in approval; Sun Tzu, from *The Art Of War*.

Li opened his eyes again. "No need to invade Hong Kong, we simply waited for the British lease to expire. We learned the dangers of impatience from watching the American debacles in Iraq and Afghanistan. There is no need for physical force. We manacle our victims with debt instead. We recruit their own wealthy elites and make them wealthier, give them a massive stake in our hegemony, just like the ancient Romans when they conquered the known world, just like the decadent Westerners who controlled the African slave trade. There's no difference between the People's Republic and the Triads, except that we do it on a bigger scale and reward our people with government contracts and celebrity."

"'It is forbidden to steal, therefore all thieves are punished, unless they steal vast quantities to the sound of the Shanghai Stock Exchange bell'," paraphrased Huang.

"Very good," said Li, "I'm sure that's exactly what Voltaire would have said if he'd lived in our era."

"And you really believe that you can change this? Which planet are you on?" As soon as the last words slipped out of his mouth Huang realised the unintended dark irony. "But this is how the world has always worked. No one consciously created this system. It evolved, emerged. You know about chaos theory? Complexity emerges from apparently simple initial starting conditions."

Ordered complexity emerging from chaotic simplicity; Huang thought about the images from the edge of space and time being collected by the giant instruments above their head.

145

"The methodology is implicit," he continued, "almost impregnable in its informality, its strength being its tacit nature. Those who wield power know how the world really works, the critical difference between what everyone agrees is supposed to happen and what actually does happen. This has been the way all throughout history. Even the so-called great democracies are simply elected dictatorships in thrall to the powerful vested interests that control the world's economy. In The West the same people circulate through the top jobs in government, the military industries and the international banks; a corporatocracy."

"And where is the difference from our Politburo?" retorted Li, angrily. "Why does nobody notice? Because the same interests also control the media. The Party's greatest success has been to emulate rampant capitalism while at the same time denouncing it as flawed and decadent."

"You sound like a Marxist," said Huang.

"Bah," retorted Li, "anyone who can see the truth is dismissed as an extremist with a discredited ideology. The stark unpalatable reality is that half the world is poised to exploit the wealth of the solar system and the other half still doesn't have access to clean water, basic healthcare and a primary education. It stinks. I'm sick of it."

Li was on the observation deck, his hands manacled behind his back, gazing at the Earth. The pale blue disc, swirled in white, hung majestically above the jagged, undulating grey lunar surface. Huang stood at an angle where he could watch the Earth and subtly observe Li's reactions. The security droids waited patiently on either side of Li, indifferent to the awesome spectacle before them.

"Magnificent," uttered Li. He turned and looked at Huang. "How many human beings have seen this first hand? We're privileged, you and I."

They stood for several minutes in reverent silence, watching their home world, a lonely, dynamic speck of life in the dark void.

"How far away?" asked Li.

"Four hundred thousand kilometres," replied Huang.

Li nodded.

"Beauty and despair," said Li. "Now I know 'why the Moon': beauty and despair. Sun Tzu said, 'All men know the utility of useful things; but they do not know the utility of futility'. You think this will succeed where all your other methods have failed. It won't."

But in the tenor of Li's voice Huang detected the tiniest quaver.

"You had a reputation as someone prepared to do whatever was required to meet your objective, no matter how extreme. Yu always went the extra *li*, and you always got a result."

Following the visit to the observation deck Huang had allowed Li a full uninterrupted eight hours of sleep. He had adjusted the temperature in the cell to a steady, comfortable level and dimmed the lights while Li slept. He had no idea if these counterintuitive measures would help to soften up his adversary, but he felt he had nothing to lose.

If Li had been affected by the subtle improvements in his living conditions he failed to show as much, maintaining the same calm demeanour as always.

"So why the anonymous blog?" asked Huang.

"I've told you why,'" replied Li.

"But you must have known that it was only a matter of time before you were identified."

Li shrugged.

"You compromised half a dozen secret detention centres, identified dozens of extraordinarily rendered detainees, revealed details of interrogation techniques that embarrassed our government and senior statesmen across the world."

"Others were doing the same. Still doing it when I was arrested and I'll bet still doing it even now. I'm not the only one unhappy with what's been going on."

"But you are the most prominent, the most unexpected."

Li shrugged again. "If there's one thing my experience taught me it's this: we know nothing about other people."

"Who helped you to escape?"

"So now we finally come to the reason why I'm here," said Li.

"Who?" asked Huang again.

"Cultivated people who consider justice foremost."

Huang narrowed his eyes. "Confucius," he muttered.

"Confucius taught that 'when cultivated people have courage without justice they become rebellious. When petty people have courage without justice they become brigands.' That's what the Party is, a band of nuclear-armed, space-faring, two-faced petty brigands."

"Who helped you?" repeated Huang.

"Dangerous idealists who've asked themselves an important question: 'How far can a society compromise its values in order to preserve them?' Can we uphold the rule of law by trampling over it?" Li shook his head. "I don't think so."

"Who are these dangerous idealists?"

"I don't know. They very sensibly keep their identities secret."

"I don't believe you."

"Of course not. But I wouldn't tell you even if I knew."

"Why do you think our political system is doomed?" asked Huang.

"Because it's inherently unstable. You can't have such a lopsided arrangement with such glaring disparity between haves and have-nots and expect it to continue indefinitely."

"Surely the entire history of humanity proves you wrong."

"The entire history of humanity is the chronicle of the consequences of global disparity – war, famine, disease, climate change, eco-disasters. We're on the threshold of the greatest leap forward ever for our species, the colonisation of the solar system, the promise of interstellar travel within two or three generations, plenty for everyone. And you just know that ninety-nine percent of the wealth will be in the control of one percent of the population, utilised for their benefit alone."

Li remained calm and defiant, but he looked pale and drawn. He had lost weight since his arrival, and his face and body had visibly aged. Huang thought that he might be close to cracking.

"How long have I been here?" asked Li.

Six months had passed, all of it spent inside the same cell, apart from the one visit to the observation deck.

"Long enough for me to do this."

Huang tapped instructions into his smartsheet. The droid that had been Li's constant companion stepped forward and released his manacles. Li rubbed his wrists and narrowed his eyes.

"Reverse psychology…?"

"Security override code Oscar Romeo three seven six five three," announced Huang. Both security droids immediately slumped into an electronic stupor.

Li stared suspiciously at Huang.

"I must confess, this one is new to me…"

"Six months," said Huang.

"What?"

"You've been here six months."

"I don't…"

"The transport ship returned today. It touched down about fifteen minutes ago. My collaborators have spent the last six months cracking the security codes and flight algorithms. I've now cut all communications with Earth."

Li simply stared.

"I'm sorry I couldn't tell you before now, but as you know this place is thoroughly wired for sound and vision. We'll be on our way before anyone at home can work out what's going on and try to wrest back control. It's all been carefully planned. When we leave I'll send a mayday message to the other lunar bases. They'll rescue the rest of the prisoners and tell the world about the true nature of this place. Launch windows are too short for anyone to intercept us. We'll land somewhere remote enough so the Party can't find us."

"You mean you…"

"We've been infiltrating the Party for years. Waiting for the right person to emerge, a leader who can take us on to the next level. That's you, Li. Your planet-side captors are not the only ones who have been observing you during your time here." He picked up his smartsheet. "My network has been too. They're all connected through this. Via me they've been silently monitoring our every move over the past six months. You're a hero Li, a new Liu Xiaobo. Come on," he said, standing, "time's tight. We have to get moving right way."

"You know, that speech was the most extraordinary rendition I've heard in all my life," said Li as he stood and walked around the table.

Huang smiled.

Li smiled too.

"Security override Oscar Romeo eight eight five nine five," announced Li. The security droids jerked back into life. The one nearest to Huang grabbed his arms, manacled his hands behind his back, marched him over to Li's chair and pushed him into the seat.

Li sat in Huang's chair and calmly picked up the smartsheet.

"They're all connected through here. That should make rounding them up a straightforward matter."

The look of shock upon Huang's face was monumental.

"'To the mind that is patient, the whole world surrenders.' That was Sun Tzu, also. As you said, I'm someone who was always prepared to do whatever was required, no matter how extreme, to meet my objective."

The nearest droid's flank opened and a jointed arm fitted with a syringe-like apparatus containing an electrode unfolded in the direction of Huang's temple.

"Let's start with the psychoprobe."

Huang gasped as a controlled pulse of compressed air fired the device deep into his brain.

"As I told you when we first met," said Li, "the Party goes to enormous lengths to achieve its ends."

Yakker Snak

Andy Remic

Dirty dog bastards. YAK YAK. SNAK SNAK SNAK. YAK FUCKING YAK. SNAK FUCKING SNAK SNAK. All fucking day. And all of the fucking night. All day all night all day all night *all day all night all day all night ALL DAY ALLNIGHTALLDAY ALL NIGHT NIGHTNIGHTNIG(‡)&⁊(*&ͽäℋ&⁊^%^*()~Φ~ HTN‡•IGHT ROUND AND ROUND AND ROUND aAND ROUNDdddddd WE GO GO GO go go* go until it becomes a blur of unreality, a blur of dementia, a blur of *obsession,* a blur of unrealised hatred and hateful sheet-clawing *insomnia...*

It's enough to make you kill, they'd say.

Enough to turn any sane person, *in*, they'd say.

And... well, they'd be damn right.

My name's Anne. I'm six feet tall, six and a half in heels, I possess luxuriant long blonde hair (slightly curled), an athletic figure (and hey, I work damn hard to maintain that figure, baby, and my breasts are completely my own), I love animals (gave +$1500 to *Save the Whale* last semester), enjoy Swizz chocolate as a luxury, Japachinese wine as necessity, and curried sweetmeats and occasional sex when I'm in the musicmood. I'm a regular. A normal. A nobody. I never fought in the Plutarch Wars (seven now, dammit, wave that banner), I don't have no unreal hang-ups on politicking, freedom, multisexuality with aliens nor the evils of oppressive Government Police. I keep my mouth shut, my brain in gear, try my hardest to be a nice person and treat those others as I'd like to be treated, and hell, get on with enjoying my life.

153

Which I do.

My life consists of working harder than hard at *Doctor Slane's Doctors' Surgery*, a title which I believe contains two doctors too many (he's only crippled sixteen people in his *waaay too*-long life, but hey-ho, such is the lot for a retired cerebro-spinal surgeon with a random chaos twitch reflex) and I love my little dog, *Fizzle*. Fizzle is beautiful. Vat-grown from finest sheep-dog gen-slush, she has a lovely long glossy black and white coat, is intelligent, intuitive, only barks when she's told to bark, fetches the paper from the front lawn-tek dispenser slot, curls up on the couch every evening to watch *Dr Meh* on TV, and purrs like a kitten when I rub vigorously behind her ears. Which I do. A lot.

My life was perfect. Note the past tense.

My problems began, as I suppose so many problems do, with my new neighbours.

I live in Hudson 57th, a small town with a school, church, pub, alien brothel, the usual. Houses are well spaced out, semis, because there's no real land shortage here unlike other continents where the Plutarch Wars made areas toxic for a million years. But shit happens, right? Thankfully, it also killed the people who would have lived in those toxic areas, meaning there was no mass illegal immigration. It was balanced. Neat. Quid pro quo.

A week ago, new neighbours moved in next door to my little slice of heaven. They were a gay couple, Hazel and China, and whereas China was quite butch, a tall strapping girl with harsh-cropped black hair, almost military in style, and a severe face like an old boot, Hazel was blonde and waif-like, drifting like a spirit across the back lawn and tending the rich red roses that reminded me so much of *blood*. Anyway, I went out, made my introductions like a good little neighbour should.

"Hello. My name's Anne. Looks like we're going to be neighbours for a while, ha ha ha." I smiled easily. Fluid. Over-friendly. After all, I didn't want them to think I was strange and occasionally violent. We shook hands.

"Hazel," said Hazel, smiling, a twinkle of angel dust in her shining eye.

"China," grunted the masculine woman, and when she shook my hand over the modest metre high fence that divided our back gardens, she nearly broke every bone in my hand. She was tough, this one.

"You settled in okay?" I asked, inquisitive but not too nosey. After all, I didn't want them to think I had a raging temper and could fly off the handle into a bloodthirsty berserker rage at the drop of a pin, did I? No. Obviously not.

"Yes," said Hazel, "we've got all the boxes in, just need to start unpacking." She glanced at China. "And you've got to pick up the dogs, right? What time is that?"

"'Bout an hour," said China, rubbing her chin with (I fancied) a sound of grizzling bristles. But then, I was always a bit over-critical. Wait till I get to know her, I thought. *I'm pretty damn sure everything will be just fine.*

I looked from Hazel to China, and back again. "Dogs?" I said brightly, not wanting to alarm my new homosexual neighbours in any way for after all I had dabbled myself during my early years, and could even claim to have been a part of the new multisexual movement in '63 when aliens were finally allowed to settle on Earth (after a fuck-load of immigration paperwork, I can tell you). Wild sex? Baby, I'd had a tentacle or two, I could tell you. I was a liberfuckinated human being! No aliophobia in my mental back room!

"Yes, we have two of the new Wonder Breed."

"Wonder Breed?" I said, still forcing my forced smile.

"Yes. Wonder Breed. The Vat Breeders call them psychopoodles."

"Psychopoodles," I said, and I could feel my smile slipping down my face like melted butter. I pushed it back up with a nudge. "Oh. Good. I *do* love dogs."

"You'll love these," smiled Hazel with her pretty smile.

"Ugh," grunted China with her butch square jaw.

"They're vat-grown, by Dr Zezeller of New Australia. He's

modelled them on a variety of different animals."

"That's nice," I said, but quite obviously it wasn't.

Later that day, as I took Fizzle on the fields outside the back of my house, I got to meet the Wonder Breed. Hazel and China hung over the back fence like bastards, and motioned for my attention like whores. I bit my lip and chewed my tongue and tried hard not to lose my temper, or indeed show any temper, for I had a bad temper and bad things happened when my temper went bad and badder than bad.

I tramped up the garden, Fizzle obediently behind me as any good dog respectful dog submissive dog should be. Fizzle sat down, panting, long red tongue going *heh heh heh*. The sun was high in the sky and I looked up. It burned my face. I allowed heat to flush through me like a pulse from a hydrogen bomb. That felt *soothing*.

"This is Ruby," said Hazel, dangling a scruffy curly-haired ginger-furred nasty piece of shit before my very eyes.

"YAK YAK," went Ruby, and panted, little evil black eyes surveying me more like a bone of ripe succulent meat than a human being. "YAK YAK YAK. YAK YAK!"

"And this is Millie," said China, bending down and hoisting up another scruffy little black-furry dog bastard type. "SNAK SNAK," went the bastard dog bastard, tiny black eyes staring at me with a totality of evil equalling nothing like I'd ever seen in the clinic. And in the clinic, I'd seen some mad shit, I can tell you.

"Lovely," I said, with a teeth-smile.

"YAK YAK."

"SNAK SNAK."

"YAK YAK YAKKER YAK!"

"SNAK SNAK SNAKKER SNAK!"

I reached out to pet Millie, and the little furry fucker snapped at my hand, sinking an incisor into my middle finger and drawing blood. "Ouch!" My hand withdrew quick and I sucked the bite wound while Millie carried on staring at me as if to say COME ON COME ON DO YOU THINK YOU'RE HARD

EH?

"Ooooooh, sorry about that," apologised Hazel, "she shouldn't have done that, she's never done that before, bad Millie, naughty Millie," she waggled her finger at the psychopoodle, "who's a naughty girl, then." Millie wagged her tail. Hazel and China turned to go back in their house. Apparently, the biting incident was finished. Apparently, the biting incident had been dealt with and done and dusted. Apparently, the biting incident was okay with a kick up the arse and a sprinkling of enemy shaving sugar.

I watched Hazel and China retreat. Millie and Ruby ran wild around the garden for a few moments YAKKING and SNAKKING then stopped, looked up at me, and stared with that evil dog bastard stare which I knew I was going to have to get *very* used to.

I stared back, then turned, and retreated into my quiet and necessary Haven.

That night, things went from bad to worse.

Hazel and China had sex. Now, in the scheme of things this is No Bad Thing. After all, people have sex, animals have sex, people and animals and aliens have sex. This is all good and fine and dandy by me. However. I was tired. I was very tired. I was exhausted, in fact, and as I lay in bed, tossing and turning, that elusive dream of sleep, that distant honey touching was *so*... close, so close, *oh so close* when they started...

"Oooh."

"Aaah."

"Ooohh aaah."

I groaned, and put my head under the pillow. This seemed to work quite well for a bit as I listened to Hazel and China ooohing and aaahing, pleasuring one another in pleasurable pleasure, gentle at first, then growing with a tattoo-beat rhythm that was actually quite soothing to the terminal insomniac. I started to become lulled by their fucking. Hypnotised by their humping. Mesmerised by this meeting of minge.

"BANG!"

I nearly jumped the fuck out of my skin. The whole wall seemed to reverberate. Echoes clanged off down the Hall of Echoes and I sat bolt upright in bed. I was awake now, that was for sure. Awake and good and mad.

"Oooh. Aaah. BANG!"

I blinked. What the hell were they doing?

"Ooooooh! Aaaaaah! BAAAANG!"

Just what the hell what the fuck were they fucking doing? And more importantly, how would I ever get to sleep? I had a long day tomorrow. Dr Slane was down in the surgery to cripple a few more innocently trusting patients with his gleaming and dangerously efficient scalpel.

I sighed. I would make a hot drink. I would ride the storm. Ride the ride, so to speak. After all, they could only shag for so long, right?

I padded through the darkness of my house, and Fizzle looked up from her basket. "Good girl." I patted her. She smiled at me with a dog smile, a curious facial gesture she'd picked up from me, no doubt – because I was happy A Lot. As I said, Fizzle was a bright dog. An intelligent animal. Judging by Ruby and Millie, it would appear cerebral ability in the vat-grown animal kingdom was in its minority/decline.

I made cocoa with hot milk. I carried this back to the bedroom. Everything had gone quiet. It was a miracle.

"Hallelujah!" I muttered, and climbed under soft covers, and sipped my hot drink. I turned the lights back down and after a while, finished my drink. I settled down. I was soothed. I was calm. Sleep crept fingers over my eyelids and pulled me down into blank velvet dreams...

The clinic. Green walls. Steel beds. Sturdy straps.

I walked down endless tiled corridors, my cold feet slapping cold tiles. I glanced left, to a window socket, and beyond the dark trees lay moonlit-rimed and framed in steel and bars. Bars. Like a prison. I carried on walking. At the end of the corridor was a plain white door with no handle. I reached the door, but how could I get out? How could I escape? I reached forward and pushed at the portal. It slid open, smoothly, to reveal-

"*BANG!*"

I opened my eyes. I groaned.

"Ooooh aaahh oooh ahhh BANG! YAK YAK YAK."

"You've got to be fucking kidding me," I said, and sat up. I admit I was scowling. I used to scowl a lot – at the clinic. Somewhere, in the distant scramble of my mind, I recognised a link – a link between the scowl, and some incarceration.

"Ooooh aaahh oooh ahhh BANG! YAK YAK YAK. Ooooh aaahh oooh ahhh BANG! YAK YAK YAK. YAK YAK SNAK SNAK YAK YAKKER YAK SNAK SNAK BANG! OOOH AHHH AHHHHHHHHH YAK AAAHHH SNAK BANG!"

I put my head back under the pillow and willed self-suffocation.

The peace of death.

I finally got to sleep as dawn tendrils unzipped the sky.

I was too tired to go to work. Dr Slane was not impressed. "Ve vill have to review ya vork record vhen ya return, young laa-*aa*dy..."

I stood in the garden, enjoying the early morning sunshine, holding a cup of coffee and sipping the sweet dark brew. In folds, my lethargy began to dissipate. Caffeine. Fresh air. Sunlight. I became enlivened. Invigorated.

The doors opened at the back of the house, and I heard the *pitter patter* of tiny claws. I did not look.

"YAK?"

"SNAK SNAK?"

And then began a howling cacophony of YAKing and SNAKing, so bad you could have mistaken the whole episode for a session at a dog torture chamber. The little psychopoodles ran around in circles, jumped at the fence, stood on the garden furniture YAKing and SNAking to their hearts' content. They were insane. I thought I'd been insane, and I'd certainly seen enough of *those wacko crackos* at the clinic, but I'd never seen it in dogs before.

I moved to the fence, and coughed. Coughed again. I coughed more loudly, slopping coffee over my hand.

A slow fury started to build in my mind as Ruby and Millie ran around in the early morning sunlight. I mean, how could this Hazel and China think this was acceptable? How could they think it was *normal* to allow YAKing muppets free rein at all hours of the night and YAKing morning, oblivious to the needs of other SNAKing residents? How could they *listen to it themselves?* It was just crazy behaviour. Who'd want to listen to *that?*

Hazel finally appeared. She had a certain glow to her cheeks. *Yeah,* I thought, *at my bloody expense!*

"A good evening?" I said.

"Oh yes," smiled Hazel.

"Break her in, did you?"

"Pardon me?"

"The house. First night, and all that."

"Er. Yes. It was wonderful."

There was the awkward silence, the kind of escalating unease when two people who don't know each have nothing to say. The silence was soon filled with YAK YAK SNAK SNAK, grating against my brain like sandpaper on raw cerebellum.

"Are they always like this?" I enquired, gesturing with my coffee mug to the insanely charging sprinting circling animals, which were behaving like lobotomised chipmunks on a speedball supercrack coke-high adrenaline cocktail.

"Like what?" Hazel said.

"Like that. Charging about. YAKing and SNAKing."

Hazel stared at me. Her lips compressed into bloodless lines. Obviously, something I said had upset her.

"*YAKing* and *SNAKing?*" she finally snarled, as if regurgitating a sausage of faeces, and her words dripped the obvious poison. "These, our beautiful psychopoodles Ruby and Millie, well, they produce dog music!"

"Music, you say?"

"Yes, a bright symphony, a glorious soundtrack, a veritable orchestral manoeuvre in the bark! It is a wonderful thing to experience! It's like the violin strings of a newborn baby; the tinkling laughter of galloomphing children; the rhythmical clicking clarity of wild dolphin song!"

"It's a fucking racket, is what it is," I said.

"How dare you!" snapped Hazel, feigning outrage. *Where are we? Eighteenth century London? Queen Elurgybreath's Royal Court? Where's the powdered wig and fake tits?* I snorted out laughter like a pile of snot.

I decided to live by the mantra: it's better to have neighbours who hate you but are quiet, than neighbours who love you but won't shut their rabid rancid cakeholes.

"Listen sweetie," I said, sipping my coffee, and now *my* eyes were gleaming, now *I* was filling up with a juicy frothing emotion, although I'm not sure how you would classify it. Probably better not to. I'd been locked up before. "Listen. I can live with you and China being unsympathetic and socially unaware arseholes. I can live with your all night shagging sessions, where you, oops, *BANG!* one another's heads offa the wall at every bite of sweet cunnilingus. I can live with that. That's fine. That's cool. But what I *won't* live with is your little curly turds making that sort of evil dog bastard racket all day and all night. It's just not on. It's socially and morally reprehensible. It's a noise violation. And it's a pain in my rosy-cheeked arse."

Hazel stared at me for a long time, then simply turned and strode in. A moment later, her voice – once all sunlight and flowery honey, now evaporated – snapped, "Ruby! Millie! In!" The dogs padded in, the door slammed shut, and that was the end of the noise! I had won! Whoo har! Git some! And all that.

Just to be sure that my new neighbours understood how thin our connecting walls were, and to demonstrate how readily I could hear their carpet munching and general sado-masochistic tendencies, I played them some music. Now, I admit I dragged my 2000 watt subwoofer so it faced the wall. And I admit, I might have used my *Watkins and Atkins 50,000i* instead of my *Klag 15* music system. And yeah, okayyyyyyy, I might have cranked that volume nobble all the way up till the walls shook like an epileptic earthquake, shook like a motherfucking motherfucker on vibe amphetamine. I treated Hazel and China to a repertoire of finer classics. I played *Grip Wrench's* "Every Bastard's a Bastard" and "Kiss My Momma's Fat Ass". I played *Ball-kicker's* "Fuck the World and All its Wriggling Maggots", and "You Wanna Come Here and Earn a Colostomy?". And I rounded off my session with *Sperm's* "KAK!" and "Let Me Wriggle Inside You (Let's Do the Fandango)." It was a fine choice, if I say so myself. It was rockin', it was boppin', the bass was a-thumpin', and the whole house felt like it might break apart.

I pulled the plug.

A deafening silence reigned. And rained.

Yeah fuckers, that's what I can give you, a bit of payback, a bit of aggro, so just you remember it. That's just a taster. All reet?

I mooched about the house all day, in a soporific zombie state due to the previous night's escapades (*BANG! YAKKA SNAKKA OOOH OOOH AAAH* – *oh how I would have paid to be a flatulent fly on the wall*).

All day, a generous silence oozed from my neighbours. It was beautiful. It was serene. It was harmony from one neighbour to another. We'd reached a hateful stalemate, but hey, I could live with constant execration. After all, I had on the battlefield.

That night, things went from bad to worse.

It began again. The "ooh" and "aaah" and "YAK" and "SNAK". Then came the "BANG!" followed by the "CLANK!" and the "BUZZ!" and the "TWANG!" and the "GAH!" like some titanic deflating sigh after a particularly heavy bukkake session.

I lay there, and I couldn't believe it. I just couldn't believe it. I just couldn't fucking believe it. I mean: How could they? Hadn't I warned them? Hadn't I fucking warned them? Hadn't I *shown* them what might fucking happen when I fucking warned them? I knew they could fucking better do better.

Every time I looked around, the walls grew in a little tighter.

I put up with it. Two whole hours I put up with it.

Sweat streamed down my body. My hands trembled. I fought it. I fought it so bad. My mouth was filled with tar and feathers. My mind was filled with swirling blood-oil. My teeth were razors. My eyeballs filled with tepid maggots. My fists clenched napalm. Hate snuggled up to me, with a big warm wet sloppy kiss.

Slowly, I got out of bed. The red mist of Anger was there, hovering, its middle finger raised and a scowl on its pugly face.

I walked out of my house, around to the neighbour's door, and knocked so hard my knuckles left imprints in the wood. Inside, there came a skittering and a howling. Claws scrabbled. There were a few ominous *thumps*. I knocked again. Across the road, several lights came on. People were starting to pay attention. That wasn't good. That was bad. Real bad. I could do without an audience. But if an audience I had, then to hell with it, an audience it would be.

China opened the door.

"Keep your fucking noise down," I said between clenched teeth.

She smiled, eyes gleaming, and said, "We are."

"I disagree," I said, teeth grinding to paste.

"I think you'll find our decibel levels were within legal limits. I know. I have a decibel monitor." She smiled again. It was mocking. She was mocking me. Her eyes mocked me. The curl of her lips. The rise and fall of her chest. The bitch was laughing at me. Laughing, I say!

"If you don't keep the yakking snakking little bastards quiet, you're going to regret it."

"Oh yes? What you going to do, Anne?" She smiled again, and a crowd had gathered behind us on the road.

"Come here," I said, gesturing as if I wished to impart a secret. "And I'll tell you."

I leant in close, and China, instinctively, as if by reflex, leant in as well. I could smell her faint perfume. I could smell her sex sweat. I shifted, a few inches closer. Closer. Closer. Closer. Then I lunged, teeth clamping, biting hard into the soft flesh of her ear, crunching through cartilage as I bit and chewed and became a suddenly furious primal animal. China screamed. And struggled. And wiggled. I did rend and tear. China flapped her arms like a suicide jumper attempting to fly. I chewed and gnashed, and fancy I perhaps made some growling sounds. China was surprisingly strong, like the butch lass she was, but I was stronger. I finally tugged, and China's ear tore away trailing long, almost elastic, strips of skin. The further I pulled back, the more each string *ping ping pinged* until I stood there, an ear in my flapping mouth, a crowd behind me in hushed and horrified silence. China clutched her head, blood pumping between her fingers. I took the ear out and waved it at her.

"CAN YOU HEAR ME? EH? CAN YOU FUCKING HEAR THIS?" I screamed into the chewed-off ear, then directly at China's horrified and teary expression. "THIS EAR IS COMING NEXT DOOR WITH ME! I WANT YOU TO HEAR WHAT I HEAR WITH YOUR EAR! YOU HEAR?"

I stomped off, ear in hand like some grisly war trophy, and sat in my living room waiting for the police.

The police came. They were very nice. They checked I was taking my medication, and upped me a couple of rainbow pills. They took the chewed and bedraggled ear off me (with a slight struggle, I confess) and returned it to China and billed one of my credit cards the price of an ear re-graft. It was all very civilised and I was very calm and because of my situation, because of my history, I didn't have to visit the cells. Better for them, really, and they knew it. Last time I was locked up, it left three murderers and a child rapist dead. They knew I had a temper. They knew I was a woman not to be messed with.

A week of beautiful silence!! It was amazing. No YAKs and certainly no SNAKs. I thought to myself, *maybe they've had the little bastards put down?* But then something untoward happened. I'd let Fizzle out for her last wee, and she was daintily squatting in the plastic grass, when there came a massive "yelp!" and she came speeding towards me whimpering as if she'd been shot in the arse, which is exactly what happened. By a crossbow. She barrelled into my arms, whimpering and yelping and leaving a trail of blood, a crossbow quarrel protruding from her rump. I felt acid and ice push through my heart. I took hold of the quarrel and tore it free with a *suckering* sound, a splash of canine claret, and to a cacophony of whimpering animal whimpers. Almost in concord, the next door YAK YAK YAK YAK started again, and was soon accompanied by the SNAK SNAK SNAK SNAK of the other evil little fucker. My eyes narrowed, I scanned the surrounding plastic fields and plastic trees, searching for the cowardly sniper. But I was torn – get my beloved pet to the Vet Surgery and have her sewn up and anti-biotic injecto-mushed, or go after the dastardly cowardly sniper myself and rip out his/her/its spleen with my flexing digits? I'd done it before. It was a wonderful way to go.

Sense won through, however, and my love for my beautiful Fizzle. I drove to the Veterinary Block on Green Gate at high speed, away out from Hudson 57th, away from my neighbours and YAK and bloody SNAK. The surgeon was a top dude with a laser, and he anaesthetized Fizzle and flesh-welded her rump back into one lump of steaming dog meat. I drove home in a slight daze, thinking weird and wild thoughts to myself. *Who would do such a thing to my beautiful Fizzle? Who would dare to fire a crossbow quarrel into my dog?* It was a bad and evil thing to do, and I had my bloody suspicions all right.

I drove fast, over the plastic moorland across winding, sweeping roads. It began to rain, a heavy dark bastard, a heavy pounding piss downpour that made the road slick under my questing, dipping, hunting headlights.

I was in no mood for fun. I was in no mood for games.

I passed the local military base, nicknamed Franco's Fun Palace after some nutcase who trained there, and I subconsciously clocked the layout and duty guards. Then we swept down from the rain-soaked moors, Fizzle and I, her snoring on the back seat, her paws twitching as if she ran in some pleasant dream, hunting down her dreg attacker perhaps, and I arrived home mentally exhausted and poisoned ready for a stiff whiskey...

I carried Fizzle from the bastard car, and realised my front door was slightly open. I frowned. Had I left it open in my panic to get to the Vet's? Or was somebody really fool enough to break into my house? *Were they really dumb enough to break into my house?*

Padding silent as a panther like, I put Fizzle in her bed, and pulled a knife from the blocky block, a big bad bastard knife with a serrated edge and a nasty gleam all too precious for one such as me. I was the sort of woman you did not fuck with! I was the sort of woman who you did not rob unless you wanted to lose a few ribs.

But if it is them, maybe they want something more? Evidence? Evidence for what? Evidence to give to the police, evidence to get me arrested, evidence to get me locked away? Yes. Locked down dark back away at The Mount Pleasant Hilltop Institution, the "nice and caring and friendly home for the mentally challenged". And I was never going back there to face the needles and hot irons of Dr Betezsh. No. I'd rather die. Or more accurately, I'd rather kill.

I crept through my house, familiar with everything in the dark, with layout and every squeak and corner and breakable. And I couldn't see them. I couldn't hear them. But somebody was there. I could *sense* them. Smell their piss. Like when you're in a forest, and you're being hunted, being stalked by some huge vicious natural predator. Well, I'd been in that situation a few times, and this felt like a very, very similar bastard...

It was when I reached the stairs. The attacker leapt from the dark, barrelling into me but I twisted, I was expecting *something*, and a fist cracked my face knocking me back but the knife slashed up and across, and I felt the blade bite flesh, felt the blade bite deep and *carve hot meat*, and then the attacker was gone and I hit the ground on my arse and sat there, stunned for a moment, but triumphant. I cut her. Whoever she was, I cut her bad.

When the spinning stars from the blow stopped, I stood up and closed the front door. The rain still splashed outside, and I turned on all the lights and cleaned up the blood. No point calling the Government Police. No point troubling them. I would find out soon enough. This was the sort of thing *I was good at.*

The YAKing and SNAKing started the next morning, and I walked Fizzle in the back garden and the back field, following a path up to where the sniper must have stood. There were footprints. Small footprints. I smiled, and returned to my garden as Hazel and China were stepping from their back door. Hazel had a huge bandage around her head, soaked a little with blood at the centre. She was scowling at me and I gave her a big middle-finger-fuck-you smile.

"Hurt your head?" I said.

"Banged it," she said.

"Looks like a nasty cut," I said.

"It is," she said.

"Looks like it was made by a knife, to me," I said.

"Maybe it was," she said.

"Shame it didn't cut your whole bloody head off," I said.

Hazel stared at me, mouth twitching, then turned and went in. China scowled at me, face a scrunched up frown, evil looking bastard like, and I kept on smiling sweetly and thinking razor edge thoughts and this what it went like, this is how it

167

tumbled like, downhill like, down a rabbit hole only no shouting queens like, just violence and blood and lots of death. I stared back, and we stared at each other, and China went in with that fearful butch scowl. Happy now, for having caused them some harm after they crossbowed my dog up the arse, I went and made a tuna and mayonnaise sandwich because I knew they hadn't found anything on me because I don't now have anything to find, I'm clean like, because I expect this chaos shit with a rampant history like mine.

I decided to go back to work, to *Doctor Slane's Doctors' Surgery*, and work hard and keep my head down and out of trouble. Fizzle was healing well with the Fast-ButtHeal™ creams and potions which cost me a pretty penny I can tell you. And I tried hard to keep my head down and do nothing wrong but I could feel my mind starting to go strange and this was weird this was what I used to feel like and I felt like an egg, an egg which had been cracked and bashed and that wasn't good, oh no, Dr Betezsh used to attach his white-hot electrodes to my nipples and I'd struggle against the straps, biting at the leather gag with all my might, and he'd wag his finger and gaze down with shark eyes, and say, "You've been bad, Anne, you've been a very bad girl."

I finished work, and it was dark and wintry bastard raining again. I drove over the moors. I stopped by the military installation and I knew I shouldn't do this but I kinda had the feeling it was going arsewards and scrotum, so I wanted some backup, and wanted some help. I went to the boot of my car, took out the bolt-cutters, and cut an Anne-size hole in the fence. I squeezed through. The rain was coming down hard like drunk piss. There were soldiers everywhere. They had machine guns. My eyes gleamed in the darkness, I knew, and this was going from bad to bad to worse to fuck. I started towards the HQ which is where I knew it was and I was challenged and, ahhhhh, well, that was where it got really bad.

The rain was easing off when I arrived home. I was carrying a black briefcase containing my backup plan, my second coming, my *protection*. I stepped into the house, and next door the fucking neighbours were at it again, but so bad I couldn't fuckabelieve it, like my ears would bleed a dark bastard blood-

"Ooooh aaahh oooh ahhh BANG! YAK Ooooh aaahh oooh ahhh BANG! YAK YAK YAK. Ooooh aaahh oooh ahhh BANG! YAK YAK YAK. YAK YAK SNAK SNAK YAK YAK SNAK SNAK BANG! OOOH AHHH AHHHHHHHHH YAK AAAHHH SNAK BANG! YAK YAK. Ooooh aaahh oooh ahhh BANG! YAK YAK YAK. YAK YAK SNAK shit SNAK YAK Ooooh aaahh oooh ahhh BANG! YAK YAK YAK. Ooooh aaahh oooh ahhh BANG! YAK YAK YAK. YAK YAK SNAK SNAK YAK YAK SNAK SNAK BANG! OOOH AHHH AHHHHHHHHH YAK AAAHHH SNAK BANG! YAK SNAK SNAK BANG! OOOH AHHH AHHHHHHHHH YAK AAAHHH SNAK BANG BANG BANG!"

I was grimacing I can tell you and thought right that's it i think i was starting to lose it and lose my marbles just like that time that time when they locked me up and i went to find something a gun or a knife or a weapon of any kind because a woman can only take so much shit and abuse and YAK YAK SNAK SNAK YSNKA YKNSKAY KAK KAK and then i stopped because there was my beloved fizzle and she'd been crucified against the wall and all her blood was running down through her beautiful black and white fur and forming a big bastard puddle on the floor and that was it no more take no more they'd killed my fucking dog killed my fucking baby and you don't do that to a woman or at least not to this woman and so i got my case and went out into the road and it smelled bright and fresh after the rain and fresh and newlike and i walked slowly to the door and the neighbours were banging and fukking and yakking and snakking and with a kikk i kikked the door off the hinges and walked into a dark hall and all the mash was upstairs in the bedroom and i could see candlelight and smell incense like poison in a deathpit and i walked up the stairs and they were there on the bed fukking and yakking and the dog bastards ruby and millie and they ran round and round my feet YAK YAK and SNAK SNAK with stupid little eyes and stupid little curly fur but i didn't punish them cos its all about the owners right and they were up to some kind of human nonsense the way humans do and the way humans can not making no sense of it all and they saw me last second in the throes of their ecstasy both on the different end of the plastic and they looked up shocked like and i punched down a fist going through hazels face and punching her teeth out the back of her head and into the bloody mush pulp pillow and china rolled off all weak and flabby like humans do and started screaming and i kicked her in the fa63756e74ce just stunning her like and opened the case and set it down on the bed.

Inside, metal glittered.

I set the timer on the Micro-Nuke™ (a bomb in bag, a nuke in a box – cue singing dancing girls dancing on TV around this beautiful war porn) and stepped back and saw the red digits flickering. I know you probably think this exc63756e74essive, using a Micro-Nuke™ to solve such a potentially simple situation but excessive is as excessive does, I always say. Leaving a blood-drooling China and the happy YAKers6675636b6572 ## with their own very personal and soon-to-be-detonated Micro-Nuke™ I went out to my car, got in it after pushing through the crowd of curious neighbours from their plastic houses with plastic lawns and plastic trees and drove away, real fast like, away over the moors and stopped by the gates of the Military Installation. The mesh gates were scarred and still flaming. Inside the compound I could see at least fifty bodies, machine guns in still, bloodied hands. I had to do it though, don't you see? Because – well, you can only push a girl so far.

And nobody *truly* knows what goes on inside somebody else's head.

In the distant valley of Hudson 57th, the Micro-Nuke™

detonated6675636b6572.

A bright orange light filled the sky and I watched night turn briefly to day.

It was beautiful; like basking for a few moments in the white hot primary beauty of creation.

Below, the town was vaporised, and as a fireball raced towards the stars I could see, I fancied, Ruby and Millie, still YAKing and SNAKing the little 0110001101110101011011001101000111001, fired up into the heavens like tiny furry shittypoodle cannonballs, their jaws working and paws paddling as the blast carried them up up UP UP UP to finally be consumed by fire, heat, inferno, eating them away into ash and beyond into component atoms until nothing NOTHING existed any more.

I sat down. It started to rain again. I heard sirens wailing.

I waited for the Government Police.

The Mount Pleasant Hilltop Institution, the "nice and caring and friendly home for the mentally challenged", opened its gates and checked the passes as the long, low black car glided inside. From the car emerged four large, serious looking men carrying large, serious looking briefcases and finding it hard to hide their large, serious looking designer killware under suit jackets. They climbed steps, were met by Dr Vago, and introduced to the Institution.

Dr Vago led the four large men down long sterile corridors, some the green of petrified puke, some the brown of flatulent faeces, and all the while a smell pervaded the air. The smell of over-strong disinfectant. The smell of piss. The smell of... *human decay.*

"Here you go, gentlemen."

"And she's been no trouble, you say?"

Dr Vago raised his eyebrows a fraction, and tucked his neat hands into the neat pockets of his white coat. "No trouble at all. After she nuked the piss out of her neighbourhood, that is."

171

"Has she explained why she did it?"

"No." Dr Vago shook his head.

"We need to understand the malfunction," said one suited man, "in order to better reprogram her mind for next time. She's an optimum combat model, you know."

"Hmm. This happened before, you say?" said Dr Vago, carefully.

The four large men exchanged a glance. "Classified," they said, in poetry-perfect harmony.

Then, one man said, "Well, has she spoken about *anything* after – the incident."

Vago sighed, and shrugged, and taking one hand from his pocket rubbed the weary bridge of a weary nose. "No. She simply utters two words, over and over again. I don't understand what she means, she won't explain what she means... it's as if her programming has fused into some kind of permanent loop. The top minds her are at a loss as to decipher her mental state."

"What does she say?"

"Hear for yourself," smiled Dr Vago. He snapped open digital locks and pushed the metre-thick portal wide.

Anne Droid v10.3.2 sat, naked, her chest panel open, lights flickering against polished chrome and titaniumIII. Her arms were round her knees, and she was rocking backwards and forwards, backwards and forwards, backwards and forwards.

She looked up as the four men formed a line, watching her.

Anne Droid smiled.

"YAK YAK," she said, and scratched the end of her nose. "SNAK SNAK SNAK..."

The Legend of Sharrock

Philip Palmer

I was sixteen years when I became a warrior. The ceremony is a simple one. I was stripped naked and daubed in red mud. My father cut a mark beneath each of my eyelids here, and here. So that I wept tears of blood. I stood utterly motionless all night long in the icy cold and in the morning the sun warmed my limbs.

Then I drank a flask of wine and ate half a prashon for breakfast.

The scars under my eyes were inked with poison from the sunbark tree, to stop them healing. Some tribes do a similar thing to their – no, you don't need to know about such barbarous acts. These are primitive customs, you understand. We honour our past by such means.

After breakfast, I was declared a warrior. And then I embraced my father Lexas. And I embraced my brother Andro. And my sister Wareel kissed me and wept; and I laughed and that made her laugh too. And finally I said goodbye to my mother, Giona.

"I will miss you, my son," she said, bitterly. And I laughed, bewildered at her evident sorrow.

"I'll be back soon," I assured her.

It was one hundred years before I returned.

And during those years I fought and suffered; and I knew the glory of war. And its horror too, for many friends of mine died; and I saw innocents slaughtered by the weapons of the enemy, and by our weapons too. Such is war; sometime it is full of honour, but sometimes it is not.

One hundred years I fought, in forests and in swamps and in spacecraft. And on four occasions I travelled through the gashes in space in a suit made of riftstuff; flying swiftly from one galaxy to another like a bird through a raging gale.

This was our great war against the Raxoan. They had formed a treaty with the Southern Tribes, who had sold them a hundred planets; all of them in fact owned by us, including Madagorian itself. The Raxoan had thus been duped, with contracts most plausible and lies most compellingly told. (Such treachery is typical, as I have explained before, of the effete and soul-denying Southern Tribes.) And though we explained to the Raxoan the error of their ways, they would not be swayed, not by our logic, nor our charm, nor our direst threats.

And thus, once they had dispatched their invasion fleets against us, we had no choice but to wage war.

Their efforts to invade us were, in truth, pathetic and easily defeated. The Raxoan had the most powerful of war craft, armed with weapons capable of exploding a star. But our Philosophers had taught us how to sow the space around our planets with gashes in reality that would destroy any untrue vessel. So time and again the vast battle fleets of the Raxoan were rent and ripped by these jagged reefs of nothingness. Their space ships blew up, and their warriors fell out of reality and left not even a particle of flesh to be mourned. The Southern Tribes knew our power of course; they knew the Raxoan would be slaughtered like helpless bleet. But that was the joke of it all for them. Their purpose was to invoke our rage, for the sheer joy of seeing us angry. The humiliation and defraudment of the Raxoan was a mere by-blow.

And after we had swept aside the great space armadas of the enemy, we invaded *them* – attacking the planets of the Raxoan with all the power at our disposal. We smashed their ships with waves of dark energy, and despatched unthingness bombs to destroy their missile silos.

The Raxoan, like the Southern Tribes, were a mechanoid-loving culture, who employed spaceships with databrain minds and warriors made of metal. And we had no problem defeating such creatures, with our remote-power weapons created out of the dreamings of our greatest Philosophers.

There was no glory to be found in such warfare. It was like hunting birds by burning the air in which they flew; no sport was to be found in *that*.

But once their mechanoids had been destroyed, or subverted with our information-snake codes, the real war began. We sent Maxolun killer-craft against their mighty fleets; and engaged their vast warcraft in glorious space combats that lit up the blackness of space with sunfire blasts and left the rubble of destroyed war craft to drift for all eternity. Our Maxolun pilots had a genius for evasion and attack; on many occasions I served as gunner to such craft, and was awed at how the pilots could leap and whirl through space and into other realities before emerging at just the perfect place for a counter-attack. Our tiny warcraft were like insects that could hunt and harry and eventually slay vast herds of karako.

But mostly I served with the Warrior Guard; the armoured warriors who flew or rifted on to the planet's surface where we fought a true warrior's war. Face to obscene bodily excrescence; flesh against flesh; Maxolun against Raxoan.

The Raxoans were, it must be said, fearsome adversaries, even without their mechanoids. Picture them. Each was larger than you, Cuzco. Multiply- bodied. And spiked; the barbs on their bodies were like an army's worth of swords raised. They lived in swamps and they swam in seas of their own shit. Their planet had a heavy gravity, which made it hard for us to walk or move. And the Raxoans' hides were impervious to sword thrusts or axe strikes. So we fought them with sunfire guns and missiles fired from death-tubes. We fought in squads of twenty. And we had spears, each four times my own height, tipped with metal forged in the fire of a sun's core, which we used to impale the Raxoans. And space armour, of course, was essential; for the air of their planet was corrosive and poisonous, and would rip the flesh off creatures such as us in minutes.

It was a vile war. We stabbed and blasted, and many of our warriors were slain by whirlpools of mud and by spikes fired from the bodies of Raxoans that penetrated our space armour as it were paper. But we slew magnificently, and remorselessly; and when we heard that the Raxoan fleet had tried to explode our sun, we slew even more of them, with even greater brutality.

One hundred years I fought, on twenty different planets, all engineered to be replicas of the Raxoan home world with its poison air and seas of shit. All war is glorious; this was somewhat less so, but glorious still. And we prevailed.

Another tale could be told of the Maxolun Philosopher called Caloud who risked his life by surrendering to their battle fleet. There, with courage and great patience, he explained to the Raxoans how they might surrender in a way that would be acceptable to the Maxolu. It took them a while to comprehend the complexity and poetry of the rituals that were necessary. But eventually they succeeded, somewhat fumblingly, in offering us homage and honour, with gifts and poems and deeds of valour, as a prelude to their surrender.

The Raxoan then appointed one of their kind as Chieftain of All the Raxoan (for they had no sense of hierarchy, which we found incomprehensible and indeed intolerable.) And this Raxoan travelled to our planet, unarmed and unescorted.

And in front of the Assembly of All the Chieftains, this monstrously large Raxoan 'Chieftain' delivered a message to us, full of ritual invective and arrogant acquiescence; and full too of the most lyrical poetry, about how his people wished to maim and murder our parents then fornicate with their corpses, and other appropriate revilements. One phrase still stays in my memory: 'your impaled and blood-puking grandmother's scream of pain shall be foregone by us, for now we would be friends.' I often wonder if Caloud helped them with the drafting of their surrender speech; for no Raxoan could write such a deliciously vicious line.

Our Maxolu Chieftains roared their approval at the Raxoan's rhetoric. And they then agreed to accept the Raxoan as our allies.

Thus, the war came to an end. And the Raxoans, from that moment on, never again had dealings with the Southern Tribes.

And then I returned home and found my father mindwild.

Does this, I wonder, happen to any of your kind? Yes? No? I see some of you are uneasy. Perhaps it does, then. But I'm not speaking here of simple madness, nor of the losing of wits with the passage of age. Mindwild is something else. It is a kind of possession by a dark fury that happens to those of us who live too long.

My kind enjoy great longevity, you see. Some argue we could live forever, if we did not fight so many wars and embrace so many risks. In days gone by, warriors often lived five hundred years or more. Now, since the Philosophers invented the paklas which give us such remarkable powers of healing, we can live for far longer; many thousands of years. Of *our* years, I mean; the time it takes Maxolu to orbit our sun, Karasheen.

My father was already an old man when he married my mother. Older still when he sired me. I have six older brothers by my father's first wife; the youngest is a thousand years old. And, as is the way with my kind, every year that passed my father grew stronger and more graceful. His fighting prowess increased. His memory became sharper and more reliable. He knew, for instance, the name of every warrior and Philosopher and home-maker and child in his tribe, and his tribe was two hundred thousand strong. But his soul, ah, his soul. It had darkened.

Mindwild: possessed by the spirit of a warrior, with no alleviating spirit of poet, or father, or lover, or friend.

Once, my father had loved my mother with the greatest and

177

most lyrical of passions. Yet now he loathed her. Sometimes, or so I was told, he beat her; on numerous occasions he treated her with contempt, in ways I shall not describe. He hated all his children by her too – Wareel and Andro and I. He hated also all those in his tribe, but he commanded them masterfully. And he had declared war on all the other Tribes of Maxolu – thirty-nine of them in all. His aim was to create a single tribe, powerful enough to launch a war to the death against the Southern Tribes on their far-flung planets.

It was a demented plan; which was to be expected, since my father Lexas was of course insane. But he was also powerful. Twenty-six great battles had already been fought; and Lexas had won them all. Not by weight of arms; nor by superior strategy. Simply by challenging the chieftain of each tribe to single combat. None can refuse such a challenge according to the honour-code of my people; and none of my father's opponents had survived these bloody and furious bouts.

Thus, twenty-six chieftains had perished in single combat; and my father now near ruled our world. All this had occurred in the last five years of the hundred that I had been away.

So when I returned to Madagorian, I was confronted with dark truths about my world and about my family. I spoke to my mother Giona, whose spirit was broken and who seemed to me as nervous and ineptly shy as a Philosopher's teenage child - this, the warrior-born who was once one of the most fearless cathary racers in our tribe, in the glorious days of her youth!

My sister Wareel told me dire tales of my father's violence to my mother; once, he staked her in the desert, so the sun beat down on her body, and left her there for days. It was a degradation indeed for one so noble and so true; and yet she whimpered not once.

Andro too had incurred my father's wrath; and now was barred from his tent, and condemned as a creature-so-vile-no-warrior-should-ever-again-be-his-friend. This is a dark naming for our kind; it meant, irrevocably, that Andro had no friends and no status within our tribe. He had to sleep in the desert or with the catharys, for no tent would offer him welcome. He stole all his food, for none would serve him meat. And when I spoke to him, Andro would not honour my eyes with his eyes, for fear of bringing shame upon me too.

I begged Wareel to speak to Andro; but she would not. She was the kindest of sisters, but she felt herself bound by the code of our kind. Even I – a warrior fresh from battle – risked banishment for speaking to my brother without permission of my Chieftain. And in truth, I did not speak to him for very long; or with any trace of our former affection.

All this was unendurable and wrong. So I sought my father out.

I found him in his tent, drunk, eyes glittering. He welcomed me coldly. I sat before him and a pretty galoit served me a glass of wine. I drained it. She poured another glass; I drained it, and smiled at her pleasantly, to honour her service. She smiled in return, but there was fear in her eyes. Her face was black and bruised; I guessed my father had beaten her as punishment for some offence, and must have done so often, for such bruises would normally heal before discolouring.

And there I sat, honouring my father, who sat before me with legs double-curled and grinning with evil unallayed; and he joined me in my drunk.

Before long the tales began.

Lexas told me the familiar, sweet and comical story of how he first met my mother. She was a champion cathary racer, as I have said, and she had defeated him in a race. His beast was the fastest on the planet; but her creature was inspired by her touch and her spirit, and she rode it like the wind driving a cloud.

The best part of the story was when, halfway through the race, Lexas had out of frustration beaten his own beast on the haunch with his whip, and it had roared and bucked and thrown him. (At this point in the tale my father mimed falling, and bashing his nose, and roaring with rage; and I laughed uproariously at his clowning.) However, rather than continuing on to victory, Giona had stopped her beast, and waited patiently as he remounted. And then she allowed him to gallop past. And – to the astonishment of all - paused a further fifteen minutes as he urged his cathary to the finish line.

Then she nudged her own beast with the gentlest of touches and the animal ran faster than any cathary in living memory; and Lexas was rocked by the breeze as they raced past him. Thus was he defeated with ease.

Later, he told me, at the celebration feast, he had toasted her prowess with words most eloquent and flattering; including eleven new words he had created which conveyed the depth of his admiration for her beauty and her skill.

Later still, she seduced him in the sands, by the light of our moons. The sands were warm, as they often are at night, and the wind was chill. And as they fornicated, with passion most extraordinary, her cathary – no, perhaps that part of the story does not bear recounting. It involves – ha! It is very funny, in fact, but only if you have ever seen a cathary piss. For the creature nuzzled up to them and then - they saw what was about to happen, and they had to flee – stark naked – to avoid the tidal wave of...

No, it's longer funny. Not after all this time.

My point, however, is that my father spoke of my mother, in the telling of this long and enchanting story, with love and deep respect; as was appropriate for a Chieftain speaking of his bride.

But then his tone darkened. He told me that I was a fool, for helping to wage a war that did not serve the interests of my own tribe. And that my mother was a fool too. A fucker-of-animals. A slut-who-should-be-caged-in-a-dungeon-without-light. And many other words. Hurtful words. Our people love invective; it is an art form for us. I cannot paint, nor can I sing, but I can call you a cunt in four thousand different ways; and of this I am proud.

But even so there are limits, strictly defined, which all should observe. And it is a point of deep principle that no Maxolun male should ever talk of his wife as my father spoke, that day, of my mother.

And no son should ever hear such words, such daggers-of-contempt, for the female who gave him life.

I should explain that for my kind fathers are – what can I say? I'm sorry – my usual flow-of-story is becoming – I'm aware you see that for some of you, love between a father and a child is not a special bond. But for us, it assuredly is. More intimate than - well, than anything.

When he was alive, my father and I were as one. He was a part of me. And every time I fought, my father's soul possessed me. I can say it no more clearly than that.

I did not *love* him. Love is too small a word. Fathers of my kind can love children of course – as I loved mine. But the feeling of a child towards a father – awe is perhaps a better word. My father was my god.

And so, it was hard for me to do what I did. Hard beyond all measure. But I did not falter in my resolve; nor did my courage fail me.

We drained our final flask, we shook hands, and we blessed our ancestors. Though my father did so with a sneer in his tone, as if he did not accept that previous generations knew more than ours. And then my father instructed me to take over the leadership of the mounted regiments of his defeated enemies. I was, he conceded, a warrior tested and proven and he would have use of me now.

However, to his utter amazement, I declined. And then, with customary Maxolun invective, using a formal phrase of such obscenity I dare not repeat it here, I spat upon the floor; and challenged my father to a single combat to the death.

It was, of course, an utterly foolhardy thing to do. For a whelp such as myself to defeat the oldest and hence the strongest warrior on Madagorian in such a combat would be a feat that staggered credulity. Many older warriors had failed before me; and it seemed most likely that I would fail too.

Yet my honour demanded that I should *try*.

And I had a deeper motive than revenge for the way my father Lexas had treated my family. For I knew there were at that time certain impetuous fools, my brother Andro among them, who were plotting rebellion. They talked of challenging my father's right to claim victory after defeating a tribe's chieftain in single combat, without testing his strength against the other warriors in that tribe.

And, as I knew, the rebels had won much support for their view among the warriors of all the defeated tribes. Andro himself had argued that if they were all to gather and defy their new chieftain, they would be an unstoppable force. My father's army of loyal tribe-warriors would be easily defeated by the hordes of the other twenty-six tribes!

However, the law of single combat was a hallowed and a precious tradition. To repeal it would, in my view, be to mock and to disgrace everything that was of value to me and my fellow warriors.

That way lay anarchy. Patricide, I truly believed, was preferable.

And so the day of our combat was assigned. My father had choice of weapon; he chose the eight-blade. A pole with four blades at each end, and a spike between the blades, like a carois in a flower. A hard weapon to use but, handled right, it could both stab and slice, and was prized for the ease with which it decapitated. I had never held one before. My father however was the master of the eight-blade; indeed, some say he invented it.

In preparation we stood naked, daubed in mud, all the long night, at the very centre of our village of tents. And we slept for much of that time, whilst standing, to preserve our strength.

In the morn we dressed in our battlewear. Armour for the loins, and boots that would not slip and slide in blood. That was all. My father's body was half again the size of mine; since our kind never cease to grow. His body was scarred, for old skin loses its ability to heal scars so well. But his arms and legs and chest were dense with muscle; and his hair was black; and his eyes glittered with evil clarity.

I felt like a child; I had to stare up to see my father's eyes.

"Let the battle begin," said Timola, once a great warcraft pilot, who was to be the arbiter of justice in the combat. He had known my father for many years and reverenced him greatly.

How to paint the picture of that scene, to those who do not know my world?

Ours is a desert tribe and our days are fierce hot, so we fought at dawn, before the sun's beams had the power to burn flesh. On all sides mountainous dunes reached up, encircling the combat arena; and at the base of these mountains of sand sat row upon row of spectators on tiered benches - my family and warriors and home-makers and wise ones of this village of my tribe. No children were allowed. No Philosophers chose to attend. Ten thousand watched, and two warriors on platforms were entrusted with ensuring there were no breaches of etiquette. A before-combat 'heaven-eyes' pose had to be assumed by each fighter before every flurry, with eyes uplifted, one arm raised, and the backs of the feet raised off the ground. Punching and biting were allowed but spitting and sneering talk were barred; and only two weapons were allowed, namely the eight-blade and the dagger. Our fingertips were inspected for poison beneath the nails. Our fists and knees were ray-scanned in case either of us had surgically implanted metal in with the bone. Our souls were pronounced pure.

And so we began.

We stood, at first, in heaven-eyes for two entire kals: near naked, each staring up at the heavens where the souls or warriors reside, balanced on our forefeet; and all this while holding the heavy pole of an eight blade in one hand.

Then we commenced. Our long black hair trailing behind us like the wake from a ship, our cold bodies warmed by the dawn sun, as we touched our heels to the ground and began our deadly dance. Our moves were fast and sinuous. Lunge. Side-step. Leap.

Shaft clanged against shaft; blades whistled close to flesh.

My father's parries were astonishingly powerful and several times he near rocked me off my feet. And his thrusts were fast and could not be predicted. But I was of the moment; I was the wind whirling against sand; I was the flurry of sand spattering against the wind.

He came at me fast; I was faster, and my blade lunged at his head; he ducked and scuttled and was behind me. But I leaped up, using air like footholds, and landed and launched a perfect spike-thrust that missed him entirely because he was behind me again, and I stepped to the right just in time to dodge his spike.

Crash! The collision of metal shaft upon metal shaft echoed through the desert; and not a sound was heard from the gathered crowed.

Crash! The collision of shafts once again cracked like thunder.

Crash! – and then I knew something was wrong. For I felt a trembling in the shaft I held, like a tide ebbing away; and an instant later it shattered entirely. I leaped backwards as my weapon turned to shards, then tried but fail to seize the blades upon the floor; but Lexas drove me back mercilessly.

I knew I had been duped, for metal does not shatter so. My eight-blade must have had a shaft made of hardened glass. This successfully mimicked metal for a while; it had endured for fifteen entire minutes of combat; but now it was broke. Fair play had not been done. My father had cheated.

But the presiding warriors on their platforms did not call foul. And Timola, my father's dearest friend, did not speak out. Even my brother Andro was silent. And then I knew that I had no friends this day.

And so I drew my dagger and attempted to live.

I could not fight my father now; I could only run and dodge and duck and dive, and leap, and roll, and parry his savage eight-blade strikes with my dagger's short blade. He renewed the attack; I ran faster, and dodged more desperately. The crowd began to boo and to mock me for my cowardice; but I was unperturbed.

Sometimes, you see, a warrior must be a coward.

Then I struck one blade of his eight-blade with my dagger and it ripped off, and I caught the blade in my hand and threw it at my father's heart. Reflexively he batted the blade away; but by then I had thrown my dagger too; and it embedded in his eye.

A brain-strike; a dagger through the eye; I truly thought I had won!

But despite my confidence, I nonetheless rolled away to a safe distance; and right I was to do so. For my father was halted in his wrath for just two long seconds; and then he renewed his swinging and lunging attack. He spun the eight-blade in complex patterns of whistling metal in the air, hoping to catch me a glancing blow. But I ran and fled and ducked and dived; pursued by a warrior with a dagger embedded in his eye. It felt as if he could see me *through* the blade and handle of my own weapon.

A brain-strike, and decapitation, are the only sure ways to kill a Maxolun warrior enraged. And yet I had failed to kill my father, though he had my dagger through his eye; such was his strength, and his resolve!

He lunged again and his spike went through my heart; I spat blood and tried to punch him, but he pulled the spike free, and lopped off my left hand with a downwards strike. And this time I did succeed in punching him, with my other – or rather only – hand. Then a blade ripped open my stomach and blood welled and gushed; though fortunately my guts did not entirely spill out of my body.

He stabbed my second heart while I was dazed. And I staggered around in pain, feeling my two hearts dying inside my body, as blood gouted ferociously from my stomach. But this time I grabbed the shaft of his eight-blade with my one remaining hand and held it tight; and struck it with my left forearm and broke the shaft. My father laughed and held the two halves of the eight-blade aloft; one weapon had now been made into two, and the humour of it appealed to him!

But as he laughed, I punched him again, in the face; and this time the punch rocked his skull, and shifted the dagger blade embedded therein. And suddenly, the light went out of his one remaining eye.

He fell. I guessed he was dead or dying, and I do not recollect what happened next.

I was, so I am told, three weeks asleep, recovering from my dire wounds. And when I woke I had a tube down my throat to help me breathe, and a machine to pump my blood; and the stump at my left wrist was covered in a growth-bag. My mother, Giona, was standing over the bedside. She had been standing there, I was later advised, for the entire month; not moving, not eating, not speaking. She saw me wake, and she stared at me.

I was her youngest child, and her most beloved, or so I had always believed. And she knew that I had good cause for doing what I did. I had slain an evil tyrant; the deranged Maxolun who had treated her and all our peoples so very ill. And thus, I had saved the soul of the Maxolu.

And yet, for all his sins, Lexas had been her husband; and she had loved him deep and dear.

I could not speak; but I implored her with my eyes for pity, and for her forgiveness.

A long moment lived between us. I could feel her regrets, and her pain. Tears dampened her cheeks; and her eyes were bright red with grief.

Then she spat upon me; thick white spit that spattered my face and left puddles. Hate for me was in her soul; and I felt it like a blow. Then she turned and left, without speaking a word.

On that day, so all the chroniclers of my kind agree, on that fateful day when I slew my father and liberated my people from his terrible tyranny, was the legend of *Sharrock* born. And since then I have lived my life with honour, as a warrior should.

And yet, because of that day, I lost a father; and I never saw my mother again, nor my brother Andro, nor my sister Wareel.

I miss them so.

The Ice Submarine

Adam Roberts

Systems were malfunctioning again. This time the fault was in insulation systems: heat was leaking into the living spaces from the superheated outer skin. The Chief Technician reported directly to the Captain to insist, for the third time that week, that the vessel be taken off active service for proper repairs.

"We follow orders, Chief," the Captain replied.

The men had stripped to their waists, their beards heavy with sweat, working with a fuggy slowness that was, the Captain was certain, pregnant with mistake. He was weary too, but always there was a cold spot at the focal point of his mind reminding him that errors in a vessel such as his could be nuclear-catastrophic. He jingled the flat metal key restlessly. His Second Officer had objected to being locked out of the missile launch, but the Captain had over-ruled him. He copied from the data log onto paper, a standard procedure in case Western anti-submarine technology should scramble the electronic storage systems. His pen worked awkwardly: *Systems malfunction, heating insulation breakdown. Temperature 48. Trouble with military contingent, who insist incessantly on surfacing. Will continue current voyage for only thirty more kms.* Blots of sweat plocked the paper. Experience told him that to wipe them away would be to blur the words. Instead he dabbed at them with the corner of the facing page. He wrote the date at the top, a last thought: *January 3rd 1440.*

Before the war the captain had been a scholar. He had specialised in Medieval poetry. Occasionally he pondered the connection between war and poetry. We might, for example, contemplate all those great soldier-poets of tradition. But his own poetry, when he had essayed it as a young man, had been small and derivative, chalky images and conventional sentiments. He had tried to capture in words the grandeur of the sky, the way the stars seemed so far and simultaneously so close; the way some evening sky-colours struck the eye as ordinary, banal, and then a tiny shift in tone would blaze the sky with a glory of red-gold that dug deep into the soul. The proximity of the numinous divine and the rounded nothingness of beast-life that most people lived. But his destiny, it transpired, had not been the contemplation of desert skies. Instead, destiny had sent him to that place that was furthest from the huge open spaces and the heart-reviving sunsets.

But now, when he remembered life before the war, he no longer thought 'I was a poet and scholar'. Now he thought: 'I was a widower'. He was still a widower, of course; but being in the military somehow altered that fact.

He ordered the engines full stop, and all was silent. For an hour there was no sound at all except the gunshot splitting noises of the ice settling around them, a series of irregularly spaced bangs. Everybody twitched with each enormous crack, even the Captain. He trusted his ship, he trusted that it had been built strong enough to withstand the pressure, but he twitched anyway. He tried to distract himself by encoding his report in random data, ready for the next surfacing. *78 South, 12.8 East, Queen Maud's Land. Pursuit of Enemy Craft abandoned after eighteen hours. Malfunction of insulation system, operating temperature unacceptably high, request orders to proceed to repair co-ordinates.* He knew this would come to nothing as he wrote it, but he continued with the formality. *In the name of Allah, the Great, the Compassionate. Victory to the Pan-Islamic People's Republic. Captain Sayyid Ali Beheshti.* He fitted the clip into his personal transmitter, and settled down to read the technical reports. The Chief, handing him another chip with a detailed technical report, grunted. "If I had proper solid bodied men working for me, it'd be good, sweat them down a bit. But the skinny lads I have, if we keep going they'll just melt away like butter in the oven."

"It'll cool down now, Chief," said the Captain.

Another microsense was sent up, wriggling through the ice to the surface. If it picked up the coded launch command, it would wriggle back down to them in twenty minutes. Never more than twenty minutes from the world's end.

The Captain sat back, stroking his beard and listening to the bangs from the ice. Reality snapping and buckling all around them. Crocodile noises. Eventually the cracks came less frequently, and finally they stopped altogether. With their immediate environment now set he ordered the sensor-probes poked out into the surrounding ice. These picked up a few possible vibrations, possibly the signatures of following moles. Maybe the whole escapade had been a Western trick, to lure the ship from its secrecy. After a few hours the vibrations died away. Could be anything. "Could be ice settling", said Gupta, the second-in-command. "Could be a battle on the surface. Could be nothing at all. Sir." He always said 'sir' a tick too late, as if in afterthought, with an unmistakable hint of implied disrespect. Increasingly the Captain found his fury at Gupta harder to block down. He had resorted to internalising a mantra: *all of us are brothers, all of us brothers.* But the words gave him little purchase on his rage. He could feel himself slipping towards an explosion, towards screaming at Gupta's surly face. It would be unacceptable for him to lose control like that.

"Could be those things, Gupta," he replied, focusing on keeping his voice level. "Could be moles after us. We sit tight."

For a day and a night, and then another day, the ice submarine lived in darkness, in blindness. Its crew turned in on themselves. Men got back into their uniforms; then into their woollens; finally into their plasjackets. The Captain, muffled up like the rest in the hellish cold, read the Qu'ran quietly to himself. Third Officer brought reports of restive behaviour among the men, and in the morning of the second day the Captain made a speech on headphone-only. In the hectic storm of this war, soldiers and submariners alike should relish the opportunity provided by an interval like this. If they were cold, they should think of the ground troops being irradiated and heat-blasted on the surface; of the oceanic submariners being blown, lasered or microwaved into nothingness by the latest Western Satanic devices. He concluded by advising his men to spend the time in contemplation of the benevolence of Allah, and in the study of the Qu'ran. But afterwards he sat with a sick feeling in his chest. At the launch, a year and a half previously, he had genuinely believed that the time of confinement would enable all his men, and the soldiers they carried too, to get closer to the One God. But the hermit life seemed only to focus their pettiness and self-concern. The soldiers were worse than the submariners. On the evening of the second day their squad-commander, Baru, clattered through to the bridge.

He spoke without preliminary: "Captain, we must move the submarine."

The Captain tapped at his beard with all four finger-points at once. His subordinate officers looked at him. The sensible thing would be to avoid a confrontation.

"Commander Baru," he said, very softly. "It would be a courtesy to me if you could let me know your reasons."

"We must rotate the submarine. My men find it uncomfortable praying to Mecca. The quarters are narrow across, but long alongways. If you twist the submarine through ninety-degrees, we will be able to pray without inconvenience."

"But if I rotate the submarine, I will need to heat it up."

"For a short time only."

"Commander Baru, a moment may be all the Western machines need to determine our position."

Baru sniffed noisily. He was scoffing, coming close to

publicly disagreeing with his Captain. But the moment of confrontation came and passed, and instead Baru turned and stomped noisily back along the central corridor.

In the night of the second day the Captain ordered movement. Any moles on their trail would have given up by now. The reactor moaned, the hull heated, and the vessel moved forward, ice subliming to steam before them, congealing back into ice behind. They moved up through half a kilometre, then cooled the hull to a few degree above zero. Their rate of progress slowed, supposedly to become indistinguishable to seismic or other spy-devices. The Captain had never really believed this, just as he never quite trusted the maps of the mountains and landscape thought to exist under the kilometres of Antarctic ice. How did people know that this was the way the hidden land lay? Ice this thick was extraordinarily difficult to sense through. Some Western Satanic satellite had passed by overhead a hundred years previously and determined that the Transantarctic Mountains lay *here* rather than a hundred metres further over. But an ice-submarine, shuttling along in its envelope of superheated steam, burrowing through the ubiquitous medium of ice at many kilometres an hour, could not afford a hundred metres of error. A collision with unyielding rock would be death.

In his meditation, in the evening, the Captain had tried to map his consciousness onto the Antarctic continent. The soul was rock, covered in the frozen ice of flesh. God might melt the latter, but the Devil himself could not thaw away the former. He ran his crew through an attack drill to help eat up the time. Only when his inner balance told him that it was the right time did he recall the microsense and order hot ahead.

They surfaced in the blackness of night, and the Captain, with Gupta and one Technician, climbed up and out onto the conning tower to breathe real air. Dust in the atmosphere hid all but the brightest stars. The blackness tasted of almonds, of grit. There was a strangely metallic decaying smell faint in the cold of the air. The ice stretched away lone and bare in the darkness on all sides, somehow sensible, even through the gloom. The Captain put his report into the stratosphere, to be picked up and decoded from its cloaking noise by Islamic satellites. Or so he hoped.

He peered at the sky.

"Battle fought recently, do you think?" he asked his second-in-command. Gupta's eyes were the only part of him to catch the attenuated starlight, but the Captain sensed the scowl, the irritation. "There's a lot of dust in the air," he replied. "Sir."

"There are anomalies to the east, sir," said the Technician.

The Captain pulled at his beard. "It has been provided for us," he said.

Back below he summoned Commander Baru. The soldier was still chewing something, presumably his supper. The insolence of it. Sayyid Ali Beheshti thought of standing on his privilege as Captain, and ordering him to get rid of it. But Baru would probably only have spat the cud straight on the floor of the Captain's cabin. That would require disciplining, and then there would be even more tension between soldiers and submariners.

"Commander," he said. "There seems to be a camp a few kilometres to the east."

Baru thought for a while, chewing, swallowing. Then: "Will you move the vessel closer to the camp?"

The Captain all-but sighed. Baru's ignorance of sub-ice tactics was deep-set, not to say depressing. "No, Commander. That would simply alert them to our presence. They will most likely be a scientific station, with few arms but much sensor equipment. If we come closer we make it much more likely that we will seismically register."

The Commander stood to attention with a smack of heels together. "Your orders, sir?"

This was mockery, but Beheshti froze his resentment deep inside. No place for it here. "Baru," he said wearily, rubbing his eyes. "Take your men out and destroy the camp."

He took his place on the platform as Baru led his dozen men over the side and onto the ice. Their dark uniforms registered blotchily in the ghost half-light. A hundred meters to the east and they were invisible. Beheshti went below and slept for an hour. Then it was time for prayers, which he took in his cabin. When he poked his head into the frosty night air again it was just in time to hear the first sounds of gunfire, hollowed and flattened by the distance and the echo-index of the ice. It was a spooky series of sounds. A hound's bark slowed down and broken into fragments, played deep underground. Devilish. Beheshti flicked little pearls of frost from his beard with his thumb. Those had been his breath only moments before.

Then there was a light, an orange bauble only thumbnail sized near the horizon. The rumble came a little afterwards. At this Beheshti almost lost his composure and swore. What was that idiot Baru playing at? The West would be all over them in minutes.

"Prepare the engines," he ordered. His number two coughed, interposed: "But the men, sir? We can't leave them on the ice."

Beheshti wanted to say *that idiot Baru has dug his own grave*, but he didn't. Instead he put through a rapid series of orders. "We'll hold as long as we can," he told Gupta, his voice pulled thin with anger. "But as soon as we detect air support for that camp, we must go under." The ship would be a quieter place without Baru and his boneheaded soldiers anyway. It was all he could do to hold back from ordering immediate going-under. The latest version of moles were faster and deadlier than any before. He needed all the head-start he could get.

But at five minutes a buzzing sound started to swell from the blackness, and a few minutes after that Baru and his men arrived back at the submarine, riding ice-buggies. Baru himself clambered up the platform and breathlessly counted his men past him. "We found a hanger-full of these little cars. They ride along on a cushion of steam, *very* fast." His breath, panting out in gouts, flickered faint in the starlight.

"Aboard, commander," ordered Beheshti. "Now."

"Yes, Captain, yes." His last man clambered up, carrying a sack over his shoulder. Beheshti thought it was a body bag, and his anger was too much. "You've brought one of your dead back with you?" he hissed. "I'll have you court-martialled."

"No, sir, no, sir," panted Baru. "No, we have no dead. This is a prisoner."

Beheshti took the vessel down to five hundred metres and a kilometre from the incident, sent up a microsense and put all his probes into the ice around him. He was angry now, and his men could see it. It wasn't the anger as such that scared them, more the fact that the Captain's famous self-control was starting to slip. He ordered the prisoner, an ice-coloured Western woman, locked in one of the toilets, and told Baru to come with him to the Captain's cabin.

"What are we to do with a prisoner, you idiot?" he demanded. His control was slipping, he could feel it. A stream of invective came from him, and Baru's piggish face looked startled. But, to Beheshti's surprise, the soldier did not give way. Instead he responded in as loud a voice as the Captain's, "It was a tiny scientific camp, Captain. They were clearly not a military base, and so they must have been engaged on some spy-mission. I thought it best to capture one of the Westerners for interrogation."

Beheshti's anger was stopped by the sheer nerve of the man. He put both hands over his mouth, trying to hold in his rage. It pulsed, then subsided. He could actually feel the anger going down inside him like something swallowed. Then he breathed.

"And what are we to do with her? Once she is interrogated?"

Baru looked a little puzzled. "After, sir?"

"Do you suggest killing her in cold blood?"

"Of course not, sir. Couldn't we take her back?"

"How long will we have to keep her locked up in a toilet? How much food do you think we can spare?"

"But, sir, how long will it be before we are recalled for repairs? Surely, given the state of the vessel..."

"The state of the vessel is my concern," Beheshti snapped. "As, now, is this woman. You are dismissed."

When his wife had died, Beheshti had been staggered by his grief, stupefied by it. His relatives tried to console him by telling him: every husband feels this when their wife dies. But he couldn't see the consolation in that thought. The realisation that others had suffered precisely this brought only the opposite of consolation. In fact it means a sort of pollution; it means both dilution and contamination of the intense, personal intimacy of grief. Rather than face their offensive expressions of sympathy, Beheshti assumed the external carapace of ordinariness, resuming his daily duties. Only the external shell, though. Inside was molten with pain.

Beheshti had the woman moved to the mess, and went to see her there. She complained a great deal, but knew only a few basic phrases in Arabic. It seemed that her shoulder was dislocated, and that her head hurt. At any rate, there was blood on her ear. Perhaps one of Baru's men had knocked the side of her head.

By the time a computer translator had been brought in, she had quietened down. The shoulder, it turned out, was only 'stretched' (Beheshti assumed the meaning was 'strained'), and the head wound was easily cleaned. Baru hovered excitedly. He was like a dog: he hated the confinement of being aboard, and loved the chance to stretch his legs on the ice above. Always badgering the Captain to surface. Having stretched his legs he would be high-spirited for hours.

"What was your base working on?" Baru asked of the

woman. She peered at the screen for the translation. Her voice, when she spoke her reply, sounded croaky, and she kept stopping, or hesitating with a weird high-pitched *err* sound. Beheshti looked at her hands. They were trembling, as if with cold. Was she cold? The ice was still clanging as it froze around them, but to the Captain the air still felt warm. Was she trembling with fear? If so, fear of what – of being found out?

The screen printed out a reply, *scientific station [ ] engaged in science [ ] [ ] studying the atmosphere conditions [ ] peaceful [ ] outrage.*

Beheshti ignored the machine. "Are you scared?"

She read the screen, and then looked up at his face. Her frowning mouth made creases in her cheeks in time to the cracking noises outside the submarine, as if her white skin were made of ice.

"What is your name?" Beheshti asked.

She read the screen, and replied: "Ann Keltner". Then she said something more. *suing kennel [ ] environmental scientist,* said the screen.

"But you are affiliated with the military," barked Baru. He leant forward.

The screen replied: *scientific expedition.*

"There were weapons and explosives at your camp," Baru pointed out.

As she was reading this and replying a crewman called the Captain away. He hastened through the corridor and up the ramp to the bridge. The Bridge Technician hurried to meet him.

"There's definitely something going on, Sir," he said. "All sorts of seismic action."

The Captain nodded. "They are after us. Ready reactor, and launch three torpedoes." Beheshti's guts were shimmying. He paused, tried to listen to his intuition. "No four. Five. Yes. I believe they have come after us in force."

The torpedoes went, steaming their way through the ice, in five directions. The Ice Submarine fell into line away and a little to the east behind one of them. He shut his eyes, tried to sense what was happening around him in the blind darkness. The aircraft launching hunt-kill moles. The moles searching for heat, for vibration, for anything to move towards. He searched for that impossible telepathy, that godlike ability to read the blank surroundings that is the ice-submarine Captain's fantasy. There was a loud thump, and he twitched in his chair. But it was evidently only a piece of rubble suspended in the ice, bumped aside as they slid past.

"Sir!" shouted the Technician. The screen showed a sudden bunching of data. One of the torpedoes had detonated. "Drop to three kilometres," he ordered. Now was the time to try and slip past these weapons, whilst the shudders and heat of that explosion masked their movements. "I want to be right down, as deep as is safe. What do the maps show?"

The technician scrabbled with the keys. They were within twenty kilometres of the coast. He entertained and dismissed the idea of driving straight out into the ocean: a good way of baffling moles, but only at the cost of making them much more readily identifiable by the Westerners. Oceanic submarines were lost nowadays at an appalling rate. That was why the war council had decreed that the entire nuclear capability of the People's Republic would be carried by ice-submarines. This only made the pressure on Beheshti the worse, of course. If the moles found him, they not only killed his men, but they broke another finger in the nuclear-hand of Islam.

"We're nine hundred metres off the rock, sir," called a navigator.

"All stop, let it freeze."

Once frozen in position, it was simple enough for an ice-submarine to settle downwards through the ice so slowly as to be undetectable. Heat the ice to 5°, and the water slid upwards past the hull to freeze easily and with minimal cracking, whilst the vessel bedded down under gravity. Beheshti sat for an hour in the Captain's chair, before going back to the mess to find out what was happening with the Westerner.

"She still claims she's a scientist, sir" said Baru. His men were sitting around looking bored now, but Baru still had the puppyish gleam in his eye. "Claims they were only affiliated to the military by force of necessity in the war. She even had the courage to lecture me, sir."

"How so?"

"She disapproves of ice-submarines. Says they are wrecking a pristine scientific site, thawing and freezing ice at all depths. Says we're contributing to the melting of the ice-packs. I told her, good, maybe we'd drown New York, but she said Mecca would also go under. That's not right, is it, sir? Mecca's a way inland?"

"She's trying to war with your thoughts, Commander. Ignore her."

"Still, there was a base there for some reason. To begin with she insisted that it was a random position. Then it turns out that there was a battle there a few weeks ago, and that she was studying the detonation patterns frozen on the ice."

Beheshti sat opposite her. He smiled at her, and shook his head slowly. She looked away.

The vessel settled slowly, sinking through a few hundred metres of ice so slowly it was almost impossible to detect the sense of slippage. Yet it was there, a liminal feeling of *going-down*. The men felt easier, Beheshti could see. The deeper the better, the defence of the burrowing animal.

Six hours in, the Captain decided they were safe enough for him to take a nap. He slept for several hours in his cabin, and woke when a distinct lurch took the ice-submarine down through at least three metres in a moment. That was a distinctly unpleasant sensation. "What is going on?" he yelled, pulling on his plasjacket and tumbling up the ladder to the bridge corridor. "What is happening here?"

The Chief Technician was blanched with worry. "I don't

know, sir, I don't know. We dropped 3.4 metres suddenly. That shouldn't..."

There was another lurch. Somebody screamed, and then was quiet. The silence was horrible. Beheshti got to the Captain's chair, positioned himself in it, when the whole world fell.

For long seconds they free-fell. The Captain watched with horrible detachment as the long hair of one of the under-Technicians, a lad also called Ali, floated upwards. Then they hit the floor. There was a terrific crash, a buckling crunch, and the yells of men, as bodies collapsed and loose equipment smashed about. Beheshti was driven down into his chair.

Then, nothing.

"What was that?" Beheshti asked. Nobody replied, so he repeated the question. "I want to know what is going on." His lips were dry, they stuck on the words as they tried to form themselves.

The Chief Technician was the gloomiest. The reactor had been so badly shaken by the fall that he was certain it was irreparable. He had sealed the fusion room. They had a few days power on conventional sources, maybe enough to move through half a kilometre of ice: which was no good to them when they were five kilometres down.

"Ice," said the Captain, twining his forefinger into his beard. "Ice, yes." The probes, poking out from the hull, were not detecting any ice at all.

Beheshti, his face masked, climbed out onto the conning platform. Behind him came Gupta, Baru. It was utterly black, but the air felt surprisingly warm. "There's no way we can be on the surface, is there?" Gupta asked. "Sir?"

"How could that be, Gupta?"

"I don't know. Maybe we were closer to the coast than we thought. Perhaps some odd ice formation, some sort of cave." He stopped speaking. "A sort of overhang, perhaps? Why," he

199

said, as if interrupting his own chain of thought, "is it so *warm* here?"

Beheshti ordered power to the ship's floodlights, and great tunnels of light suddenly filled the darkness. They reached through blackness to end in great white ellipses. Beheshti angled them in various directions, but wherever they pointed the same white ellipses ended their beams at roughly 500m. The ellipses bulged, shrunk, deformed as the beams moved up, down, around.

The Captain sent out exploratory parties to check out the strange bubble, or cave (he didn't like the way Baru called it a 'bubble'; the word sounded too fragile), and it was one of the men on such a team who discovered the air was breathable. He must have taken his mask off in a spirit of curiosity, which angered Beheshti: had the atmosphere been toxic he would have died. But it seemed true, though hard to comprehend. This space under the ice had a high level of oxygen.

"It can't be a natural formation," insisted Gupta. "Sir. The oxygen proves that. It must have been constructed by the Americans. It is some sort of anti-submarine base."

"But why, then, is it deserted?" The searchlights could find nothing; only a huge arching ceiling of ice over a flat ground of flattened pebbles. The only feature was a low saddle of rock reaching up out of the ground, to a height of less than a metre, a quarter of a kilometre from where the ice-submarine had fallen.

"I don't know sir, but I must advise caution. As your second-in-command, it is my duty to advise caution."

"Caution, Gupta. Yes."

"Sir, if this is a Western site, then they could be on us at any moment. I must insist, I must *beg* you, Sir, to relinquish single control over the missiles. Give me launch privileges again, as a precaution."

Beheshti angled a searchlight directly up. The white spot on the roof was perfectly smooth, blank. "Yes, Gupta, the missiles. But would the missiles even fire, here? They are, after all, encased in ice-torpedo shells. They are designed to burrow through the ice and only when they reach the surface fire into the atmosphere. I doubt it they are of any use to us at all, in our present condition." Nor could Beheshti send up a microsense, or know whether the People's Republic wanted him to launch an attack.

By the second day, the men had grown used to their strange new environment. Beheshti had authorised the setting up of a few floodlights, positioned on the shingle. Men off duty played football, their shouts echoing weirdly in the great chamber. The Captain himself strolled, his feet crunching on the pebbles. It was amazingly warm, considering that they were buried under so much ice. Considering that the temperature on the surface so far above them could be anything up to sixty-six below. He hunkered down to his haunches, and picked up a pebble. It was a black stone, flattened and worn smooth. By the ice? But ice didn't make pebbles. This must have been a beach at some time. Most of the stones were the same dolomite as the Transantarctic Mountains, but some were a paler, yellow stone, and some were pitted like old sandstone.

Why was it so warm? And why didn't the temperature melt the ice above and bring the great weight of material over them crashing down?

After working all night the Chief Technician thought that he might be able to work the reactor turbines for up to six hours before the whole thing became dangerous. Six hours was probably enough to get them to the ocean, where they could travel for days more on battery power as a conventional submarine. But six hours of reactor power or six thousand hours was equally irrelevant to the vessel in its current situation, beached on Antarctic shingle, with the ice half a kilometre distant in every direction. "We need to be actually in the ice, or on it," the Technician reminded him. "It's not enough our nose is pressed against it."

"So we need to do more than drag the vessel to the ice," said

201

Beheshti. "We need to dig a tunnel and push the vessel *into* it. Yes?"

"We should start soon," said the Chief Technician. "The oxygen in that bubble out there – God knows how it got there in the first place, but it won't last for ever. Our boys are breathing it up. We'll need to get into breathing packs in a day or too, and that'll make the digging harder."

When Beheshti asked about dragging the ice submarine over the shingle the Chief Technician had literally thrown up his hands in horror. "It'll *wreck* the underside, just *wreck* it. But there's no other way."

Beheshti walked back to the submarine. And, for a moment, in the shadows at the feet of the arclights – half-seen, but undeniably seen,, he saw: his wife. She was standing, and looking at him. He knew it was her, although (in his head, straightaway, he corrected himself) it could only be the ghost of her. He stopped, and gawped; but looking straight at the light assembly he could no longer see her. A trick of the light? A hallucination? No, he knew in his heart, no: neither of those explanations was right. Trusting to the automatic process of his external carapace, he resumed walking to the submarine; but as he walked he was thinking: death. We have broken into a grave. That is why she is here.

All available hands were sent to the nearest face to begin burning and digging a tunnel, but twelve hours work produced only a feeble-looking indentation in the side of sheer ice.

Baru brought Ann Keltner, the Western woman, out on the second day, and she was as astonished by their environment as any of them had been. Beheshti didn't think she was pretending her surprise. She clambered down the side of the submarine and scrunched about on the pebbles.

Gupta said: "Sir, you are going to make sure that she is guarded at all times?"

But Baru was dismissive. "Where can she go?"

Gupta was eager to make his point. "Sir, we don't know. This *may* be an American base, of some kind. There may be some sort of equipment that can summon the Westerners here. We should keep her in view."

"Do you want me to pull soldiers off digging detail to babysit her?" asked Baru, with an unpleasant edge to his voice.

But Beheshti interposed. "I don't like the idea of the woman wandering about by herself," he said. "Commander, I want two of your men detailed to be with her, to make sure she doesn't get up to mischief."

"Where can she go, sir?"

Later in the day, Baru reported to him on the bridge. "Perhaps you should come and take a look at this."

The Westerner had been exploring the 300 square metres of black rock that poked up through the shingle. With only a hand torch, and with both bored guards sitting on the edge of the rock-formation smoking, she had seemingly stumbled through a crevice. Her leg had gone into the crack up to the thigh. Her cries had brought the guards, who had helped her out, and brought her back to the submarine, but not before peering into the crack themselves. "They think it's worth going down into," Baru told the Captain.

"Down *into?*" echoed Beheshti. "Is there something down there?"

He went out personally with a torch into the blackness beyond the arc-lit area of the submarine itself. The women and her two guards followed. Away over to his right, the digging area splashed a puddle of light in the darkness. He teased away the strands of hair from the corner of his lips where they were straying into his mouth. Was it his imagination, or was the oxygen already being used up? And so *warm*.

At the rock formation, they paused. There was no doubt but that the rock was warm to the touch. Not by much, but it was warmer than Antarctic rock had any business being. The Captain didn't know how it could be. Was this outcrop somehow heating the ice and creating the bubble? But what about the oxygen?

He let the Westerner go forward, and followed her. They came to the crevice, and went down on their haunches to look inside. It was less than a metre across, a black slash in the rock that bent round to the right, boomerang-shape. The Westerner was already lowering herself into it, wriggling with her legs to see if there was any purchase. Beheshti's first instinct was to stop her, but when she found a ledge and stood grinning with only her head and chest poking over the top, he instead lowered himself down to follow. They stood side by side, bathers in a weird rock-sea. One of the guards got in beside them, but there was no room for the other. When the Westerner ducked down and disappeared, it took a moment for the Captain to summon the courage to follow her.

They crouched and followed a sharpwardly down-leading slope. After a few hundred metres the ceiling lifted, and the sense of space returned. Beheshti could see the Westerner's torch beam flicking and dancing away ahead of them. It turned towards them, and moments later she was by their side, gabbling her gibberish with tremendous energy. She kept pointing and pulling.

They were in a bell-shaped chamber, apparently formed by nature itself; but when Beheshti lifted his torch he saw the reason the space had been preserved under the rock. The roof was tiled, a vault of what looked like bricks, aged and blackened.

It took a while for this to sink in.

The woman was pointing to the ground. There seemed to be the broken remains of a wall, antique-looking, and a pile of what looked like bones. "How strange," he said to the soldier. "It's archaeological."

"It looks old, sir."

The woman was chattering away, talking rapidly to herself. She seemed to be gathering bones, cradling her arms around a whole mess of rubbish. Beheshti slapped the stuff out of her grasp. Her voice rose, and then stopped as the soldier angled his gun. Her expression was distorted; it looked like rage, like pain. Beheshti could imagine her complain, without needing to decipher her gibberish. *A whole civilisation buried under the ice, the archaeological find of the century, we must explore it.* But there was no time for such things in war. Nor did he really see the need for scientists, archaeologists. It was all known to Allah, and nobody had to wait very many years before meeting Him.

Back in the submarine the Westerner was increasingly agitated. When they brought her the translator she spoke at length. *Antarctica thought to be iced for three million years [ ] discovery of these archaeological remains of the highest significance [ ] at least twelve thousand years old [ ] imperative these results be communicated to international community.*

Beheshti sat opposite her pulling at the two chief strands of his beard alternately with each hand. All his rage felt pure now, focused, brought to a shining point. It wasn't Baru, it wasn't even Gupta. It wasn't the faceless Westerners manning the American ice-submarines, trying to kill him. They, after all, were doing a job. As he looked into the eyes of this woman, he understood the point of the hate, and that in itself it was a clean thing. It was not going to provoke him to violence. That was not the way it worked. It would instead inspire him, bring a new strength of will to his work. That this woman could sit here with a defiant expression on her face, as if some ruins underneath the ice were more important than the war being fought. He could lecture her, but what would be the point in that? They were fighting for no small extension of territory or material greed; they were fighting for the actual souls of humanity. For God, and God would answer all scientists' questions soon enough when they encountered him. Did actual people, real souls, matter less than some old bones and bricks?

"Tell her," he said to Baru, "that if God had wanted people to discover this old rubbish he would not have buried it under five kilometres of ice." He stood. There was some shouting coming from above, in the bridge.

The voice of the Chief Technician came from overhead. "Sir, sir." Beheshti scrambled up the ladder.

Gupta was out on the top. "Sir," he bellowed through the hatch. "The roof is tumbling."

Even as he climbed out to see for himself Beheshti was struck by the odd literariness of Gupta's *tumbling*.

For a moment it wasn't clear what was happening. But out past the spaces illuminated by the arc-lights Beheshti could see that torches, each one marking a man, were scattering from the ice-face. Streaming like fireflies back towards the submarine. There was a shuddering thud, and then another one. A huge hunk of ice appeared from above in one of the lit areas, and crashed to the floor with a strange elegance. The body of the block seemed to flex as it struck the earth. The sky was breaking to pieces, and the huge weight of the five kilometres of ice overhead was forcing destruction downwards. "Back to the submarine," yelled Beheshti, straining over the lip of the platform to shout to his men. They needed no telling, were swarming back to the ship, but the words were bursting from the Captain's mouth, like an explosion, like the ice blocks shattering into shards of ice-shrapnel. "Back to the submarine! Run! Run!"

If you trace the western Antarctic peninsula from Queen Maud Mountains in at the Ross shelf, along to the end of the western peninsular and the last of the Graham mountains, it spells نعم, the Arabic for 'yes': *na'am*. It is the world, it is affirmation. As he runs through the ruins of a place forty times older than the prophet, the captain hears a voice inside his head. The voice is reciting the Qu'ran, the eighty-first sura, about the end of the world. And is the world not ending? And all he can think is: *it is her, it is the Western girl, it is her.* When the sun is overthrown, and when the stars fall, and when the camels big with young are abandoned, and when the wild beasts are herded together, and when the seas rise, and when souls are reunited, and when the girl-child that was buried alive is asked for what sin she was slain, and when the pages are laid open, and when the sky is torn away, and when hell is lighted, then every soul will know what it has made ready.

What has he made ready? Yes, he thinks. Yes, he thinks. He has almost reached the flank of the submarine when the first piece of the ceiling strikes him.

Welcome Home, Janissary

Tim C. Taylor

Escandala came out of her feint to deliver a sweeping kick at Horden's legs, pivoting on a gauntleted hand attracted to the *Osman Bey's* charged outer hull. She committed all her momentum to this one attack.

Horden jumped out of the way, an instinctive reaction strong enough to break the electrostatic attraction sticking his boots to the hull.

Escandala felt the natural human chemicals of release flood her body because in this zero-gee duel fought without thrust packs, Horden had already lost. Gravity's tendrils plucked at him from Akinschet, the gas giant thousands of klicks away.

Reinforcements always forced change. When Horden's four hundred human marines had arrived to fill the squadron's gaps, they had brought trouble too. Dangerous ideas about helping Earth were spreading through Commodore Gjalp's human contingent.

No!

Horden had exaggerated his leap. He was only a fraction of a meter off the hull, but Escandala's leg still followed its arc toward him. She scrabbled for a firmer hold, grunting with effort. Horden was fighting for prestige and influence but for Escandala this was all about her son. She *had* to win.

But she had already converted all the tension stored in her limbs into the thrust behind her kick.

Horden locked his legs around hers. His added mass slowed her scything motion then snatched away her weak grip on the hull and flung them both into space, circling each other as if dancing.

Inside her EVA suit, Escandala felt her shoulders slump when she traced forward the pattern of their dance and saw Horden's victory there. When time caught up with the inevitable, Horden grabbed hold of the communication boom and released his grip on her legs.

Escandala drifted away from the *Osman Bey*, her cramped world for the last eight years. She tumbled into the void in nothing but her EVA suit.

All the humans in the squadron watched her defeat.

She stealthed her suit and drifted away. As victor, Horden now commanded them all. She had no concerns about his ability as commander; the Jotuns would never have let him challenge for leadership unless they considered him fit. Horden's perverse attitude of allegiance to Earth bothered her far more.

The people of Earth had sold the ancestors of every human here as breeding stock, the price of patronage demanded by the masters, the White Knights. President Horden had signed the Accession Treaty on behalf of all humanity. Now his many-times descendent harboured dangerous ideas for the slave-soldiers.

"Please, little bird. De-stealth so we can bring you home quickly." The voice relayed through her helmet speaker belonged to One-Ear, the alien officer responsible for training human marines on the *Osman Bey*. His Jotun palette clicked as he tried to articulate human speech, sounding like a human boy with his throat half ripped out. "I am sorry you must relinquish command."

"Horden is welcome to that burden." Escandala was happy to let her voice betray her position. Hiding was not a serious proposition.

"That is good," said the Jotun. "You have seven months remaining in defence of Akinschet. Then we return home to Tranquility where you must give up your son, Zenothon. Horden's victory means you can spend more of those last months with your boy."

She laughed, a cracked sound that swamped her helmet with bitterness. When they had taken away her previous two children, to train and deploy as slave-soldiers, her aching loss had been buttressed with pride. With Zenothon her feelings were too tangled to interpret.

Six years ago, breathless and sweat-drenched, she had shared an irrepressible smile with the gurgling, messy bundle floating nearby in the birthing cocoon. Still secured by a natural umbilical tether, their bond had been unconditional. Since then, not only had the servants of the White Knights cut the cord, they had done things to her boy.

"Did I speak inappropriately?" Poor One-Ear sounded worried, though who could really guess what an alien felt?

Gunner Valthrudnir, as One-Ear insisted humans address him, had always been kind. And the Jotun officers were just as much slaves of the White Knights as the humans. She pictured the two meter high furry hexaped, good ear erect in concern, contorting his throat painfully to converse in human tongue.

"Your words are not inappropriate," she replied. "Merely inaccurate. I was fighting for my six-year-old boy, all right. Fighting to keep away from him. He frightens me."

"Don't you want to play with the other *Osman Bey* kids?" Escandala nodded toward the children rampaging back and forth over the gravitoid's hillocks with the kids from the *Garuda*, the other TU currently docked with the Sleeve. Giggles and simulated explosions vibrated through the thin belt of atmosphere coating the artificial worldlet.

"No, Momma," said Zenothon, frowning gravely. "Not just yet. This might be the last time we spend on the gravitoid before

211

we go to Tranquility and the Jotuns upgrade me to become a man. I can feel this worries you."

Escandala suppressed a shudder. Zenothon's augmentations allowed him to read her feelings like a viewscreen and write his own at will. What was it like to sense and interpret sweat and body temperature and other physical tells, considering such analysis to be as natural as his other senses? The kids even communicated using targeted nano-packets which delivered tailored cocktails of hormones. *Gifting*. That's what Zenothon called it.

"I have made you a model," said Zenothon. "Do you like it?"

Escandala guessed her son issued some kind of command signal from his head. From behind a hillock, a half-meter long model of a Sleeve floated toward them, taking up a holding position above her head. The Sleeve itself was a container vessel, a hollow mesh tube holding the spherical tactical units and the gravitoid. A flattened bulge around the middle of the tube contained the command and FTL communication section. Globular engines for interstellar travel took the rear, and the cone-shaped nose housed the gravity lens shield which prevented the seemingly empty vacuum of deep space from turning into a lethal radiation bath at near-lightspeed velocities.

Zenothon's model Sleeve shepherded six spherical TU's and a similar sized bumpy globe with a shimmering illusion of atmosphere.

"It's *our* Sleeve," she said. "Very impressive."

Zenothon moved the model in front of her face. "Look. There's the *Osman Bey* in front." Green letters on the hull spelled out the name. "Then behind us, we've got *Thermopylae* and then the new TU's that joined us with Mr. Horden: *Dreamwalker*, *Jade Buddha*, and *Great Cycle*. And at the end, the gravitoid where we are standing right now."

Escandala tried to smile but then quickly dropped the pretence. Zenothon was more perceptive than a human had any right to be. She made to give him a hug, but decided the time for such human affection had passed. She squeezed his shoulder instead. "You'll be moved to a real planet soon."

"Tranquility. I wished I was being moved to Earth. Everyone's talking about that. Christophe even showed me pictures Mr. Horden sneaked past the knowledge filters."

Escandala sucked in her breath sharply. "Let's not take things that don't belong to us. Especially from that man. He'll cause trouble, mark my words."

"I'm sorry Mr. Horden bested you, Momma."

"That's not important."

Her little boy looked up and shook his head, disappointed. "Please don't lie, Momma. I can interpret the micro-tremors in your voice. I know you are fibbing. Please, hold my hand."

Like the rest of his generation, Zenothon carried a matrix of subcutaneous implants and these now injected a small army of nanobots through Escandala's skin, seeking her hypothalamus to deliver their cargo of effector triggers. Her glands began to sing to each other in a harmonious cascade of wellbeing that resonated through her bloodstream.

Her mind rebelled. These feelings were not her own. She had been *programmed*, and by the thing her son had become.

"How can you do this?" she shouted, snatching her hand away. "You're not even human."

Zenothon said nothing, merely observing as Escandala backed away. Then, just for a moment, his eyes reddened and moistened. But the emotion was quickly repaired. Zenothon spoke calmly. "I am sorry if you feel I have failed you in some way. I was never trained to socialise with humans who have your... limited means of communication."

Escandala did not even want to know what Zenothon meant. "You're only six," she wailed. "You shouldn't think like that."

"You talk of 'six subjective years', as if everyone's mind works to the same clock. That may have been true for earlier

213

generations. The meddies told us that…"

Escandala did not hear what the medics had to say. "You aren't human," she said quietly. "I don't want anything more to do with you."

And then she was running, fleeing her son.

The two war fleets faced-off across the corridor through the minefield surrounding Akinschet and its moon, Utgard. The safe passage was filled with laser-blurring aerosol. Soon, Escandala's tactical unit would break the lull by bursting through the corridor from the planet side.

Her squadron was here to ensure the mining operations on Utgard continued to slingshot chunks of refined heavy elements around the local star and out along the interstellar trade routes to fulfil supply contracts, a journey of a thousand years. It scared her to think how the White Knights operated on such inhuman timescales.

But then so too did their enemy: the Muranyi Concord.

Escandala studied the Muranyi deployment in the tac-display beamed to her helmet, but that only deepened her unease. It was all wrong. Why was the enemy floating there, as if waiting?

Survival in ship-to-ship combat depended on speed, and the ability to change velocity rapidly. Instead of shooting through the corridor at a respectable fraction of c, the seventeen enemy vessels had slowed to a halt just outside, like an ancient blockade of a narrow water channel.

The White Knight's little empire had been fighting this border war with the Muranyi Concord for seven centuries, but Escandala had never seen tactical records of attacking ships sitting still.

This had to be a trap.

She waited hour upon hour, alone in her grey launch chamber. Overt physical needs were catered for by plumbing directed inside her body openings, yet she still suffered anguish from the pain of forced inaction. Every primitive instinct demanded she fight or flee, and still she waited.

Zenothon wouldn't have to live this nightmare when his turn came to wait in an EVA chute. With his freaky control over his body chemistry, he had been engineered to feel whatever he wanted, or had been ordered to feel. This, according to the Jotuns, was the principal reason why the White Knights reworked their client species. The Jotuns left dark hints too of the White Knights' obsession with forced mutation, speculating that Utgard might be sprinkled with mutagens.

In order to protect this mining world, Gjalp had detailed three of his Sleeves to attack the enemy directly. The rest of the squadron kept a fast orbit of Akinschet.

After Escandala had waited twenty-one hours in the launch chute, events unfolded in rapid escalation. In the tac-display etched into her visor, narrow blue course projections sprang toward her from the enemy markers. They fattened steadily as the Muranyi ships sped up.

The *Osman Bey* set off, the violent acceleration slamming her back into the buffer gel in her suit, and pushing her suit against the semi-intelligent amniotic fluid that filled the launch chamber. Despite all this protection, several marines would black out at some point during hard manoeuvring. She was determined she would not be going into combat unconscious.

The tac-display reported the enemy ships hurtling through the aerosol corridor to be Type-47 cruisers: big ships but constructed many objective centuries ago, and no match for the nimble TU's. The intruders wouldn't have floated there in space unless they possessed some secret advantage, a trap that Gjalp had tasked *Osman Bey* to spring for the greater benefit of the squadron.

A missile lock alarm pinged in her helmet, followed by an image of green missile attack paths zigzagging their way toward her.

Escandala ignored the missiles. Not her problem. If they hit, they hit.

She concentrated on the shape of the Muranyi box formation. Two ships at each vertex and a larger Type-60 'colony buster' in the centre.

Eight of the eleven marine TU's were each paired with one of the enemy ships that made up the nearest face of the enemy's box. The *Osman Bey*, though, was to destroy the colony buster, running the additional risk of crossfire. This was not completely a forlorn hope because *Thermopylae* and *Dreamwalker* hung back alongside *Osman Bey* to act as her shields.

The first wave of TU's ejected a constant confusion of chaff as they split up to close with their target assignments. Escandala tensed when they left the safety of the aerosol corridor and sheltered instead behind the chaff thrown out by *Thermopylae* and *Dreamwalker*. An orange flash bottom-left of her display warned that her EVA suit had administered a medical patch.

Immediately, she needed to kill.

Doubtless this battle lust was inspired by a crude hormonal adjustment forced into her endocrine system.

Defensive munitions obscured the TU's. The Muranyi tracking lasers couldn't find the clear path they needed to trigger the massive increase in beam power that would burn through armour.

A blue shimmer grew around the *Osman Bey* in her tac-display. Gunner Skaldi must have initiated a sweep of *Osman Bey's* Fermi cannons.

Fermi levels surged in all matter caught within the focus of the beams. Electrons imprisoned for centuries within predictable energy functions frolicked in hitherto unobtainable conduction bands. The semiconductor materials in the missile guidance systems suddenly became conductors, ruining them utterly. If chance brought the now aimless missiles too close, *Osman Bey's* defensive munitions would clear them away.

Osman Bey and its shield maidens accelerated toward the Muranyi flagship, zigzagging to the limits of their crew's physiology, still desperately throwing out chaff.

Thermopylae disappeared from the tac-display. It could have been due to a hidden missile or momentary weakness in her chaff system. Whatever the cause, forty-eight humans and five Jotuns, Escandala's comrades these past eight subjective years, were dead.

She tried to care, but couldn't. All she wanted was to kill.

The pressure on her back ceased momentarily as the *Osman Bey's* outer propulsion shell spun through 180 degrees, then the crushing force smashed her chest and transfixed her groin. After a thirty-second torrent of hammer blows came an instant of blissful weightlessness, before a squeezing sensation rippled through her as she was vented into chaff-filled space. The shower of amniotic fluid froze instantly into a glittering amber halo.

Then the TU's accelerated away, leaving Escandala in hard vacuum a few hundred meters away from an enemy warship powerful enough to sterilize an entire planet.

She was alone, cut off by strict communication silence from the thirty-five other marines sphinctered from *Osman Bey*. Stealth suits rendered them invisible. Even the exhaust from her needle gun and the thrust pack pushing her toward the nose of the target ship were cooled to ambient temperature, with the accumulating excess heat stored in energy batteries.

She could stay hidden this way for hours before the batteries would be fully charged, and hiding was something Horden had ordered her to do. She was one of ten marines ordered to act as a reserve, responding as they saw fit to enemy anti-personnel defence.

There came a flicker in her peripheral vision. She tilted position and magnified the image. It looked like a ripe seed pod exploding its contents in a gust of wind, but the seeds were jagged scraps of ceramic accompanied by the fragments of frozen blood and viscera from her comrades caught in its blast.

More flashes now, but the deadly blooms around the hull of the enemy ship did not contain human corpses this time. The enemy was firing at random.

"They're making a sally out onto the hull," said one of the marines though her helmet speaker. "Sweeping from aft —"

The voice cut off abruptly. Escandala flew from her position near the ship's nose to hover over the dimpled cylinder that was its main hull section. From the far side of the ship, white suited quadrupeds — Muranyi marines — had attached swivel-mounted heavy weapons to the hull and were spraying the area in front of them with a hail of lead slugs and dye. A half dozen human marines, made visible by the sticky yellow dye, were now dancing under the lash of the slugs.

She shouted a primordial battle-cry in the privacy of her helmet and then took off to close with the enemy.

Below her, Muranyi marines were moving to clear the hull of bacteria bombs left by the humans. She headed for the enemy slug-and-dye weapons now aiming their fire into space. Their aim was random, defeated by the stealth suits.

Escandala showered them with black needles of death from her gun. The enemy went limp, but some hadn't died at her hand. There must be another human here, as invisible to her as to the enemy.

She trained the enemy's heavy slug thrower on their own troops, brushing them off like the wind sweeping snow from the branches of the trees outside her shore leave quarters on Tranquility.

The thought of a planet with weather and seasons penetrated her combat numbness for long enough to remind her that she did have something worth fighting for: her son's chance for a few years of peace on a real world. Perhaps that would put some humanity back into Zenothon. She supposed she should feel ashamed that only now did she think of her son in the shielded crèche at the centre of *Osman Bey*.

Escandala took the bacteria bomb from her hip, secured it to the hull and activated. As she punched the vacuum in triumph, an injection of atmosphere and nutrients awoke trillions of bacteria from diapause. Hungry, they began to feed on the metal in the ship's hull. The population was predicted to attain critical mass at about six minutes for this class of vessel. After that, nothing could save the ship from rupture.

She moved up off the hull seeking a better position to defend her attack.

A bomb placed earlier by another marine cracked the outer hull, launching a geyser of gas and enemy bodies forced through the narrow breach.

A few minutes later her bomb caused its own explosion. With nothing left for her to do, she withdrew a klick from the doomed ship. Now she must wait, hoping her side would win.

The stratagems of Gjalp's slave squadron were already proving successful. The tactical units from the three attacking Sleeves had eliminated half the enemy fleet, and now swarmed around the surviving Muranyi, probing for surprises.

Finding none, the uncommitted squadron reserves spun away from orbit and wiped out the enemy the easy way, imparting their velocity to kinetic torpedoes that accelerated to near-relativistic speeds before impact.

From the initial acceleration through the aerosol corridor to pickup by the *Osman Bey*, the entire operation had taken forty minutes.

Afterwards, *Dreamwalker* hosted the Sleeve's victory celebration on her briefing deck. There was plenty of space: of the six TU's in her Sleeve, only *Osman Bey* and *Dreamwalker* remained.

Escandala stood near to Zenothon while Gunnlod, senior Jotun commander of the Sleeve, called out the names of those who had sacrificed all in service to the White Knights. Escandala wept, blaming her emotion on the combat drug toxins, but conscious of how close Zenothon had come to becoming a fleet casualty statistic.

"You'll be fine, Momma," he told her after the ceremony and moved toward her as if for a hug.

She backed off and walked away, unwilling to have him

programme her feelings. It wasn't as if anything she said or did could upset the thing that had once been her son.

Gjalp ordered the squadron to examine the enemy ships and corpses, looking for explanations for their strange behaviour.

There wasn't much left to be examined.

Horden manipulated assignments so that he examined one of the largest chunks of dead metal along with Escandala. Once they were out of direct sight, he unexpectedly grappled her. She reached for her knife but when their helmets kissed, Horden initiated a conversation the old-fashioned way: using sound waves.

"None of us will ever go home," he said.

"What?"

"I was an observer at the last Jotun strategy briefing. The Muranyi are using outdated materiel and expendable convict crews to wear us down on the cheap. There's a major offensive on the way in this sector. No one will be going home to Tranquility. Ever. We'll be off to our next battle soon. Our Sleeve has just suffered seventy percent casualties. If it's not our turn to die next, then it will be the time after."

"But you can never be sure. There's always a chance."

"Mathematical possibilities."

"So what? We were bred to die. We've always known that."

"That is exactly how they rely upon us to think. Why else would they be so open about our prospects at the briefing I saw?"

"I suppose your Earth-supreme credo gives you a better idea. What do you suggest we do, mutiny?"

"Yes. And the offensive means time is short."

Escandala struggled to absorb this. Mutiny had never seriously occurred to her. "Even if we secured the ships without being killed, what would we do? Turn them around for the ninety-year trip back to Earth?"

"All I need is a few minutes to myself."

"What good will that do us?"

"For us, nothing. But for Earth, a little. Think of the advantages that our augmentations give us. Our children more so. They can will their metabolism into the hibernation state for interstellar travel. We require complex machinery to achieve the same, but Earth natives can't even manage that. Think how this one advantage will benefit our species. I have the augmentation designs on memory crystal. These augmentations might not seem much in comparison with the huge advantages the other species have over us, but I believe in human ingenuity. All I need is to gain access to a powerful enough transmitter or the quantum telegraph. With your help I could do that. The Jotuns trust you. Think how we can turn this to our advantage against –"

"Our? Keep me and my son out of this. You might impress little boys by stories of embattled Earth, but the planet can rot for all I care. Never forget they sold our ancestors into slavery."

Suddenly, alarms pierced the fleet with sound, vibration, and scent alerts. Engines fired up and began to accelerate ships from standing.

Escandala didn't understand the panic until she heard a single phrase over and over: *Projectile assault! Projectile assault! Projectile assault!*

She watched an onrushing arc of dancing lights. They offered teasing hints of their form, twinkling briefly in Akinschet's illumination before winking back behind the veil of darkness.

Escandala guessed the instrument of their doom: broken fragments of a proto-comet, too small to detect remotely but fast enough to penetrate ship armour. The trap must have been set months or even years ago, waiting for Gjalp's squadron to be lured into a precise point in space and time.

Horden jetted away, aiming for the biggest gap between the ships.

Escandala followed.

The first exploding TU was quickly followed by the rest of

its Sleeve. TU's with enough velocity scattered, abandoning the slower Sleeve frames.

Too late.

A cluster of cometary debris shot past. She didn't even know it was there until the glare of light from a passing TU's engine lit the scene.

A TU passed close by. *Osman Bey*. She prayed to the Creator that Zenothon had been allowed the time to reach the shielded crèche at the heart of the ship. If he was caught in some connecting tube he would be pinned by the acceleration, unable to grab onto the adult-sized handholds that led to the acceleration protection dotted about the vessel.

She straggled behind the *Osman Bey*, which accelerated from brisk to flat out. In a few seconds, the zero-point engines would kick in and deliver near-relativistic velocity. Zenothon was now either in protection or he was dead.

She saw the rock moments before it hit *Osman Bey*.

The resulting fireball engulfed her mind.

Fragments of the ship spun outwards like a cracked helmet visor blown out by explosive decompression. She closed with a section tumbling toward her.

Horden bumped into her from behind and slowed to match her velocity.

"Is anyone there?" asked Horden, speaking through the general comms network. "Please notify."

She expected no reply and got none.

They waited.

She repeated Horden's plea until finally trailing into stillness. They were alone. Even the comet fragments had finished their assault and vanished into the darkness.

"Come on," said Horden. "We only survived because we're tiny in comparison with the ships. They didn't stand a chance, but that's no reason to think there are no survivors."

What was the idiot talking about? She surveyed the wreckage of broken ship fragments plunging through clouds of frozen air, blood, and meat.

"Just because there is no signal doesn't mean there are no survivors," said Horden.

"But no signal means no one in a suit. That means all are dead."

"Unless they are in a crèche."

She guessed the origin of the *Osman Bey* shard that had passed them and accelerated toward that point. The crèches were pressurized, armoured and shielded. It was just possible that Zenothon was alive.

"All secure," said Horden. "Let's go."

Secure was an optimistic way of describing the lash-up of mag-clamps and webbing the two humans had improvised from insulated-encased power cables. But wrapped in this embrace was the *Osman Bey's* crèche with its cargo that might be Zenothon and six other children, or might be corpses. The crèche was connected to a salvaged Sleeve vessel, *Pheidippides*, which still possessed a little rigidity in its shell, and retained functioning communication equipment. Gaping holes in the Sleeve's control section meant they had no way to pressurize *Pheidippides*, let alone produce a breathable atmosphere.

It might not hold and there may be other survivors. No matter. Either way, they had to seek help amongst the mining settlements on Utgard.

Escandala engaged the engines, and felt a jerky vibration through her grip on the control panel. The engines were only vector adjusters for fine control during slow manoeuvring such as docking. Thrust was pitiful, but the engines were fixed securely and the result moved them toward Utgard.

Horden had strapped himself to a communication console, looking childlike in the vast expanse designed for the hexapedal Jotun frame.

TU's carried short range radio and microwave transceivers, but all the Sleeves in their squadron held communicators

223

quantum-entangled with Severin, their supply depot orbiting Tranquility, 43 light years distant. Had they possessed the codes to activate the equipment, they could have asked Severin to request rescue from Utgard. As it was, they had to hope the miners were intrigued enough to investigate what would look to them like drifting wreckage.

"I know what you're thinking," said Horden, fiddling with the controls. "If only we could get this communicator to work, it would give the children a chance. But there's more. Geirrod, my old Sleeve commander, explained that he could use Severin as a relay to patch communication to any receiving station in the network. I could get an FTL message to Earth."

But that was impossible. Humans bred for the fleet were denied access to the interstellar communications network. One-Ear had explained that this was to protect them from distractions, but his mouth had been gaping, indicating heavy irony.

"Why bother?" asked Escandala. "We have at best three hours air left in our suits. If all the children still live, they have maybe a couple of days before they too run out of air and water."

"Done," he said, giving no sign he had heard her. "I've set up a distress signal of sorts which should reach Utgard, although there's no reason to hope they'll be listening. It's a sequence of primes. Not very informative but clearly artificial. Best I could do with no understanding of their language. It's the children's best chance."

Escandala grudgingly admitted she was impressed. She said nothing, though, conserving oxygen instead.

Utgard's sulphurous globe looked so far away to Escandala, yet it was close enough for a shuttle to launch from the mining port and rendezvous with them within about forty minutes. Not that there was any reason to hope for such a deliverance.

Her suit diagnostic reported two hours of air remaining.

"Still no response," said Horden. He looked up from the communications console and threw out his arms in frustration.

"Let's face it, no one's coming."

"Your timing is impeccable," said Escandala, jabbing her finger at a point behind Horden's shoulder. "Someone *is* coming."

The fast growing speck came not from the moon, but from the jumble of debris that had been two opposing fleets a few hours before. She laughed maniacally. Horden with his big ideas of being an Earth hero! This must be a Muranyi follow-up to eradicate any survivors.

She zoomed her visor display upon the ship. But this was not an attack. It was a bulky six-legged figure in a fleet EVA suit, a Jotun riding an inspection disc.

"Identify," came the command in the whistle and plosive yodelling of the Jotun speech.

Horden and Escandala obeyed.

"Would you believe it? It's my little hatchling, Escandala, and our friend Mr. Horden."

"One-Ear!" Escandala spoke his human nickname in the Jotun tongue, and hugged him as tightly as the suit allowed.

"You have done well," said One-Ear, "for such a—"

"How did you see us?" interrupted Escandala, peering into One-Ear's visor. "You're..."

"Blind. Yes, I thought you might notice that. Caught a heat flash when 'E' gun exploded. Melted my eyes and didn't do the rest of me much good either."

"You haven't answered Escandala's question."

"Well, Horden, you need to understand that we Jotuns have many faculties even you know nothing about. Despite your frequent ransacking of restricted parts of the data store, we still have our secrets."

Even under the layers of his suit, Horden exuded unease. "I have never —"

"Let's get word to Utgard, shall we?" said One-Ear. "We can talk directly to Severin through the quantum link, and they can route a message to Utgard. We'll have you and your hatchlings down there in no time. Here's how to operate the quantum telegraph."

Horden followed the blind Jotun's instructions to patch One-Ear through to Severin base.

"They will order Utgard to send help," said One-Ear after completing his report. "Looks like the mining life for us," he said. "Perhaps for the next few decades. I expect they'll send a fleet to defend or retake the mines – can't leave them to the enemy – but the nearest reserves are forty-three objective years away. Not so bad in a ship, but *we* would have to live those years the old-fashioned way. So please don't forget your old friend and tutor, or I would be ever so lonely."

"You silly old flea colony, of course we won't forget you."

"It's just that... Well, I know you humans too well. With nothing much else to do you'll start breeding within a few days, and not stop until you die."

The humans turned to each other and laughed.

"You humans! For such a fecund species, you exhibit a bizarre coyness about the actualities of your breeding. It would be different if Jarnsaxa had survived to be with me."

"Jarnsaxa?" Escandala allowed herself to relax and enjoy One-Ear's revelation. "Are you telling us that you were in love with Captain Jarnsaxa?" She giggled, surprised she could still feel such levity.

She stopped abruptly. Her guilty amusement was raw loss to One-Ear.

The Jotun said nothing for an uncomfortable while. "If you must know, I did have some fantasy of an impossible companionship. It hardly seems worth denying now she is a cadaver. She survived the initial attack, but wreckage from our ship pierced her pressure seal. By the time it self-sealed, enough blood plasma had vaporized to cause an embolism. She died in my embrace."

"I am sorry," said Escandala, using formal grammar.

"Don't be sorry; be grateful. Jarnsaxa felt our victory was

too suspicious for our entire squadron to be sitting stationary in one clump. Gjalp was too busy gloating over her victory to act like a proper squadron commander. Jarnsaxa disobeyed Gjalp's order to power down the point defence systems. We shot up most of the comet fragments they threw at us. Not enough, but we suffered less damage than the other ships. That's why your hatchlings could be alive."

"Jarnsaxa sounds like a great leader," said Horden, entering more instructions into the communications console. "Perhaps she should have been squadron commander?" He withdrew a memory crystal from a hip pouch. "Did Severin tell you anything about the rest of the war? The Muranyi must have been planning this for decades. It cannot be a –"

"Radio silence. Now!"

It took a moment for One-Ear's command to penetrate. She looked to him for instruction. He pointed to Utgard.

Escandala looked where One-Ear pointed, could see nothing, so magnified the image until she saw a flash on the surface of Utgard. Then there was another; it was an attack on a mining settlement. Scanning for the source of the bombardment, she saw a pair of Muranyi monitor ships: unarmoured weapons platforms with poor manoeuvrability. Perfect for nuking defenceless worlds into glassy slag.

She noticed Horden insert the memory crystal into the console, ignoring the slaughter around him.

Millions lived on the moons. Aliens, it was true – she couldn't even remember the species – but they were her wards.

"Horden!" One-Ear barked the name in the human tongue, prompting Escandala to turn to her mentor. "Do not make that communication to Earth." He had a sidearm aimed at Horden.

"I won't stop," said Horden. "You will have to kill me."

"Do not make me." One-Ear ground his teeth in irritation. He reasoned with Horden in the Jotun language, "We were told the Earth-loyalty meme sweeping through the humans on Severin was to be tolerated, a harmless morale booster. The White

Knights will be very disturbed if they even suspect one of their human slaves had contacted Earth. When they are disturbed they lash out. Their punishments are severe and indiscriminate."

Horden stopped, looked at Escandala, and then turned back to his task at the communication console.

One-Ear stiffened the grip on his weapon.

Horden spun around, his combat knife arcing toward One-Ear's throat.

One-Ear fired. A jet of plasma burrowed through Horden's chest, out his back and into the vessel's communicator, which sparked and went dim. Twin plumes of crimson steam erupted from the holes in Horden's suit, freezing instantly.

Escandala looked to One-Ear. Horden's knife was buried deeply into the Jotun's throat.

Both were dead.

She alone was responsible for the children now. There would be no last-minute rescue from the radioactive ash on Utgard's surface.

Her suit reported only seventy minutes of air remaining.

Their remnant of the *Pheidippides* never did reach Utgard orbit. Instead, it began yielding to the pull from the mass of Akinschet. When the Muranyi monitor ships passed around the far side of Utgard, Escandala relaxed into a final hour to be spent in appreciation of Akinschet's murderous beauty. With her boots wedged in the Sleeve frame, she hitched a ride on the *Pheidippides* only tens of metres away from the crèche with no way of knowing for sure whether anyone lived inside. Until a child's voice spoke in her helmet.

"We heard everything you said. You and Mr. Horden."

Distortion scratched at the transmission but there was no mistaking the voice was her son's. "How can you—?"

"No time. Christophe is eldest and most augmented. Do you know, he can launch processing threads in his cognitive implant up to a limit of eight teraflops? Still took a while to rig a short-range transmitter. Listen, we can effect Mr. Horden's plan, though we must do it the hard way."

"Explain."

"We will deliver the design of our augmentations inside our desiccated corpses."

"But... Zenothon!"

"No, it's all right, Momma. Christophe has found a way to pump a semi-inert atmosphere by reversing components of the air scrubbers. That might prevent us from decay and the crèche will shield us from cosmic radiation."

Zenothon mistook her again. How could she explain? She didn't want them to succeed!

"Christophe has been hacking into the navigation system for the last three subj-years," said Zenothon. "Calculating a couple of slingshots around our star to aim at Sol is no sweat."

"What? In this?"

"Yes."

She did not doubt them. Not their capability but she did doubt the rightness of forcing their change upon Earth. If the child corpses ever did get to Sol, no good, nothing *human* would come of it.

"Good luck," she said. She lied, knowing the children would detect her lie.

Then she let go. A quick burst from her thrust pack and her velocity diverged enough from the *Pheidippides* to watch the twist of silvered metal drift away.

"We need your help," said Zenothon.

Escandala ground her teeth. She did not wish to give her help.

"We need two of the engines shifted to the port side, aligned with the others. Doesn't have to be precise but we need this soon."

The engines already on the port side burst into a violet-blue flare for ten seconds.

"Please..."

Another burst of fire. The *Pheidippides* was pulling away, shrinking against the churning disc of Akinschet.

"We can't do this alone."

Escandala felt her thumb on the thrust control trigger an impulse in the direction of the children.

A long sigh escaped her lips, fogging her faceplate until the environmental systems cleared the obstruction away.

She recalled harsh words to her son on the gravitoid. "You are no longer human," she whispered. "But I am."

She gave freely of her fuel until the *Pheidippides* drew nearer. In her heart, she knew that her Zeno, however corrupted, deserved hope and purpose in his breast when he died.

To realign the vector adjustors to Christophe's requirements was a simple task of minutes.

"Thank you," said Zenothon. "We can go home."

The engines she had positioned began a series of short calibration bursts. Escandala released her grip on the *Pheidippides*, letting go of the children.

"You imagine your home is Earth," she told them. "Mine was always here, in vacuum lit by someone else's world, fighting another's war."

Overriding the safety, she took off her helmet and freed herself to the void. Air exploded out of her open mouth; her tongue prickled as its moisture boiled. The cloud of steam erupting from her mouth obscured forever her view of Zenothon's vessel as it began the long journey home.

About the Authors

Dan Abnett is a novelist and award-winning comic book writer. He has written over thirty-five novels, including the acclaimed *Gaunt's Ghosts* series, and the *Eisenhorn* and *Ravenor* trilogies. His latest *Horus Heresy* novel *Prospero Burns* was a New York Times bestseller, and topped the SF charts in the UK and the US. His combat SF novel *Embedded*, for Angry Robot, will be published in spring 2011. He lives and works in Maidstone, Kent. Dan's blog and website can be found at www.danabnett.com. Follow him on Twitter @VincentAbnett

Tony Ballantyne has written many short stories and five novels, the most recent being *Blood and Iron* (Tor UK 2010). In 2007 his novel *Recursion* was shortlisted for the Philip K Dick Award, while his short fiction has been shortlisted for a BSFA Award and featured in 'Years Best' anthologies. He is currently sitting at his computer typing this bio; he may go dancing later on tonight. He doesn't really like to talk about himself.

Lauren Beukes is the author of the muti noir *Zoo City* and *Moxyland*, a neo-apartheid cyber thriller set in a dystopian future Cape Town. When she's not writing stories about art monstrosities attacking Tokyo, murderous illegally-modded robot pets or aposymbiot plagues in Johannesburg slums, she writes TV shows, directs documentaries and occasionally falls back on the dirty journalism habits of her former life. She lives in Cape Town, South Africa, with her husband and daughter. ("Unaccounted" owes a huge debt to Philip Zimbardo's real-life account of Abu Ghraib in his book *The Lucifer Effect: Understanding How Good People*

Turn Evil)

Eric Brown sold his first short story to *Interzone* in 1986. He has won the British Science Fiction Award twice for his short stories and has had forty books published. His latest include the novel *The Kings of Eternity* and the children's book *A Monster Ate My Marmite*. His work has been translated into sixteen languages, and he writes a monthly science fiction review column for the *Guardian*. Eric's website can be found at: www.ericbrownsf.co.uk

Colin Harvey is the author of six novels, the latest of which are *Winter Song* and *Damage Time*, both published by Angry Robot Books. He has also sold some twenty or thirty short stories, to magazines such as *Albedo One*, *Daily Science Fiction* and *Interzone*, and various anthologies. Colin edited the anthologies *Future Bristol* and *Dark Spires*, both regional SF and fantasy from the West Country. He lives between Bristol and Bath with his wife and cocker spaniel.

Steve Longworth became an SF junkie after reading Ian Watson's *The Jonah Kit* in 1975. Thirty-odd years later, in 2007, Steve had his first story published in the 'Futures' column of the science journal *Nature*, a feat repeated last year. He has also appeared in the Newcon Press anthologies *Subterfuge*, *Shoes, Ships and Cadavers* and *Fables from the Fountain*. Steve works as a full time GP and part time Hospital Specialist in Leicester, where for the last 25 years he has been battling the bureaucratic zombie conspirators who have been trying to reorganise the NHS to death.

Philip Palmer is the author of four 'pulp' science fiction novels, all for Orbit books: *Debatable Space* (2008), *Red Claw* (2009), *Version 43* (2010) and *Hell Ship* (2011). He is also a screenwriter, script editor, teacher, and film producer. His screen writing credits include the BBC 1 film *The Many Lives of Albert Walker* and

The Bill, and his radio dramas include *The King's Coiner, Breaking Point* and *The Art of Deception*. He currently works part-time as a screenwriting tutor at the London Film School and can be found online at the website Debatable Spaces: www.philippalmer.net

Stephen Palmer first came to the attention of the SF world in 1996 with his debut novel *Memory Seed*, followed by its sequel *Glass*. Further novels followed, including the critically lauded *Muezzinland*. His most recent novel is *Urbis Morpheos*, the reading of which was described by one reviewer as "…the obtuse gift it is, to wallow in this utterly striking universe that Palmer has created... a supremely odd yet deeply rewarding experience." Stephen lives and works in Shropshire.

Gareth L. Powell is the author of the novels *The Recollection* and *Silversands*, and the acclaimed short story collection *The Last Reef*. He is a regular contributor to *Interzone* and his work has appeared in a number of recent anthologies. Gareth has given guest lectures on creative writing at Bath Spa University; and has written a series of non-fiction articles on science fiction for *The Irish Times*. Gareth can be found online at:
www.garethlpowell.com

Andy Remic is a larger-than-life action man, sexual athlete, sword warrior and chef. His writing pushes the boundaries of science fiction and sexual deviancy, all in one twisted whiskey barrel. When kicked to describe himself, Remic claims to have a love of extreme sports, kickass bikes and happy nurses. Once a member of an elite Combat K squad, he has retired from military service and claims to be a cross between an alcoholic Indiana Jones and a bubbly Lara Croft, only without the breasts. Remic lives in Lincolnshire and enjoys listening to Ronan Keating whilst thinking lewdly about zombies. Andy's website can be found at www.andyremic.com and his ebook site at www.anarchy-books.com.

233

Adam Roberts is a writer and an academic at the University of London; he lives a little way west of the metropolis with his wife and two children. He is the author of an ever expanding portfolio of published short stories and some twenty novels, including *Yellow Blue Tibia* (Gollancz 2009), *New Model Army* (2010) and *By Light Alone* (2011). His work has been shortlisted for the Arthur C Clarke, the Philip K Dick, and the John W Campbell Awards.

Kim Lakin-Smith is a science fiction and dark fantasy author whose work focuses on urban dystopias, steam/gaspunk, and the notion of the outsider. Kim's debut novel, *Tourniquet*, was published by Immanion Press in 2007. Recently, she has completed a young adult action adventure novel, *Autodrome*, the adult slipstream novel *Cyber Circus*, and sister novella "Black Sunday". Kim's novella "Queen Rat" will appear in Echelon Press's 2011 anthology *Her Majesty's Royal Conveyance*. Her short stories have featured in *Interzone, Black Static, Celebration* – the BSFA's 50th birthday anthology – *Myth-Understandings* and several other venues. Her story, "Johnny and Emmie-Lou Get Married" was shortlisted for a BSFA Award 2009.

Tim C. Taylor recently began a sabbatical from the software industry to be a full-time writer. He hopes this will also mean a restart to his home brewing operation but suspects that his son will have other ideas, centering on the construction of various Lego edifices. Tim has had half a dozen stories published in the small press and one in NewCon Press' *Shoes, Ships and Cadavers*. Currently he is working on a novel linked to his story in *Further Conflicts*.

NEWCON PRESS

Celebrating 5 year of publishing quality Science Fiction, Fantasy, Dark Fantasy and Horror

Winner of the 2010 'Best Publisher' Award
from the European Science Fiction Association.

Anthologies, novels, short story collections, novellas, paperbacks, hardbacks, signed limited editions…

To date, NewCon Press has published work by:

Dan Abnett, Brian Aldiss, Kelley Armstrong, Sarah Ash, Neal Asher, Stephen Baxter, Tony Ballantyne, Chris Beckett, Lauren Beukes, Chaz Brenchley, Keith Brooke, Eric Brown, Pat Cadigan, Simon Clark, Michael Cobley, Storm Constantine, Peter Crowther, Hal Duncan, Jaine Fenn, Neil Gaiman, Gwyneth Jones, Jon Courtenay Grimwood, M. John Harrison, Leigh Kennedy, David Langford, Tanith Lee, James Lovegrove, Gary McMahon, Ken MacLeod, Ian R MacLeod, Gail Z Martin, Juliet E McKenna, John Meaney, Philip Palmer, Stephen Palmer, Sarah Pinborough, Christopher Priest, Andy Remic, Alastair Reynolds, Adam Roberts, Justina Robson, Mark Robson, Sarah Singleton, Martin Sketchley, Brian Stapleford, Charles Stross, Tricia Sullivan, Una McCormack, Freda Warrington, Ian Watson, Liz Williams… and many, many more.

Join our mailing list to get advance notice of new titles, book launches and events, and receive special offers on books.
www.newconpress.co.uk

BSFA

Don't just read Science Fiction…
Don't just watch Science Fiction…
Don't just play Science Fiction…
Be a part of it.

The British Science Fiction Association
At the heart of science fiction for more than half a century.

Publications

Vector, our critical journal, full of book reviews and essays, offering a comprehensive insight into modern SF; *Focus,* the magazine for writers, offering advice on improving the quality of your work and how to get it published. We also produce a wide range of *special edition* publications, both fiction and non-fiction, throughout the year.

Orbiter

Writers groups for workshopping your fiction and receiving excellent feedback and advice – both online groups and postal – an essential service for aspiring authors.

Events

The BSFA organises regular monthly meetings in London and other events during the year.

Contact

Join the BSFA online at www.bsfa.co.uk.
Or email: bsfamembership@yahoo.co.uk.